Good Night, My Darling

INGER FRIMANSSON

Translated by Laura A. Wideburg

A CARAVEL BOOK
an imprint of
PLEASURE BOAT STUDIO: A LITERARY PRESS

Good Night, My Darling

By Inger Frimansson
Translated from the Swedish by Laura Wideburg

Copyright 2007

Frimansson, Inger
Good Night, My Darling / Inger Frimansson
ISBN 9781929355372
First U.S. printing

Design and composition by Susan Ramundo
Cover by Al Kamp

Library of Congress Control Number: 2006935351

A Caravel Book

Published by Pleasure Boat Studio: A Literary Press
201 West 89th Street
New York, NY 10024
Tel/Fax: 888-810-5308
e-mail: *pleasboat@nyc.rr.com*
URL: *www.pleasureboatstudio.com*

God natt min älskade was originally published in Sweden in 1998.

Printed in USA

Pleasure Boat Studio: A Literary Press is a proud subscriber to the Green Press Initiative. This program encourages the use of 100% post-consumer recycled paper with environmentally friendly inks for all printing projects in an effort to reduce the book industry's economic and social impact.

My thanks to Karl-David, who let me use his blowpipe as much as I needed.

Prologue

The plane touched down at Arlanda airport at six fifteen in the evening. The first leg had been late to London, which meant that they missed their connection. All the planes to Stockholm had been fully booked. They would not have gotten a seat until the next morning, if the woman from the Embassy had not gotten angry. Her name was Nancy Fors and she had been calm and a bit melancholy the whole trip. The unexpected explosion surprised Justine.

They were the first to leave the plane. Two plainclothes policemen came on board and guided them out through a back way.

"The press has already figured out that you were coming, unfortunately," one of them said. Justine didn't quite catch his name.

"They're real hyenas with all their chomping and slurping, but we'll fool them."

They took her into their car.

The light hit her, that pure, cool light and the delicate greenery. She had forgotten that nature could look like that. She mentioned this to Nancy Fors: "Don't you miss home? How do you manage to live there in that heat?"

"I know that it's temporary," she answered. "And this is still here, here at home."

They passed the Sollentuna-Upplands Väsby exit. It was seven-thirty.

The policeman behind the wheel said, "You know . . . that girl Martina. Her parents want to meet you."

"They do?"

"It's important to them."

She turned her face toward the window. She saw a little clump of trees with white trunks.

"Sure," she said. "That's fine."

part one

Chapter ONE

That sharp, pure cold. Grey water like a living thing, silk.

No sky, no, just no contrasts, she couldn't stand that, that hurt her eyes. The gathering clouds, getting ready for snow.

And the dry snow would come from the skies, swirl like smoke over the roads, and she would remove her clothes and let herself get completely misted.

Over there she had tried to imagine exactly this, the sensation of ice crystals. Her whole body tense, she would close her eyes in order to bring forth the sound of a Nordic stream one spring day when the ice had begun to melt.

She never succeeded. Not even when the fever chills were at their worst and Nathan covered her with clothes, rags, curtains, everything he could find.

She had been freezing with the wrong kind of chill.

She ran forward, forward.

You never saw me like this.

Forward, forward, force the massive body, feet light in jogging shoes. Justine had tried them out at a sports store in Solna, clinically tried them out, with a young man having bright white teeth and slick wavy hair. He had her run on a treadmill and videoed her foot movements. While she was running, she formed her fists tightly, so tightly, afraid to lose her balance, afraid that he would find her ridiculous. An overweight, forty-five-year-old woman, afraid he would see something desperate in her way of pressing her knees together.

He watched her sternly.

"You pronate."

She looked at him uncertainly.

"Yes, that's right. But don't worry about it, lots of people do; almost everyone does actually."

She got off the treadmill, the hair on her neck somewhat damp.

"This means that you run lopsided. You rotate your foot like this, which is why you wear out your soles on one side."

He lifted her old winter boots and showed them to her. "See for yourself."

"But I never run. I've never done it."

"It doesn't matter. You pronate anyway."

"Promenade?"

An attempt at a joke. He laughed politely.

She bought the shoes, which cost just under a thousand crowns. He gave her a bit of a lecture: better to invest in quality, you could hurt yourself jogging with the wrong kind of shoes, tear something, overstretch something, especially if you were not used to it.

The shoes had the brand name Avia. She thought of flying when she saw them.

Of fleeing.

To reach distant horizons.

With her dark blue stocking cap pulled down around her face, she began to go up Johanneslundtippen. She ran, bent forward, and small flocks of green birds flew up from their grass nests. They were silent but accusing. She had interrupted them in some important task with her flailing human body and her heavy, whistling breath.

We're drifting apart.

No!

You should see me now, you'd be proud of me, I could follow you to the end of the world and you would turn and look at me and really see me with your sky-blue eyes, Justine is the one I love, she can climb the walls like a fly.

Or a louse.

High at the top, the wind was strong and forced tears from her eyes. Beneath her, rows of houses were spread out. They looked like cardboard boxes placed in the maze of streets and cul-de-sacs, surrounded by rose hedges. The original plaster architect's model must have looked exactly like this.

She nearly stumbled into some remains of fireworks, glass and plastic bottles. A group of people had been up here in order for the fireworks and themselves to be seen better on New Year's Eve, shooting them up higher than anyone else, and then drunkenly stumbling down, finding their way home.

Sometimes she took the car to the new riding stables in Grimsta. There were plenty of parking spots during week-days. She seldom saw any horses in the muddy field. Well, once she saw some long-legged animals with their muzzles to the ground like vacuum cleaners, but she could not see a single blade of grass.

Justine was overcome with the impulse to clap loudly so that one of them, the leader perhaps, would roll his eyes wildly and run off as fast as he could without realizing that he was enclosed on all sides by the fence; panic would make him forget everything but the attempt to flee, and all the others would follow him, out of their minds with fear, and they would thunder back and forth in the mud, completely losing all sense of direction.

Of course she didn't do it.

Left of the ice rink, a path of electric lights began. She fol-lowed it just part way. She cut through the waterlogged fields below the apartment houses, passed the parking lot at the Maltesholm baths, and noticed that one of the windows on a trailer still hadn't been fixed. She kept going toward the water and then ran for a while along the edge.

Four ducks waddled silently away. Although it was January, the temperatures were above freezing and it had been raining without a break for over a week, but this afternoon, the sky was bleak and white.

She drew in air through her nostrils.

Heaps of leaves lay along the slope, and the decay process appeared to have stopped. They were brown and slimy, not at all like leather.

Just like over there.

No sound, no birds, no raindrops, just the muffled thudding of her rhythmic steps as she forced her way up the slope, then echoing as she came to the boardwalk, where she almost fell. The water's dampness had made a treacherous cover that made the Avia soles slip.

No, don't stop, no weakness now; her lungs burned, a caustic, silent wheeze. She drove herself now, as if she were him. Nathan.

You were supposed to be proud of me, to love me.

Safely inside her house, she stopped, leaning against the wall just inside the door to undo her shoelaces. She threw off the rest of her clothes, the red, windbreaker suit, the long johns, the sports bra, the panties. She stood with her legs wide apart, her arms out and let the sweat drip off.

The bird flew in from somewhere up inside the house. The sound of his rustling wings. He screeched and muttered, going on and on. He settled in her hair, holding tight with his coarse, shiny claws. She turned her head, felt him as a warm heaviness on the top of her head.

"Have you been waiting for me?" she said. "You know I always show up."

She petted his back and took him down. With an angry little chatter, he disappeared into the kitchen.

She stretched on the thick, dining room rug, as she had learned from an exercise class on TV. She never cared for group activities. Shy, Nathan called her. In the beginning, that was what had attracted him the most.

She was still tall, but the time over there had sculpted her; she looked thinner, even though the scale still read 171 pounds. She stood for a long time in the shower, rubbing her stomach, limbs, the backs of her knees with a sponge.

Over there, not a single day went by where she did not long for clean European showers, long for a floor to stand on and tiles on the wall.

She and Martina had cleaned themselves in the yellow river water, but the smell of decay and mud seeped into their pores and could not be scrubbed away. In the beginning, she had a hard time getting in it, she thought about what may have been swimming about underneath the surface—snakes, piranhas, leeches. One morning they were forced to go through the rapids with all their clothes on since there was no other path. After that day, she was no longer afraid.

She dried off carefully and smeared on some body lotion. The Roma bottle was almost empty now, the one that looked like the Leaning Tower of Pisa. She cut it open with scissors and scraped out the rest with her finger. She looked at herself for a while in the mirror, flushed from the heat, no longer young. She painted lines around the eyes just as she had done since the sixties. Not a single person could make her stop.

Not even Flora.

Dressed in her green housedress, she went into the kitchen and poured herself a bowl of soured milk. The bird had settled on the window sill; he stared with one eye and muttered as if he were displeased. A blackbird strutted on the path outside, fat for winter and ruffled. Its call changed during the winter and became one shrill tone, as if someone were trying to pluck a too tightly wound guitar string. The other song, the one that was both melancholy and jubilant, usually stopped near the end of summer and did not return to life until late February, from the top of a very high tree.

For her entire life, Justine had lived in this house, by the water next to Hässelby Villastad. It was a narrow, tall little stone house, just right for two or three people. There had never been more than three, except for the short time with the baby.

Now Justine lived by herself. She could change the furniture just as she liked, but for now, she left everything just as it was. She slept in her childhood room with its faded wallpaper since she could not imagine moving into Flora's and her pappa's master bedroom. The bed was made, as if they would return at any time, and a few times a year, Justine would shake out the bedcover and change the sheets.

Their clothes were still hanging in the closet, Pappa's suits and shirts on the left side of the bar and all of Flora's little dresses on the other side. There was a thick layer of dust on the shoes. At times she thought about dusting them, but she never got around to bending down and picking them up.

She wiped down the dresser when she was in the mood to take care of things. She cleaned the mirror with window cleaner and she moved the hairbrush and the tiny perfume bottles around. Once she picked up Flora's hair brush and held it to the window, staring at the gray strands of hair. She bit herself hard inside one cheek and quickly ripped away one of the strands. Then she went to the balcony and set it on fire. It burned with a pungent odor, rolled itself up, and disappeared.

It was already getting dark. She was in the upper hallway now, and she pulled a chair to the window, poured herself a glass of wine. The water of Lake Mälar shimmered out there, waves bobbing up and down, gleaming from the neighbor's outdoor light, which was on a timer that began at dusk. There was seldom anyone at home, and she did not know the people who lived there now.

Just as well.

She was alone. She was free to do anything she decided to do. Everything she had to do to become whole, strong, a living person, just like everyone else.

She had that right.

Chapter TWO

He had spent Christmas with his parents. Quiet, uneventful days. Christmas Eve had been beautiful with all the trees covered in frost. His mother had hung a light in the old birch tree, just as she had done when they were small, and he remembered his and Margareta's giggling eagerness, which began the minute they woke up on the morning of Christmas Eve.

His mother usually asked that he return for Christmas. And what else would he be doing? Even so, he played hard to get, let her ask and plead, as if he constantly needed to hear how much he meant to her.

He had no idea what his father thought. Kjell Bergman was a man who seldom revealed his emotions. Only once had Hans Peter seen him lose his cool, seen shades of pain glide over his large, bulging face. That was the night the police came when Margareta had driven off the road. That was eighteen years ago, and Hans Peter was still living at home.

His sister's death meant that he had to postpone his plans to move out. He was the only child now, and his parents needed him.

He was twenty-five when it happened, and right in the middle of trying to plan his future. He had studied theology and psychology at the university. Something within him longed for something higher; he saw himself in austere black vestments and experienced something resembling peace.

He stayed with them for three years. Then he packed his things and moved out. His parents had begun to talk with each other again. In the initial period they had been silent, sat like statues in their TV recliners and said not one word, as if they wanted to punish each other, as if they, in some irrational way, considered it the other one's fault that Margareta had driven off the road.

She had had her driver's license just one week and she was using their car that evening, a 1972 Saab. No one ever managed to find out why she had driven off the road close to Bro and right into a cement block.

The car was totaled.

Her room stood unused for many years. His mother went in sometimes and shut the door behind her. When she came out, she would usually go to her bedroom, get undressed and creep under the covers.

Hans Peter suffered from that, so he slowly, cajolingly, tried to convince them to let him go and clear it out. Finally his mother gave in.

He had cleaned out everything from his sister's room. He carried her private things up to the attic, and claimed her bed and the neat little desk as his own. His parents did not react. They didn't make a peep, not even when emptiness gaped from the spotless room. Yes, he had been thorough: he had washed the walls with soda and water, used a wool mop on the ceiling, scrubbed both the windows and the floor.

His mother had always mentioned having a dining room.

"Now you can have it," he said. "I've prepared it for you."

And he threw the IKEA catalog on the coffee table, and finally convinced them to start looking through it. His father gnashed his teeth a bit, pressing his molars together silently. His mother had cried. But finally they accepted it. He had forced them to accept that Margareta was not going to come back, and it would not be a blot on her memory to change her room into something more practical than a museum.

However, they only ate in that room when he came home, in order to make him happy. Hans Peter thought that they never had guests. They hardly had them before, so why should they now, just because they had a dining room?

It seemed they could just barely deal with everyday burdens. His father was tired constantly. Previously he had worked as a sheet-metal worker, but he had been retired for many years, his back ruined.

His mother had been a high school teacher.

Hans Peter remembered a time when Margareta had complained to their parents that they isolated themselves too much. She was about thirteen then, had started to rebel a bit. His father had grabbed her by her shoulders and pushed her against the wall.

"We live our own lives our way, and if Little Missy doesn't like that, she can move out. We don't like folks sticking their noses into our business."

That was one of the few times he showed anger.

He began to avoid them. He found an apartment in Hässelby Strand, which was close to the subway, close to nature, and he liked to walk and move around. He kept up his studies, even though it didn't lead to anything. When he began to worry about his student loans piling up, he started a series of part time jobs such as delivering mail by bicycle and doing surveys for SIFO. They didn't bring him a lot of money, but he also didn't have a lot of needs.

At Åkermyntan's library, located in Villastaden's shopping center, he met Liv Santesson, a recently graduated librarian. Eventually, they got married. It wasn't a question of passion on either side. They just liked each other and that was enough.

It was a simple wedding, a civil ceremony at City Hall and then lunch at Ulla Winbladh Restaurant with their nearest relatives.

Her brother ran a hotel in the city. Hans Peter took a job there as the night clerk. This was an unfortunate choice for a newlywed who was not able to take care of his wife in a suitable manner.

They didn't have any children, and eventually they stopped having sex as well.

"We just have a different kind of relationship," he told himself, convincing himself that she agreed.

She didn't. One Saturday evening, four years after their marriage, she told him that she wanted a divorce.

"I've met someone else," she said, nervously pulling at her earlobe, shying away a bit, as if waiting for a blow.

He was completely calm.

"Bernt and I fit together in a different way than you and I did. Just to be honest, you and I have never really had all that much in common, other than literature. And you can't live from literature alone."

A feeling of sorrow entered him, light and fluttering, came and went.

She embraced him, her little frozen hand on his neck. He swallowed, and swallowed again.

"You're fine," she whispered. "There's nothing wrong with you, nothing like that . . . but we never see each other and Bernt and I, we . . ."

Hans Peter nodded.

"Forgive me. Say that you forgive me."

She was crying now, the tears traced their way down her cheeks, hung on her chin, fell and were soaked up by her sweater; her nose was red and shiny.

"There's nothing to forgive," he said, as if his mouth were full of oatmeal.

She sniffed.

"So you're not angry with me?"

"More like disappointed, that it didn't work out."

"Maybe we needed a little more . . . fire."

"Yes, perhaps we did."

The next day she moved out of the apartment. She only took essentials with her, and moved in with Bernt. Later that week she returned with a moving truck which she had rented from a garage. That surprised him. She never did like driving.

He helped her carry out her things. He kept most of the furniture and the kitchen utensils. Bernt already had a completely furnished apartment in a building on Blomsterkungsvägen.

"Can I offer you a cup of coffee or something," he asked when they were done.

He didn't want to ask; he really wanted her to go as soon as possible so he could be alone. He didn't understand why he asked, the words just fell from his mouth.

She hesitated a moment, then agreed.

They sat together on the sofa, but when she wanted to lay her arm on his shoulder, he steeled himself against her.

She swallowed.

"So you're really pissed off at me, aren't you?"

That was the first time he heard her use bad language. That surprised him so much that he burst out laughing.

Many years later, he ran into them at Åkermyntan. They were weighed down by grocery bags, and they had children, though he forgot their names right away.

Her new husband was tall and strong, with well-trained abs. He was wearing a jogging suit.

Stupid jock, he thought, but without any real aggression.

Liv had cut her hair. It was curly now.

"Come over for a drink sometime," she said, and her husband nodded.

"Sure, do that. We live in Baklura, you just take bus 119."

"OK," he said without much enthusiasm.

Liv touched his sleeve.

"I wish that we wouldn't lose each other totally," she said.

"No," he answered. "We won't."

Sometimes his mother reproached him, although indirectly. She wanted grandchildren, which she never said directly, but she would do things like pointing at a picture of a child in the newspaper or make some kind of sorrowful comment. Or she would turn the television on right when the children's programming was starting.

This drove him crazy, but he never let on.

He would go out with various women. Sometimes he brought them home and introduced them to his parents, mostly to give his mother a bit of hope.

He knew his parents were disappointed in him. No real job, no family.

You really couldn't blame them.

Everything would have been different if that accident with Margareta hadn't happened. He would not have lost his own bearings.

On Christmas Day it began to rain, and it kept raining all week. His mother did her best to pamper him. She prepared breakfast trays, and when he lay in bed waking up, he heard her careful knock on the door.

"My big boy," she murmured, as she placed the breakfast tray on the bedside table.

Then he'd want to hug her and cry, but that gave him a bad taste in his mouth, so he lay still under the blanket, not moving.

He stayed until the day before New Year's Eve. Then he couldn't take it any longer: their breathing, their chewing, the sound of the TV at the highest possible volume. They were both over seventy. One of them would be dead soon and he didn't know which one of them would have the hardest time being alone.

They had known each other since they were in their twenties.

He longed for his own cool apartment, where he could uncork a bottle of wine, solve the crossword puzzle, and listen to his own choice of music, Kraus and Frank Sinatra.

He told his mother that he was invited to a New Year's Eve party.

He barely made it in the door when the phone rang. One of his women friends. *Dammit*, he thought. *I can't take more of this.*
"How's it going?" she said girlishly.
"Fine. I just got home."
"Were you with Kjell and Birgit?"
She had only met them once and already acted as if they were close.
"Yeah."
"I thought so. I've been trying to reach you."
"Uh-huh."
"Hans Peter? Can I come over tomorrow evening? Can we celebrate New Year's Eve together?"
He thought about telling her that he had to work at the hotel, but couldn't bring himself to do it.

She came over, and she had taken an effort with her clothes and make-up. He hadn't remembered that she was so cute. He understood that she had made an effort, just for him, and it made him feel guilty.
They had met at a mutual friend's place, and had gone out for a while since then. Sporadically. Nothing steady. But she had been one of the women he had taken to meet his folks in Stuvsta.
"You don't think that I am being too eager, do you?" she asked directly. "A woman is not supposed to take the initiative. Or so they say."
"Don't worry about it."
"Well, I'm here now."
She had two grocery bags full of food, wine, and champagne.
OK, he thought, *this is how she wants it.*

There was something about her that made him excited, more than he felt with anyone else. Something in her way of putting her head to one side and looking a little bit guilty.

He was frightened of his own strength.

Afterwards, she got right out of bed.

He knew that she didn't like it, that he had come too soon.

He wanted to explain, but couldn't find the words.

We'll just do it again, he thought. *Later*.

They set the table together, and she didn't say much, but after she drank half a glass of wine, she began to cry.

"Sweetie, what is it?" he asked.

She didn't answer and began to cry harder.

He threw his fork on the table.

"I'm a real asshole!" he exclaimed.

She turned to the side and didn't look at him.

"Little sweetie," he said. "Why did you want to come here, anyway?"

"I like you. I was longing for you the whole damn Christmas holidays."

He got up and walked around the table, took her into his arms, lifted her out of her chair.

"Should we just finish the food, then?"

She took out a tissue and nodded.

After dinner, she fell asleep in the sofa, leaning on his arm. She breathed heavily and noisily. He was uncomfortable, but didn't want to move, afraid that she would wake up and demand more from him.

A feeling of desolation crept over him.

Chapter THREE

Nathan had been wearing the green fatigues which were too tight for the jungle. He didn't know that when he bought them; he just thought that they were practical and cheap. "Economical," he said. Justine remembered his exact word.

No one saw him go to be by himself for a few moments. No one but Justine.

He probably screamed, more from surprise than anything else, although it probably stung a little. He tumbled outward immediately. The rapids and the waterfall drowned every sound, and they were so powerful that whatever became caught in them would be dashed to pieces.

Sometimes she thought she heard that scream. She was home now, at home in her house, but even so. . . . And when she heard that scream, she also saw the body, how it turned once while falling. She saw his arms and his hands that she had loved.

Her house was narrow and tall in an almost Dutch kind of way. Originally it had been built with just two stories, but to get more room, her Pappa had had someone remodel the attic. But they were hardly ever there. In the summer it was too hot, and in the winter too cold.

Her father had never been an entirely practical person. He had hired carpenters, young men with suspenders. They had rushed up and down the stairs and formed their lips in silent suggestions whenever she came out in her nightgown.

She had been confined to her bed. She lay in bed and listened to their steps and their hammering, and slowly she began to realize that she wasn't a little girl any longer.

The oil heater was down in the basement. The driver of the oil tanker used to mutter about how difficult it was to reach it properly when it was time to refill it with oil, as the house was down so close to the beach that it was impossible to get the hoses stretched that far. Pappa used to bribe him with a bottle of whiskey, and this was something that Justine continued to do, once she was alone. Naturally, it was no longer the same driver. This one was bony and ill-tempered, and he spoke a dialect that made it almost impossible for her to understand his words. She felt herself shrink when she heard the sound of the oil truck. For a time, she thought about discontinuing oil delivery, but she didn't know any other way to warm the house. There was a fireplace on the second floor, but it wasn't big enough to heat the entire house. The raw chill of the lake seeped straight into the walls and floors.

In any case, she only had to deal with the trucker once a year. She always placed the whiskey bottle near the basement window, tied with a paper bow.

"Thanks for bringing the oil," she would write on a slip of paper that she placed under the bottle. The piece of paper would still be there afterwards, the ink smeared.

The basement also held a large old-fashioned washing tub, which Flora had insisted on using. Twice a month Flora did laundry down there, and on those days both Justine and her father would feel ill at ease. She made herself look really ugly on those days, Flora, as if she enjoyed changing herself into a repulsive washerwoman. She knotted a handkerchief around her hair and wore her smelly patterned skirt which had missing buttons. It was a kind of reverse Cinderella transformation, and her fingers left stinging damp marks on Justine's cheeks.

The hall was minimal, but they still had to store their outerwear there. Everywhere in the house there was a shortage of wardrobes. Once she became an adult, she had sometimes wondered why her pappa, with his wealth, had decided to continue living in that small house, even if it was adjacent to Lake Mälar. Something to do with her mother, something nostalgic.

Justine had stowed Flora's capes and blue fox fur, packed them away in plastic garbage bags. Pappa's loden coat, his caps and hats were stowed in another bag. She had decided to give them away to charity but she changed her mind at the last minute and carried them into the basement. Just the thought of meeting a strange woman wearing Flora's fur gave her a feeling of distaste, as if her stepmother's eyes would be staring at her from the strange woman's face. Nail her to the pavement, force her back.

Just off the hall was the blue room, which they had used as a dining room. Everything there was either blue or white, from the wall-to-wall carpet, to the silk draperies, the flowerboxes in the window with its Saint Pauls and its Browallias. The flowers had not survived her sojourn to that hot country. She had soaked them with water prior to her departure, and placed layers of brown cardboard over the dirt, but it hadn't helped.

The bird didn't suffer. She let him live in the attic and set him up with bowls of seeds and water and a whole basket of peeled apples. He was having a grand old time.

Even the pictures on the wall continued the blue and white theme: a winter landscape, sailboats, and a weaving from silk rags that took up an entire wall. Justine's mamma had woven it long before Justine was born. It had always hung there, an extension of her being.

She only had a few fragments of memory about her mother.

A rumbling rain, a covering under which they sat close together, old sour socks sticking to her toes.

The smell of fluffy flowers, something hot with honey.

Against his will, her father told her.

Her mother had been standing, cleaning the windows. It was the window that faced the water on the second floor and the day had strong sunshine and the strong call of seagulls. The wind was still, and the ice was still lying thick over the water, but it was beginning to thin out, and perhaps she was happy about that, and perhaps she was humming to herself in the sunshine, perhaps she was even planning to go out on the balcony after she was finished in order to sit with her face turned toward the sky. She had quickly taken to this Nordic ritual. She had come from Annecy, a little town in France near the Swiss border, and he had taken her from there, against her parents' wishes, to be his bride.

It was a Thursday. He came home from work at seven minutes after four. She was lying on the floor, with her arms outstretched as if she had been crucified. He could see right away that there was nothing that could be done.

"How could you tell?" Justine asked. She was in a period where she had to know as much as possible about her mother, obsessing about her.

He couldn't answer.

"Perhaps she was still alive. If you had called a doctor right away, maybe he could have saved her."

"Don't accuse me," he said, with a wry twist at the corner of his mouth. "Once you've seen a dead person, you will know what I mean."

First he had thought that she had fallen from the step-stool and broken something important, but the autopsy showed that an artery in the brain had burst, and her life had run out with it.

"Aneurysm!"

Pappa pronounced that word slowly and clearly every time during Justine's youth whenever the subject came up.

Sometimes she worried that it could be inherited.

She asked about herself.

"Where was I, Pappa? What was I doing?"

He didn't remember.

She was just three when it happened, three years old and a few months. How does a three-year-old react when her mother falls off a stepstool and dies? She must have been somewhere in the house, she must have called and cried, she must have been terrified at her mother's sudden change.

Sometimes she woke up from a dream that her forehead was aching as if after a long hard cry; she looked at herself in the mirror and saw her eyelids swollen and glassy.

Fragments of sinking, of mud and of flowers which never had any odor.

A pappa standing on the ice and screaming.

She saw pictures in the photo album of the woman who had been her mother. The strange face did not resonate with her. Thick hair combed back, curly on the sides. Justine did not look like her one bit. There was distance in the woman's eyes, which did not match Justine's memories.

A steep narrow staircase led up to the second floor. Up here is where her mother had stood to clean the windows. To the left was the bedroom, to the right the hall widened and created a living room with a view toward Lammbar Island and beyond Lake Mälar. Bookcases covered the walls, but there wasn't much furniture: a stereo, an oval glass table and two armchairs.

Those had been Pappa's and Flora's.

Many times Justine had been offered a great deal of money for the house. The real estate agents hassled her, stuffed their information into her mailbox, and even called her from time to time. One of them was especially pushy. His name was Jacob Hellstrand.

"You could get a few million for the place, Justine," he chatted away, using her first name as if they had been close friends. "I have a client who wants to rebuild it. He's always dreamed of that location."

"Sorry, but I don't really want to."

"And why not? Think of what you could buy with that money! A single woman like yourself, you can't just sit and rot out there in Hässelby. Buy yourself a condo in the city instead and live life!"

"You don't know a thing about whether I am living life or not. Maybe I'm already living life."

His laughter came through the handset.

"You're right, of course. But admit it, Justine, admit that there's something to what I'm telling you."

She should have gotten angry, but she didn't.

"Just let me know when you've decided. You have my cell phone number, right?"

"Of course."

"It's not easy for a single woman to take care of such a big house. All by yourself, that is."

"If I decide to sell," she said, "I'll give you a call."

She didn't have a single thought of selling. She didn't need any money either. Pappa left a great deal when he died. She would live well on that for a long time. In fact, as long as she lived.

And Flora wouldn't ever be able to demand a single penny of it.

Chapter FOUR

The most difficult thing to endure was the smell. Flora remembered it from that summer long ago when she moonlighted at a hospital for mentally ill women. The mix of floor polish, unwashed hair, and flower water. Now she smelled like that. Despite what she had most feared, the nights weren't all that bad. Rather, the night belonged to her. She could count on being left alone: no one tried to communicate with her, no question of her taking part in things.

My thoughts are my own and you'll never get at them. I am inside them. Me, Flora Dalvik, a person with an entire name, an individual, the human being Flora Dalvik I will defend with my human body, however decrepit and atrophied it may be. It still has a functional brain and thoughts as all other people have; it is a living being's body.

The young women, and they were all young in relation to Flora, had impatience in their movements, as if to hurry the working day along and get it over with, so that they could hurry to the changing room, hang up their smocks and pants, and become private. Go home to their own things.

Of course there were caretakers during the night, but they weren't all that bothersome. They came in like shadows and turned her during the night. She usually knew when they would be coming, and she was ready for them.

They started appearing more often since a young girl from Polhemsgården in Solna had raised the alarm on the mistreatment of the elderly. TV showed close-ups of bedsores and blackened toes, and the girl, who was an employee of Polhemsgården, received some kind of an award for bravery, and civil courage was spoken of quite a bit.

This event, for Flora's part, meant that the white-coated assistants got her out of bed every single day, even on the weekends—in fact, especially on the weekends, since visitors could show up unexpectedly then—seated her upright and tied her to the wheelchair. They combed her thin hair and made two braids from it. She had never braided her hair. That wasn't her style.

What had been her style?

More and more, she was beginning to forget it.

She was thirty-three years old when she moved into Sven Dalvik's home. His daughter was just about five. Flora worked at his firm. Or, more exactly, she was employed as his secretary in order to assist Director Dalvik with everything he could possibly need.

Head secretary. Did that position even exist these days? She had been proud of her job. She had gone to vocational school in business administration and then gone to BarLocks. Such ambitions were rare among her acquaintances. Most of her contemporaries had gotten married and had children as soon as they finished high school.

And what did she do? Why didn't she find some nice young man and get married at a reasonable time? She had no answer. The years went by, and Mr. Right had not shown up. Of course, she had gotten some offers, quite a few, in fact, especially during the time that she went dancing and danced everywhere in town or at Hässelby Baths. Young men came there from all over Stockholm, and she knew all the tricks. She could have pulled anyone to some dark corner if she had decided on it. Just like her friends did.

No, that was too easy. And she was worried about what those city boys would say behind her back. They'd think she was just any old country girl.

She was not. She was different.

She lay on her back and stared at the ceiling. The woman in the bed next to her was in the midst of dying. The assistants had placed a screen between the beds, but the sound of approaching death could not be screened. They probably thought Flora didn't realize what was going on.

She listened to the labored breathing, each breath coming at longer intervals. The dying woman was old and had been in bad shape ever since she had arrived fourteen days earlier. It was time for her to leave the earthly plane; she was well over ninety.

The woman's son was somewhere in the room. He walked around, had trouble sitting still. He was also old. When he first entered the room, he nodded at Flora, unsure of whether she could notice him or not. She could nod back, even though she couldn't lift her head from the pillow.

He had mumbled something to the assistants about a single room, and they had explained and apologized. Lack of space and over capacity. Then they lowered their voices and Flora understood that they were talking about her.

The son appeared to be in pain; she heard him groan behind the screen. Every time he did this, his mother's breathing quickened, became shakier, as if she longed to be back in the time where she still could comfort him.

This evening, they had put her to bed early. She would be disturbed, as the assistants would be running in and out all night to see to her roommate. They would be speaking in a softened tone, as if they would not be heard just as well. They would be turning on flashlights, and the smell of coffee would drift in to her from the personnel room.

It would hardly be a good night.

She thought about Sven and thought that it was unfair. His death had gone so quickly. She also would have liked to die in such a painless, sweet way, just leave everything behind and be on her way. Instead she stayed here as a living piece of luggage, and she was demeaned and violated just like a child.

She and Sven had felt sympathy toward each other from the very beginning. And he asked her to address him informally with her, which was very unusual at the time but helped their work atmosphere quite a bit.

She quickly discovered his incompetence in various spheres, but she did her best so that he would not discover what she knew. He was hardly a company head, and Flora became aware that he had taken over the family business without much enthusiasm. He did it because it was expected of him; he had been raised his whole life to do just that. His father, Georg Dalvik, had built the concern; he was the one who had created and launched the candy named Sandy, which was now famous world-wide: "Sandy Candy fine and dandy."

Sven was not exactly the kind of man she had been dreaming of when she was young, but he was sweet. He believed in her; he turned to her when things became difficult. He also would ask her opinion whenever he wanted to buy a gift for his French wife. Because of this, she thought that she knew him and his family fairly well, even though she had never met either the wife or the daughter. He had a photo of them on his desk, a dark-haired woman, somewhat chubby, with a laughing child on her knee. The child reached behind herself to embrace her mother's neck.

Sometimes, when he was abroad, she would go and look at that photo. It was taken outdoors, in Hässelby, where he had recently bought a house. You could make out one of the gables. Flora knew exactly which one.

Sven would tell her about his gardening difficulties. He had been raised in Karlavägen, in the middle of Stockholm, and he had no experience with green things. He would tell how his wife asked him to dig a patch for vegetables, and he just raised his palms in defeat. Once he complained about the raspberry bushes, which had been hit by a mysterious illness.

Flora asked him to describe this.

"Well, some kind of brown spots on the leaves and the shoots, and it spreads and it gets spotty and gray. And there aren't any raspberries; they just shrivel up. I am so disappointed. We were going to sit on the balcony, my wife and I, and have fresh raspberries with cream."

She knew just what it was.

"I'm sorry," she said, while a warmth spread in her middle. "It's a fungus and unfortunately it is the absolute worst thing that can happen to raspberry bushes."

Her boss stared at her.

"Yes, absolutely true," she continued. "You will have to dig them all up and burn every one that has been stricken with it. Then you have to spray the rest with copper calcite fluid and copper sulfite."

"Damn, what you know!"

It was not like him to swear, but he did then.

"You've forgotten my parents had a garden center. I've been raised with copper sulfite!"

He laughed and gave her a hug. That was unusual. They hardly ever touched each other.

They only touched each other two other times. The first time was one evening when they were working overtime. Flora made tea and sandwiches for them. When she placed the tray on his desk, he embraced her waist, but he took his arm away again quickly. She understood that he had thought he was at home for a minute. He was tired. He turned red.

The other time was at a crayfish party, which had been organized for all the employees out on one of the islands. They both became drunk, both she and Sven, neither of them used to drinking so much brandy. They sat at the top of a hill and held hands, nothing more.

When Sven's wife died, he was very strong. He came back to the office after only one day. He had left his child with his parents.

He was changed, on the outside it looked like he had dropped a few pounds overnight. Otherwise, he seemed the same, but a bit quieter, a bit sorrowful.

Flora placed a pot of St Paul's in his window. Blue was the color of hope and consolation. She did not know if he even noticed it. She asked if there was anything that she could do. He turned his head toward her without looking at her.

After the funeral, he started talking about his child. Her name was Justine. She was in a difficult stage. It certainly didn't help that she had lost her mother.

"My parents can't deal with her," he said. "They've never had much patience with children. And my father has a heart condition."

Flora listened patiently. The whole time she just sat and listened, without being pushy, without giving too much advice.

The first year, he employed housekeepers, who took care of both the house and the child. Sometimes he thought about selling the house, but his wife was in the cemetery in Hässelby, and he went there a few times a week.

"Do you think that she would want me to sell it?" he would ask her. "She loved that house so much. I bought that house for her sake."

He had trouble hanging on to housekeepers. Perhaps it was too lonely, down at the beach? Too isolated?

That the girl could be behind the problem with housekeepers was a thought that never once entered into his poor, thick skull.

Chapter FIVE

The trees began to appear out of the fog, becoming black, visible. It was morning. Justine had slept the whole night sitting in the armchair, she was thirsty and her shoulders were stiff.

The same feeling as over there. But not.

Over there:

She could still feel her relief which poured through her when she finally could make out the contours of things. The thick, tropical night had begun to move off, retreat; she lay with open eyes and took it all in. How everything reappeared, the tree trunks, the leaves, how they grew and took their forms as day came. And relief spread through her, made her limbs soft. She had been awake the whole night, and finally she fell into a light sleep, just as the others began to stretch and move around in their sleeping bags.

Justine went downstairs, holding onto the handrail like a tired old woman. Yep, just like Flora used to shuffle up and down between the floors before she had to move to the hospice. She would have never gone there voluntarily, but after her stroke, she no longer had any strength.

Down there, the kitchen was dark. She lit the stove and put on a pot of water. Her dress was all wrinkled; she must have been sweating while she was asleep. She hadn't even noticed that night had come.

Was dying like that?

While leaning against the kitchen wall, she drank her tea in slow sips. Her ears strained for a sound. A sudden longing for words. Anything but silence. She called the bird. He was probably sitting on his branch and sleeping with his head turned backwards and his beak stuck under his gray feathers. He didn't come and he didn't answer. He was sitting in silence somewhere, remembering his wild origin.

The house was walled in: this chill and brooding silence like insulation. It was in the stones, the foundation, the basement, the walls. Even a sunny August day could not force in its light and life.

There. In the jungle. No silence existed there. Everywhere was living, creeping, crawling, peeping and trickling, as well as the rustling of leaves while it was all going on, an eating, chewing, steaming rot, millions of small masticating jaws that were never satisfied, the screams and the rush of rain, the howl of a saw.

She asked Nathan, "Can they really be working here with tools, isn't that called the destruction of the rain forest?"

He did not answer her, forcing her to ask again. Then he turned and his eyes were just as changed as they had been since the day that Martina had joined the group in Kuala Lumpur.

The sound was an insect. Such an insect that could make that howl, going straight to the marrow of her bones, and she froze, even though she was too hot.

Martina . . . she wasn't much bigger than an insect herself. Keep thinking like that. You grind insects under your heel until they are squished. Insects like Martina are not worth much more than that. That's what she had to keep thinking.

She herself was like the house. Made of silence and enstoned.

As if her words took time to construct, they had to search for a pathway that led out of her.

People got tired of waiting.

Nobody likes to wait for words.

Some people thought it was a sign of shyness. Others of a sense of self-importance. Her teacher used that exact word, *self-important*, about her, after only a few weeks of class. The next morning, when she thought about it, she was overcome by dizziness and sank to a squat with her head between her knees.

Flora was standing on the rag rug, right in the beige square, or maybe it was the Isabella-colored square; anyway, there she stood with her heavy, brown-lined eyelids, opening like small shutters.

"Get up, Justine!"

No. She sank deeper, into the rug. Flora was wearing boots, fine leather boots with stiletto heels. She saw the heels clearly from her position on the floor, how a tiny leaf had gotten caught in one of the points.

Flora's hand on her head, at first lightly, as if reassuring her. Then the fingers bent, the nails, her hair, like ice in their roots when she was lifted up, ooowwww.

"So, at least you can open your mouth!"

Like a pendulum, back and forth, the short, delicate strands, how they burst.

Flora put her down. It was cold, she had stayed in her bed, and heard how Flora returned through the front door. In just her nightgown, she then went down the stairs.

"Do you know what your teacher, Miss Messer, said to me this evening? She said that you were stubborn and had a sense of self-importance. Stubborn and proud. That's what she called you. I was forced to say that I was sorry, but she was absolutely correct."

"That's not true, that's not true! She hates me!"

"No strong words, Justine. No one hates. This is called raising a child and it is her duty according to the law to contribute to the raising of a child."

"Forgive me then, but tell me what I am supposed to do to get her to like me. . . ."

"If I hear a single complaint from your teacher again, I will do such things to you that even your father won't recognize you."

Justine covered her ears, her eyes turned inside out, ugly and cold in her whole body, ugly and burning. Turned her face to the floor. The same rug, that one again?

Flora's little booted foot, yes, it was little; she had heard her father say so when she stood in the hallway one night when they thought she was sleeping. She glimpsed Flora, nude and thin, like a girl, wearing her boots on the clean sheets.

Now the rug pressed against her temples, every bump and uneven spot, the smell of stale food. Flora pressed lightly with the sole, ground her foot against Justine's cheek.

"I want you to say it loud and clear. That you are a disgusting repulsive child that no one likes."

She couldn't do that.

"That you are a spoiled, nasty and lanky child that no one in the entire world could love. Say it!"

She fell unconscious and everything was gone.

The bird came, his wings whistling. She boiled a couple of eggs, gave one to the bird and ate the other one. He was a large, well-shaped creature. He peeled the egg with his beak and shook the shell and bits of egg all over the kitchen.

"Fritz?" she said, not paying attention. "Is that your name?"

The bird screeched, flapped his wings, and flew to her shoulder. She stuck her finger against his gray stomach, and felt that his body was like a warm, living broiler underneath his feathers.

"I should get you a friend," she said. "We are too lonely, you and I."

He nipped her finger, lightly, lifted it, pecked it away.

He arrived at the house the day that Flora left it. Justine saw an ad in the newspaper: "Bird for sale due to change in family circumstances. Friendly and tame."

Change in family circumstances. That was her case, too. Without thinking about it for long, she grabbed the phone. The bird was at the other end of town, Saltsjöbaden, and at first the car wouldn't start, but after a few sprays of 5-56 under the hood, she managed to get it going. It was an old Opel Rekord, and she always felt nervous using it, as it wasn't very dependable.

She drove the wrong way at Slussen, and drove in circles for a while until she found the exit for Nacka. She had drawn herself a map, using large ink lines, and thanks to that, she finally was able to arrive at the right place.

The villa appeared well taken care of, and pleasant, just like all the other houses in the area. She parked outside the gate and rang the bell. After a minute, a man came and answered, she had spoken to a woman on the phone. The man was her own age; his face was terse and reserved.

Divorce, she thought.

He knew at once who she was, and asked her to come on in. Inside the house was complete chaos. There were half-packed cardboard boxes placed throughout the hallway, a little farther in she could see the living room floor. It was covered with books, as if someone in a fit of rage had torn out everything in the bookcases. From the kitchen came the smell of something burning.

The bird was also in the kitchen, in a tall, ornate cage. It was dozing, ignored her totally.

"Is that him?" she asked. "For some reason, I thought he was a parrot."

"Why would you think that?"

"Maybe because parrots are more common pets."

"I guess. So you're not interested any more?"

"No, no. It doesn't matter what kind of bird he is."

The man took a glass coffee carafe off the stove.

"Dammit, I forgot all about this."

"Oh . . ."

He gave her a crooked smile.

"It's been kind of crazy around here."

She should say something, ask about the creature's habits and what kind of food he ate. She couldn't get the words out. There was something about the bird's ruffled, black gray appearance that made her feel like crying. As if she were hunched inside that cage, left for others to take on.

The man cleared his throat and pulled out a cardboard box.

"We're breaking up," he said.

"Yes . . . I understand."

"Yep, that's it. After so many years together, one day comes where you're no longer a family. You've taken it all for granted! Hey! Don't take anything for granted, OK?"

"I don't take things for granted."

"Well, many people do. Like me, for example. I've done it . . . up to now."

She didn't know what to say. The man was silent for a while, and then he said.

"OK. Here's the bird. He has lived with us for many years . . . he was part of our family. My wife found him out in the garden when he was young. He'd probably fallen from his nest. A cat had gotten him, a cat that wanted a toy. Know what I did with that cat? I shot him."

"You shot him?"

"With an air gun. It died on the spot."

"Is that allowed?"

"Fuck that. It's my garden and I can do whatever I want in my own garden."

"And the bird?"

"We took care of him and raised him. Well, like I said, now we're heading off in different directions, my dear wife and me. And the bird needs a home."

"He looks a little . . . scraggly. Is he healthy?"

"You know, he feels more than we think. He's listened to our discussions for months. He's sad; he knows it's time to go. He's always loved my wife. She couldn't bear to be here when you came."

"Do you think he'll be all right living with me?"

"I think so. He wants to be with whoever will have him. He knows that by instinct, and he won't be too distant from those people."

They stood next to each other and watched the bird. The man swallowed, traced his finger on one of the bars.

"Some birds live as pairs. They are faithful to each other until death!" he burst out, and saliva drops shone on his chin. "The macaws in Brazil, they're faithful to the death!"

She nodded carefully.

"All right, if you want him, take him. Take him at once. I can't deal with this. And I have to . . . keep packing."

"How much do you want for him?"

"Just take him, he's yours."

"But the ad . . ."

"Take him! Fuck the ad! I don't want a thing, not even for the cage!"

"I don't think I can take the cage."

"No cage?"

"It won't fit in my car."

He took a step to the window, looked out. When he turned back to her, his eyes were red. He took a deep breath, got ready.

"Well, I'll have to throw it out, then, or try and sell it. No, the hell with it, I'm not going to deal with any more damn ads. And we have to clip his wings, or he can be taken by impulse and fly away, and he won't last a minute with those magpies out there; they'll hack him to pieces."

Justine cried out softly.

"No . . . we can't."

She took off her scarf. It was long and thin, and she had wrapped it a few times around her neck.

"Don't cut his wings. Let me try this . . . instead."

She twisted the cage door open, and slowly, stiffly, stuck in her arm. She was a bit afraid, the man was making her nervous; she'd rather be alone. The bird opened his beak, which was black and somewhat bent. He gave out a small sound.

"Come," she whispered. "Climb up on my arm and sit down."
The man moved behind her.

"You're familiar with animals, right?"

"Yes," she mumbled, which was more or less true.

The bird took a hesitant step toward her and then sat at once on her hand. He was heavy and warm. She drew her arm back to herself. The bird kept sitting.

She placed him on the kitchen table and slowly wrapped the scarf around him. He made no attempt to escape.

She took him into her arms like a child.

"Soooo," the man whispered. "Sooooo . . ."

He was almost singing with a one-toned voice, he then turned his lips to the ceiling and gave a sound that was almost like a *yoik*. Justine burst out in sweat on her back.

She went to the door and tried to get her shoes on.

"I'll help you!" The man fell to his knees in front of her, pressed her feet into her shoes and tied the shoelaces with strong, double knots. He was silent now. He opened the door and followed her out. While she was getting in the car, he bent over the bird and kissed him loudly on the beak. Then he turned toward her, with a feeling of dismay.

"He usually strikes back when I do that. It usually works."

"Uh-huh."

Justine laid the bird down on the front seat. He looked like he was sleeping.

"Look, it's like a head of cabbage," said the man, and she noticed that he stopped using "he" and said "it."

While she started the engine, he left his hand on the open car window. It was a narrow and somewhat childlike hand.

"Well, gotta go," she said, and shifted to first. The man's knuckles turned white.

"OK then," came from somewhere above her.

When the car started to move, he let go and made a gesture as if he were waving her back. It wasn't until she got on the highway that she realized that she forgot to ask the bird's name.

She let him live in her room. She brought in a tree from the garden and placed it in a Christmas tree stand. She anchored the tree with a hook in the wall. The tree became the bird's sleeping perch. After a few hours, he had pecked off every single leaf on the branches.

He liked to be in the kitchen or come to her when she was sitting and looking out over the water. She began to find his droppings everywhere. At first she was careful to spread out newspapers and clean up after him. Now this happened more sporadically, when she realized that the house was hers and hers alone, and she must take care of it because her things were worth taking care of.

And so was she.

The roots of the fallen tree. A child could crawl underneath, even if the roots could fall, it never did happen, and she sat there and let earth fall onto the back of her neck.

The animals: small animals, with snouts, shimmering fur tufts. Or the deer, standing still right where the forest met the meadow, wet nostrils, the whites of its eyes. On the other side of the shading roots, they surrounded her, circled in, and she was Snow White, left behind by the Hunter. She thought of him and a light swelling arose between her legs; she had already had her first blood, but she was still a child, and yet.

And he led her into the forest and lifted his rifle. Aimed right at her left breast.

She sat next to the dead deer once he left, she looked at its wound. He had dug around in there, taking its heart with him. What was a deer? She did not know, but the body was mangled and now the Hunter was carrying its heart to the woman who lived in Snow White's home.

I did what you asked me with the girl.

Sudden fragility, then the mirror, looking at her reflection.

Satisfaction.

The foxes came, and the mice. And like snowflakes, the feathers of the owls fell upon the place where Snow White was sitting, warm and covering snow.

Animals made Flora ill, made her shudder and feel nauseous. A cat sneaked into the front hall, and she chased it out with a broom, its fur and tail straight up.

When Pappa said good night, Justine told him about it.

His face melted and he stroked her hand weakly, for a long time, but weakly.

Every evening for evenings on end, she asked Pappa for a pet. A cat or a dog or a bird. Maybe he would have liked to give her one, but Flora's moods controlled him completely.

"They are flea-covered, filthy things," she would say and her painted, porcelain eyes would stare without mercy. "Bacteria. Smells. Animals are animals and should not be in human homes."

The blue fox fur was another matter. It was dead. She received it one day in the middle of winter, a conciliatory gesture. Flora often needed to be appeased.

Chapter SIX

Berit Assarsson was late getting out for lunch. She didn't know where she wanted to eat, her hunger had dissipated, but she still needed to stuff something into herself if she was going to make it through the rest of the day.

She was editing a book on sailing. She really didn't know all that much about sailing, but since the book was going to be published and she had been given the job of making sure that it was ready to go, she didn't want to reveal her weaknesses to all and sundry.

Tor had had a boat when they met, and of course it was nice to glide out among the islands and seek night harbor in a protected cove. But all the rest of it. He lost his temper easily and expected her to keep track of all the ropes and their ends, and in a crisis he always forgot that she just couldn't do it. So there were always arguments and hard feelings.

They sold the boat and bought a summer place instead. For a summer place, it was fairly large, a house built at the end of the nineteenth century situated on Vät Island. It had been winterized, so they were able to celebrate Christmas there, which they often did. This past Christmas, both of their sons brought their girlfriends with them.

Berit went into the food halls at Hötorget. It was just past one o'clock in the afternoon, and the worst lunch crush was over. She ordered an avocado salad with shrimp and a large café au lait and sat down at one of the tables near the flower department. Such wonderful tulips you can get nowadays, what wonderful colors! If only the weather would change to be just a bit colder so that snow would come and lighten things up a bit.

The avocado was somewhat hard. She thought about going back to the counter and complaining, but she didn't. How many times had she sat here in the food hall and eaten lunch? At least once a week during all the years she had been employed at the publisher's. She tried figuring it out in her head: 46 weeks a year times fourteen years would be, would be, would be . . .

As a matter of fact, she had been traveling when she turned forty-five last year. Tor had surprised her with a round-the-world ticket.

"Couldn't you have waited until I turned fifty!" she exclaimed, practically alarmed over his sudden generosity.

He had hugged her quickly and clumsily.

"Who knows whether we'll still be around then."

So they went and were gone for almost two entire months. So that was eight weeks and therefore eight times when she didn't eat in the food halls. She dug around in her purse for her mini-calculator, but didn't find it. She had to take out a ball-point pen and work it out just as Miss Messer had taught them during their schooldays so long ago.

Six hundred times or more she had had lunch here in this little restaurant near the bottom of the escalator. Over six hundred times!

Well, Berit, this is your life!

More and more often she felt sad over her condition. She felt that her life had passed its peak, and quite a while ago at that, and now everything was too late.

Everything, what everything?

She sometimes talked about this with Annie, who had the office next to hers. They had both begun at the publishing house at the same time, both had been home with the kids for a while before then, both had sons.

Everything . . . you've been waiting for, everything that was supposed to happen.

Annie agreed. Even though she was four years younger, she was thinking the same thing.

I wonder when it ended, she thought. *I wonder when that change came, the change from a young, hopeful human being to a robotic machine.*

She was far from being old. Sometimes men still looked at her with that special look in their eyes, but usually only after they had been introduced. Otherwise, she was hardly ever visible. Of course she took care of her body, took care of her face, never left her house without her make-up on, not even in the countryside. Every fifth week she went to her hairdresser, a handsome black man, who knew exactly how best to cut her hair.

Too bad he's gay, she thought. *I've never done it with a black man.* She turned red from shame at the mere thought.

She let her eyes wander around the food stalls, as she almost always saw someone she knew while she was here, and sure enough, here comes Elizabeth, gliding across the room. Elizabeth had an unusual way of sashaying so that everything that was in her way was swept aside.

She saw Berit, and turned her mouth to a smile.

"Darling Berit, here you are all alone; can I join you for a minute? What are you having . . . café latte? I'll take one as well."

"I have to go soon, but go ahead and sit down. I don't have to rush."

Elizabeth also worked in the publishing business, at Bonniers, in the big white building on Sveavägen.

"How are you, darling, you seem a bit pale?"

"I do?"

"Oh, that's probably just the light here, nothing to worry about."

"As a matter of fact, I am a little tired."

"You are? We've had a few weeks off, but maybe you had to work through Christmas?"

"No, no. I'm not that kind of tired."

"Oh, I know exactly what you mean. It's this eternal gray weather. If only we had a bit more chill, so that the ice would come; I am so longing for the ice this year. We have not yet been skating one single time. And in the middle of January! Do you think it could be this El Niño thing affecting us all the way here in Scandinavia?"

"I haven't the vaguest idea."

"Well, it's dull, dull, dull, that I know. Tell me, anything new?"

"Not really. How about you?"

"Lots of work, as always."

"Same here. Same old same old . . . I'm thinking that it could be last year, or the year before, or the year before that, even. Everything the same. I think I'm getting burned out."

"Oh my dear, dear friend. Isn't it fun any more?"

"Fun is as fun does."

Elizabeth leaned closer over the round, white iron table.

"I've heard them say . . . Curt Lüding is thinking of selling?"

Curt Lüding was Berit's boss. He had started the business in the middle of the seventies, and he belonged to the young opposition, the kids who fought at the barricades. In those days, he published underground literature and socially critical novels. He was done with that now. Times had changed.

"The same old rumor," even as she said it, she felt her stomach lurch.

"You haven't heard anything specific?"

"No. You?"

"Nah. Nothing worth noticing."

"Bonniers wants to take over?"

"Well, yes."

Berit poked at a piece of corn with her fork, put it in her mouth.

"It's not at all pleasant with these rumors going around," she said. "Maybe that's why people are feeling down. That uncertainty. I'm really going to ignore work all weekend long. I'm not going to think about it for one minute! I'm going to try and get out instead, maybe take a long walk this Saturday. Maybe I'll go out to Hässelby and see to my parents' graves there, and then take a long walk through nature out there and feel some nostalgia. I haven't been there for who knows how long."

On the way back to work, she sneaked into a shop for luxury lingerie on Drottninggatan. She tried on some bras and decided on a red shiny one with underwire and a pair of matching panties. The sharp lighting made her thighs and stomach look like dough.

My body, she thought. *Just like an autopsy report.*

Six hundred and ninety crowns.

What you do for a minute of happiness!

She longed for some chocolate and walked hurriedly past the Belgian chocolate shop. She had bought some hand-made chocolate snails there for the boys' girlfriends last Christmas. Those girls were thin as sticks; they could use a little more weight on their bones.

She felt strange around them. They resembled each other: awkward, blonde, flat-chested. They hung on the boys the whole time, pawing them and whimpering like spoiled children whenever they thought no one heard them. She never would have acted like that with Tor's parents! His mother would have driven her from the door.

Helle and Marika. Helle was Danish, how she ended up in Stockholm was anybody's guess. Berit had tried to chat with them, find out a bit about their backgrounds. They were sullen and silent. Or maybe just shy. She kept up her humor for the sake of her boys.

Now it had really started to rain; she opened her umbrella and used it as a shield against the wind. When she was passing the Russian restaurant, she was forced to cross the street. The locale was being scraped bare, an excavator was in the middle of the sidewalk. She wondered what was coming next. She had eaten there a few times. Full-bodied stews and piroges. It had been cozy and warm and, whenever she was really depressed, she had eaten there and gathered her strength.

The elevator to their floor was out of order. She walked up four flights of stairs, trailing a wet line after her umbrella. She hung up her things and went to her office. It was unusually quiet everywhere. Was there a meeting that she had forgotten? No, Annie was sitting at her desk, her arms were hanging down and she wasn't working. Just sitting there with a lifeless look on her face.

"What's going on, Annie? Something happen?"

Annie motioned her over.

"Come on in."

Then she got up and closed the door.

"Now things are going to change!"

A shudder went down Berit's spine.

"What do you mean?"

"Curt's up to something."

"Up to what?"

"He's calling an employee meeting. Not today, not tomorrow, but on Monday of all the damn days of the week."

"Employee meeting?"

"Yep. Apparently something he wants to tell us all together."

"Is he going to fire us?"

"Who the heck knows."

"But . . . where is he now?"

"Going to a meeting. Gone the rest of the day. Gone tomorrow, too."

"Oh, Annie . . . what are we going to do?"

"Do? Nothing we can do until Monday. Just wait. All day tomorrow and wait all weekend, too."

"Why did he bring it up now? Why couldn't he wait until Monday then?"

Annie shrugged. Her hair was a mess. She ought to do something with it.

"What did he look like? How did he make the announcement?"

"Like always. A big port-salut cheese for a face."

Berit took a paperclip from the desk and began to twist and turn it, bend it backwards.

"I met Elizabeth at lunch, you know, that blonde who works over at Bonniers."

"That little gossip."

"Oh, she's not that bad. But she was cryptically hinting that Curt was going to sell to Bonniers."

"We've heard that one before, and nothing's ever come of it."

"Well, what if now is the time? Why do you think he's calling for an employee meeting?"

"You think. So we can be Bonniers employees."

"You would be. You're still fairly young. But me, I'm turning forty-six this year. I'm not so sure that The Big Boys will take on an old lady like me."

Annie was silent for a moment.

"But . . . if he's selling the company, he's selling us, too, like, we're part of the deal," she exclaimed. "I mean . . . we go, too. Otherwise, he has to buy us out somehow. Some kind of employment termination amount."

"Ha! Do you have a golden parachute I don't know about?"

"No."

The paper clip broke and snagged her thumb.

"What is everyone else saying?"

"Same stuff. They're scared shitless. Lotta even got a stomach ache and had to go home."

Berit went to the kitchen and started a pot of coffee. It was messy and cluttered as usual: dirty coffee mugs, an empty Lean-Cuisine package. She picked that up and tossed it into the garbage, and exclaimed, "Goddamn pit, this place!"

"Come and have coffee," she angrily called out into the hall, as if it were an order. Everyone came, silent and worried.

The publishing business had twelve employees, including Carl Lüding himself. Non-fiction was their best seller. Or had been. They had one real best-selling author, Sonja Karlberg, who wrote old-fashioned romance novels that, strangely enough, were hits with contemporary readers. She appeared to be a mild and fragile old lady, but Annie, who was her editor, began to feel ill the moment that Sonja Karlson called and said she was on the way in. Sonja Karlson could be furious over the slightest correction and once threw a galley down so hard that both the galley and Annie's keyboard broke apart.

Silently, everyone took a seat, sipping from their coffee mugs. Outside, dusk was coming, and raindrops had begun to hit the window panes. Berit glanced at the pots with the green plants in the window and noticed that no one had watered them. They were withering. Her stomach knotted. She loved all of this, all these faces around the table now heavy with worry, the mess, the bundles of manuscripts, the stress, the books off to printers, everything that was a part of her work.

She had studied languages at the university. She had no idea what she wanted to do, and chance brought her to the world of publishing. A teeny-tiny ad from a teeny-tiny press that wanted an editor. The house was Strena, and it had since gone out of business, but for a few years, Berit corrected manuscripts for thrillers, and that proved lucrative during the time she married and had children.

At an office party, she began to talk with Carl Lüding. As it turned out, he was expanding his business and he hired her on the spot without demanding a formal degree. But that was the way it tended to turn out for most of them in the publishing world, the hand of chance.

Berit's husband Tor was an accountant. The first few years, they lived in his cramped, one-room apartment on Thulegatan. It was a challenging time. When the boys were two and three, the family could finally move to a house of their own in Ängby.

Now the boys had moved.

Out of the nest.

She sometimes was sad about not having them home any longer. Now they were grown men and they were lost to her forever.

She left the office early that day, at four in the afternoon. On the way home, she bought two ox fillets and a bottle of red wine. Tor had not come home yet. She changed clothes and set the table in the dining room, using candles and the linen napkins.

"He's going to think we have something to celebrate," she thought bitterly.

When she heard him drive in the garage, she put butter in the frying pan and uncorked the wine.

He opened the outer door and hung up his coat, and she heard the thud of his shoes as he untied them and kicked them toward the wall. He came to the kitchen, looking weary.

"I thought we could cheer ourselves up a bit," she said.

"Well, all right, but why?"

"Why not?"

"Something special? An anniversary or something?"

"Not that I know of. But shouldn't we have the right to have a cheerful dinner on an average Thursday evening?"

"All right, then."

They ate their dinner in silence. Berit drank quite a bit of wine, which went to her head and made her tipsy.

"What's going on with you?" he asked.

"What do you mean with me?"

"Something's going on, I can tell."

"Tor, tell me the truth. Are you still attracted to me?"

"Berit!"

"Come on! Do I make you hard and horny?"

He pushed away his plate.

"Why are you blathering about that now?"

"I'm not blathering. I'm asking you a straight question and I want a straight answer. Is that so damned strange?"

"You're my wife."

"That's exactly why I'm asking!"

She got up and went around the table, behind him, and placed her hands on his head. He had just begun to go bald right on the top of the skull, she caressed him right there, then let her hands glide down to his shirt, his middle.

"Berit," he said. "I want to finish eating."

On Saturday she took the subway out to Hässelby. It felt strange to be riding the subway on the weekend instead of the usual work day, its totally different kinds of passengers, many children and their parents, a different kind of light, other colors, other sounds. She noticed how dirty and rundown everything looked. The floor of the car was blotchy with particles and dried fluids; many of the seats had so much graffiti they looked black.

Snow had come during the night, and it had stayed. She got off at the final station and her memories washed over her, memories from her teenage years. While she walked to the bus stop, she noticed that the area surrounding the subway had been renovated and renewed. The Konsum grocery store was gone. Instead there was a budget store with flashy red sale signs.

She had planned walking to the cemetery, but since the bus was already there, she rode the few stops. The sun glistened on the snow cover, which made her eyes water. She should have brought her sunglasses!

The cemetery looked idyllic, practically countryside, with its snow-covered gravestones and the blue titmouses chattering in the branches. On the right side of the chapel, there was a heap of snow-covered wreaths. Friday was a typical funeral day. Both her parents were buried on a Friday, first her mother and then, two years later, her father.

Except for the occasional car going by on Sandviksvägen, it was peaceful and quiet here. The graveyard is the resting place of the dead, as the sign on the entrance stated; here you weren't supposed to disturb the peace by being loud. The dead had had enough of that in life and now they had the right to rest in peace.

She was alone. She looked around. In one of the apartments back there on Fyrspannsgatan, a young daughter of a doctor had been held prisoner by a psychopath. That was over a year ago and she suddenly remembered the details of the story. The girl had stood at one of the windows and hoped that someone would see her and take action. But who would take action by seeing a girl in a window? Even if she were screaming and calling for help?

How was it going for that girl now? According to the papers, she escaped with her life, but what about her psyche? She must be psychologically damaged for ever after?

Berit wondered about which window it had been. The evening tabloids had certainly shown pictures of the house with a circle around the window in question. Curious onlookers had definitely come by just to see the place and try to understand what it must had been like to be caught in the hands of a psycho.

A thought entered her mind to produce a book about the girl. Convince her to write a diary about the awful time she had been imprisoned. She was surprised that Melin & Gartner hadn't done that already, as they usually were the first to publish books of that sort. Criminals and victims, suspects and police: those were the kinds of books that sell.

Here she was, thinking about work again! Even though she told herself she wouldn't do that!

She felt her way along the shoveled and sanded little path. Over there to the left, the family grave, which would probably only ever hold two people. Family grave, an idea from previous eras, when people lived among their folks.

The grave was covered with snow. She brushed the snow off with her mittens and said the names of those two people who had been her parents out loud. Her conscience nagged her; she really ought to come here more often.

She had bought two grave candles, one for each.

"One for Mamma, one for Pappa," she whispered, while she tried to light the two votives. It was harder than she thought, as every puff of wind blew out the matches, even though the wind wasn't that strong.

"I think of you anyway," she whispered, "even if it doesn't look like it. Even if I don't come here so often. I think of you both from time to time, and you must know that. If you see me now, if you are moving above me invisibly, keep a watchful eye on me. Right now I really wish you could do that."

Both of them had died of cancer. Her father had been a big smoker. His labored breathing returned to her, his scratching at the throat opening when he didn't get enough air.

"Whatever you do, my girl," he would say whenever she came to visit him in the hospital, "don't ever start smoking!"

He didn't know that she had already been smoking for a while, and the sight of his emaciated body on the sheets could not bring her to stop.

Her mother had skin cancer, the same kind that took Tage Danielsson's life in the early eighties.

They were already old when they had her, just as old as she was now. They could have died of simple old age. Her mother had told her that she thought she was barren, but when she began to throw up her breakfast every morning for a whole week, she realized that she wasn't.

Berit left the grave with the votive flames barely visible in the January sun. She followed Hässelby Strandväg and walked past the house she had lived in when she was growing up. It hadn't changed. She wondered who lived there now, but she saw no sign of life and the walk was white from snow that hadn't been shoveled.

She had gone this way from her house to the school every day when she was little. There were more houses, but nevertheless, time seemed to have stood still here. She didn't have any contact with her classmates now, and she barely remembered their names.

Part 1: Chapter Six

Lake Mälar was smooth, a bit of mist rose slightly above the surface. She longed for ice, longed to put on her skates and skate right out to the horizon, away from everything that surrounded her, everyday life, people, away from her own self. She suddenly noticed that her hands were freezing and she had left her mittens at the grave.

She found herself standing in front of a narrow stone house. An inner picture of the house remained in her head from her childhood.

Justinn försvinn, Justinn försvinn.

Get lost, Justine. Get lost and stay lost!

A chorus of high voices, and she was a member of that chorus and her own voice was one of them.

Justine went in, Justine went out, when she went in, she pissed again.

The sound became louder to the point she got dizzy.

A woman was standing by the door. She had short, curly hair, and was wearing pants with a flower motif. Something about her was familiar. Berit waved.

"Justine?" she said doubtfully. "Justine, is that you?"

The woman came down to her. Her eyes were green and her look was straightforward.

"Berit Blomgren! How strange! I was just thinking of you."

The words echoed inside her.

"You were?"

The woman laughed.

"As a matter of fact, I really was."

"My last name is Assarson nowadays. . . ."

"Oh of course, you've gotten married."

"Yes."

"I was just going to get my old kick-sled. These days you can't use a kick-sled that often, but at least today it looks like winter."

"We had kick-sleds, too, when we were little. I got a red one, which my pappa painted for me."

"Mine was just varnished. It's out in the shed. But why don't you come in for a minute? You look like you're freezing."

"Hmm, maybe I am. I just came from the cemetery. I must have left my mittens there."

"Would you like some *glögg?* I have some left over from Christmas."

"*Glögg?* Sure, that would be great. *Glögg* warms you from the inside out."

The sun flowed over the floor. Berit sipped her *glögg* and felt warmth return.

"How many years has it been?" said Berit softly,. "since we last saw each other?"

"1969, when we finished grade school."

"Must have been."

She thought a minute.

"Jesus, that was over thirty years ago!"

"Yep."

"You've lived here . . . still here in your parents' house?"

"Yes, indeed."

"You've been here the whole time?"

"Uh-huh."

"Are they deceased? I remember seeing something about your father in the paper. There was quite a write-up, I believe."

"Oh yes, my pappa is dead. Flora is in a nursing home."

"Flora, yes, that was your mother's name. I always thought that it was such a pretty name. She was really beautiful, your mother, and she always smelled so good."

"She wasn't my real mother."

"I know."

She took another sip of the *glögg*. It was strong and well-spiced.

"My parents are buried over in the graveyard there. They were very old, you probably remember. I didn't stay here in Hässelby very long. I had to get away from here. I met my husband soon after that. He's called Tor, by the way; he's an accountant. Sounds dull, doesn't it?"

Justine smiled. "Have some more *glögg*. We might as well finish it up, Christmas is over."

"*Skål.*"

"*Skål* yourself. To our meeting up again."

"But really . . . why were you thinking of me today exactly? That sounds so odd. The exact day when I am here in Hässelby, you think of me and then we meet up again, like fate."

"It really wasn't fate. You walked here yourself."

"Yes, but . . . I was just wandering around thinking about the past."

"*Auld lange syne.*"

"Maybe so."

"Do you have any children, Berit?"

"Two. Boys, twenty-one and twenty-two. They've moved out now. We're just by ourselves now, Tor and me. Now we can really be there just for each other. What about you?"

Justine shook her head.

Then she stuck her fingers in her mouth and whistled a sharp short whistle. There was swishing behind them, the room shrunk, it squawked and something sharp scraped her skull, caught in her hair.

"My God! What the hell!"

She screamed and leapt to her feet, spilling her mug of *glögg* all over her pants.

Chapter SEVEN

An animal was lying in the forest. An animal that looked like a dog.

First she saw just his head; around him were leaves and moss. She just saw his head, but she wasn't afraid, and she went home without being seen.

She found the washtub in the basement, where Flora was keeping clothespins. She dumped them into a corner, filled the washtub with water, and returned.

The animal drank. Some water ran out onto the moss, but the throat moved and it swallowed. She saw that the animal had been without water for quite some time.

Was it a dog? She touched the tangled fur. It wrinkled its nose and showed its yellow teeth.

The animal didn't have a collar. The body was in the moss and the twigs of the lingonberry bushes were bent and red.

"You can't come home with me," Justine said. "A witch lives in my house and she will put the evil eye on you. But I will come back and bring you food and water, I promise."

He was rough all around the neck. She gave him a name.

She said his name as loud as she dared, but he did not move his body, and his tail could not be seen in the moss.

She took meat with her the next day. Without Flora noticing, she took a piece of her cutlet and wrapped it in a handkerchief.

The animal was still there, like before.

She could no longer see his eyes.

When she placed the bit of meat next to his nose, his tongue came out a bit.

But he did not eat.

She never saw him again.

Pappa came up to her room one evening.
"Do you want to say your prayers with me?
"Ourfatherwhoartinheaven," she began.
He leaned over her, kissed her behind her ear.
"And who are we thinking about now, just you and me, just us two."
"Mamma," she whispered.
His face fell and he looked sad.
"I also have to tell you that tomorrow when you wake up, I won't be here."
"No!" Justine flew out of bed.
He pleaded with her, but that just made her angry.
"You have to stay here!"
"But I must travel to Switzerland."
He lowered his voice.
"You know, that's close to where your mother came from."
"Then I want to go, too!"
"My sweet child, that's not possible. You understand. It's a business trip. And you have to go to school. I have my work; you have school; we both have our daily duties."
She beat against his hands, against his stupid legs.
He placed her back in her bed, and left the room.
He was gone in the morning.

She thought about the animal. The animal could be her daily duty.
But Flora came to get her at school, which she hadn't expected.
Flora was dressed in her little black dress and pearls. A purse dangled from her wrist, held by a bronze chain.
"We're going to Vällingby," she said. "We are going to a café.

They began to walk down the hill.

"You could try to be happy. For once!"

Flora held her hand and minced along the way ladies do when they want to appear beautiful.

Flora was beautiful.

"Tell me what you did in school today," she said.

"I don't know."

"Of course you know."

"We read some, I think, and did addition."

Her hand was hard around Justine's fingers.

"Read some and did addition, you think!"

Justine had to pee. She wanted to pull her hand from Flora's, but Flora would not like that. Flora was her mother now, and she had to be Flora's child.

Once they arrived in Vällingby, Flora went shopping. Justine had to hold her purse while she tried on clothes.

A bare arm came out.

"Miss, this one is too big, could you bring me size thirty-four instead?"

The imperial ways of the shopkeepers, how they swept in and out, carrying the clothes. Flora came out wearing new dresses, twirled around and showed herself.

"Well, Justine, what do you think? Shall I take this one? Do you think Pappa would like to see me in this?"

First then did the shopkeepers notice her. Their expressions softened. Your mother certainly is lovely, isn't she!

Once they reached the café, she was finally able to go to the bathroom.

When she came out, Flora had already ordered a cola and a pink and puffy Napoleon pastry.

Flora didn't eat anything, just sipped her coffee from a very small cup.

The tables had checkered tablecloths. The place smelled strongly of smoke. Next to their table there was a child the same age as Justine who was with an older lady who was just spitting some saliva into a napkin in order to wipe the child's face.

"Oh Grandma!" said the child, but she didn't squirm. She bit into her bun and stuck her tongue out at Justine. It was covered with doughy clumps.

Flora's red nails.

"Eat, now, Justine! Eat!"

At a different table, there was a man with a newspaper. He looked toward them. He smiled at Justine and winked. His hair was shiny black like a chocolate cake.

When Flora shook a cigarette out of the package, he was there right away with a light.

She bent her neck gracefully.

"Eat, Justine!" she repeated. "You have to eat the whole thing. I'm warning you. I'm not going to buy pastries just so you can leave them half uneaten."

"Children are funny, aren't they?" said the man.

Flora blew out smoke. Her lips left a red mark on the cigarette.

"They can also be a pain," she said.

Justine took small bites. She had already eaten the pink, raspberry inside. All that was left looked like fat, creamy porridge.

She thought about the animal. She was not going to make it there today.

The man had pulled his chair closer to their table. The other girl and her grandmother had left.

"Can you sing?" the man asked, smiling at Justine. His lips were dry and thin. His tie was fastened by a dark green stone which shifted color when he moved.

She stared at her spoon. It was sticky all the way up the handle.

"All girls can sing," the man continued.

Flora giggled. She sounded like a child, her white teeth as tiny as a baby's.

"If you sing, I'll give you a crown," said the man, and he placed his hand on the table. His hand had short black hair and wide flat nails. He drummed a bit with his fingertips.

"Child!"

Flora's iron pinch on her chin, the skin forced together.

"Show the man that you can sing!"

She pulled herself free.

"What is her name?"

"Justine."

"Strange name."

"It's French."

"So maybe she does not understand what we are saying to her?"

"She just has the ability to turn off. But she understands all right. And if she doesn't finish her food, she knows what will happen when we get home."

"What will happen then, Madame?"

"She'll get a thorough spanking."

"From you?"

"From me indeed!"

"So Madame is a strict person?"

"Yes, strict is the word."

"Are you from there yourself?"

"Excuse me?"

"Are you French?"

Flora giggled again. She said a name that sounded like Bertil.

By now the man had pushed his chair between Flora and Justine. He sat so close that Justine could smell his aftershave. It was so strong, stronger than perfume, that her nose began to itch and run.

"Shooo-stine," said the man.

She did not dare to look at him, but looked at her plate, the surrounding flower design and the gooey mess in the middle.

"Haven't you finished yet!"

Flora's porcelain eyes, eyelashes long and painted in numerous layers. Every morning she stood in the bathroom and brushed on layer after layer with a short, strong brush.

"I . . . can't!"

It came out as a scream, though she didn't mean to. She had meant to whisper, but the word came screeching out in spite of herself. Her tears burned against her hand; her mouth changed the scream into a howl.

Flora hit her. Right in the middle of the café, Flora gave her a hearty slap. The howl cut right off.

"Justine is a bit of a hysterical child," she said. Her red lips had also left their mark on the coffee cup.

"Her French nerves?" the man said with a fake French accent.

Flora's new little laugh, sultry and cooing.

They took a cab home. The backseat was filled with shopping bags. The driver joked about the bags: did you buy up all of Vällingby, ladies? Flora joked back. The perfume of the man followed them into the taxi.

Once they arrived home, Flora unpacked all the clothes and hung them on hangers in the bedroom. There were two dresses, a blouse and a skirt. Her movements were twitchy. She pulled down one dress and threw it on the bed.

"Why did I buy this one! In this light, I can see this color doesn't fit my skin one bit! I'm sorry I bought it! This is all your fault, Justine! You've put me in this mess. You are spoiled rotten!"

She grabbed Justine's ankles and spun her around, faster and faster, until her body was off the ground, the blood left her brain, and she felt like vomiting. Her leg hit the side of the bed, and Flora lost her balance and fell over. Justine ended up next to the wall with her knees tight against the molding.

Flora took her into the basement. She poured water into the wash tub. Justine sat on the edge of the counter in just her panties and a camisole.

"Do you know how we get the laundry clean? Have you watched me do the laundry? You've seen how I boil the water so that the clothes get completely clean. But first I set the clothes to soak."

And she lifted Justine with her cold fingertips, and set her into the tub. The water came up to her stomach. She hugged her legs, holding them against her belly button.

Flora had gone. She had stomped her way up the stairs and Justine heard her turn the key two turns. When Justine carefully adjusted her position, the water splashed against the wash tub's rough sides.

The water was cold now, but what if Flora came back and fired up underneath it? How much heat could she stand? Would she be like a frog lying on the serving tray with white eyes? Would her flesh get so tender it would fall off her bones when they lifted her up?

Flora wouldn't dare.

Once when Pappa was gone, Flora locked her in the basement until late at night. She came down in her robe, waved matches around, but then put them aside. She drained the water and picked Justine up onto her knees. Justine's feet were spongy and wrinkled and her toenails felt like they were going to fall off.

Flora had brought a towel and Justine's pajamas. She had dried Justine off right there in the basement and put on her pajamas. Then she carried Justine up the stairs and laid her in her own bed and pulled the covers up over them both. Flora's arm had lain across her chest and she had felt Flora's angular pelvis against her back all night long.

Now she sat completely still. She thought she heard voices. She thought that Pappa had come home and now he was going to be really angry. But then the voices drifted away.

She could climb out of the wash tub, but she couldn't get down off the counter. She would have to grow a bit more for that. She saw a spider crawling along the wall. She was afraid of spiders and stared at it until it turned around and went back to its hole. One of her shins hurt where it had hit the bed when

Flora was whirling her about. Flora said that people who tended toward hysteria would be made better by twirling them about properly. Once she had taken hold of Justine's ankles and spun her until she did not know up from down.

"This is what doctors did in the olden days for people who were sick in the head. Blood is forced to the brain so that they get more oxygen. If you throw up, that's even better, because you get rid of the craziness that way. I'd spin you even more if I had the energy. But you're getting much too heavy."

Pappa came back from his trip. He gave her an instrument, shiny as gold and decorated with tassles.

"When you're big, you can lead an entire orchestra."

She had to be outside with her instrument, far away in the garden. She blew into it and a sound came out. Her father came down to listen to her. He called to Flora, and the two of them stood under the apple tree and listened to her blow into the golden horn.

"That's not easy, I swear. Clearly she has a gift. Do you hear her? I should make sure she takes lessons."

"Girls aren't supposed to play the trumpet!"

"It's not a trumpet, Flora, it's a horn. An old mail horn from Lucerne."

Neither he nor Flora could get a squeak from that horn. Justine took a deep breath. Her lips lost feeling.

Pappa was able to fasten a hook into the wall above her bed. He wasn't very handy and he usually became angry when he had to screw things in or hammer a nail. But now the horn was hanging on the wall, held by its red silk ribbon.

He forgot about the lessons. Now and again, Justine reminded him of his promise, but he only said, Drat! I've forgotten that again. She would stand by the edge of the water and blow her horn. She imagined herself in a parade, wearing a jacket and pleated skirt. All the streets in town were closed. Justine went first, the other musicians following her like rats.

Chapter EIGHT

After working the night shift at the hotel, Hans Peter usually slept until ten-thirty the next morning. If things were light, he sometimes could take a catnap during the night on the cot behind the curtain at the reception desk. He often thought he was a wealthy man. He had an abundance of time.

He used his time to exercise and read. Once, on the back page of an American magazine, he found a list of the most important classics of literature throughout world history and he got the idea to read them all, from the *Iliad* to *Das Kapital*. It was impossible to buy all those books, even at used bookstores, so he often was forced to go to the great City Library on Sveavägen in order to find them. "Forced" was the right word. The atmosphere in the library was somber, though he couldn't figure out why. Those people taking care of the books, daily confronted with book-hungry patrons, shouldn't they be just a little bit more cheerful? Couldn't the books light up their lives? Each time he showed his library card and named the book he wanted to check out, he felt assaulted, as if his mere presence created difficulties for the woman behind the checkout counter. They were worse than the cashiers at the department store in Bucharest, where he had visited once in the eighties before the fall of Ceausescu.

Even when he was a boy, he felt that taking out books was awkward. He picked out a great heap of books, but the librarian informed him that he could only take out three at a time. And so she held up each book: this one or this one? He got so confused that he did not go back for many years, and he had asked his mother to take the three books that he finally had chosen.

Right now he was reading *Don Juan* by Lord Byron in C.V.A. Strandberg's translation. It was a thick and remarkably funny book in verse, and he had found it in a used book store. It had been published by Fitzes Bokförlag in the year 1919 and there was an *ex libris* plate on the inside flypaper which revealed that the person who once had owned it was named Axel Hedman.

Things like this tickled Hans Peter's curiosity. Immediately he began to research who this Hedman was, and eventually he found out that Axel Hedman had been a former instructor in Latin who was condemned for the murder of his housekeeper a few years after this book had been published.

She was certainly not just his housekeeper, thought Hans Peter. The woman had been fairly young, as he discovered in an old newspaper from the time which had published a photo of the dead woman. She had thick, pronounced lips and appeared sensual. Instructor Hedman had defended himself by saying that the woman had used him and was after his savings. Apparently, the court didn't put much stock in that.

Perhaps instructor Hedman had been sitting in his cell on Långholmen and reading this very book? Right now Hans Peter was sitting at the reception desk with the book open behind a newspaper, which he used to cover it the moment anyone came and needed his help.

This didn't happen all that often. Actually, each guest could be given a key to the outer door so that they could take care of themselves and that would have been fine. But Ulf, who owned the hotel, didn't want that. He wanted class at his establishment. And there was no class in a place without a night receptionist.

The hotel was called Tre Rosor and was centrally located in the middle of Drottninggatan. It had ten double rooms and the same number of single rooms. The standard was simple, a washbowl in the room with the toilet and shower down the hall. Many of the guests were regulars, and a fifty-year-old man seemed to have moved into one of the rooms for good.

"He's all right," said Ulf. "He pays and takes care of himself. He likes living in the middle of the city without worrying about the responsibility of his own place."

Sometimes, middle-aged couples came who were definitely not married to each other. Hans Peter was good at noticing the signs. They paid in advance, and at midnight, they often departed, with a different bearing—eyes more shiny, they spoke with softer voices.

"We're just going to take a little walk," the man might say as he placed the key on the desk.

But they didn't return. At any rate, not that particular night.

Ulf owned many different hotels. Every once in a while, he asked Hans Peter out to lunch or dinner; he probably thought he had a bit of responsibility toward him, since they had been brothers-in-law.

"You bookworms," he said, indicating his sister the librarian.

Ulf didn't much care for reading.

"Made-up stories, what's the point? People that some guy just thought up. Shouldn't you care more about real people in real life?"

"The one doesn't necessarily exclude the other."

"I don't know about that. Wouldn't it be better for you to get out more and find yourself a new little lady that you could throw in your lot with?"

Sometimes he came to Hans Peter's place and was always surprised at the number of books. He stroked the spines and wondered how many volumes Hans Peter had.

"Have you really read all these?"

"You ask that every single time."

"How many hundreds and hundreds are there?"

"Hundreds? You mean thousands!"

They were very different types, but they got along well. Ulf was also divorced and some time after Hans Peter's

divorce, they took a trip together to London where they pub-
hopped and talked about life.

He had found a good job. Ulf was a great boss. Even if
there was no real status in being a night clerk, the most important thing must be what he himself felt about it.

At the end of January, it turned cold. A great deal of snow
came and Hans Peter started taking long walks when he woke
up right before lunchtime. Sometimes he thought about getting a dog. Maybe a boxer or some other kind of pleasant dog.
The problem was that he couldn't take the dog to work.
People had allergies; the hotel would lose customers.

He thought about the dog he had once taken care of when
he was a boy. His family had rented a summer cottage on the
island of Gotland. Next to them was an older couple with a
little roly-poly dachshund which looked like a sausage, and for
the first few days, Hans Peter was afraid of it. The woman
showed him how to hold out his hand with a piece of sugar
cake and tell the dog to sit. Then the dog bent her hind legs
behind her and sat; he could see her long tummy and her small
white teats. She would not touch the sugar cake until Hans
Peter let her. "Here you go," you were supposed to say. Then
she put her head to one side and gulped down the cake.

He forgot what the dog was called, but he remembered
that the woman would let him take the dog out on a leash. She
would sink up to her tummy in the sand and whined and
wanted him to carry her. Margareta was there, too; she was
little, maybe two or three. She would grab the dog with her
small, hard hands and the dog would yelp, but the dog never
hurt Margareta. She understood that Margareta was herself
just a puppy.

He sat in his chair behind the reception desk and the snow
blew like smoke outside on the street. It was dark, and all the
shops had closed. If he had a dog today, he would name her
Bella and she would be at home in his bed waiting for him,
warming up the bed. He usually had frozen toes after sitting at

the hotel all night long. Could you leave a dog that long? Well, why not. Dog owners usually didn't have to get up in the middle of the night to take out their four-footed friends? Would it be the right thing to do? What if Bella missed him? And what if she started howling, night after night? How would that go? He could lose his apartment and then where would he be?

The reception area was not very large, but it was pleasantly decorated with a set of wicker sofas and cushions that had a large flower design. On the glass table, there were some magazines: *Allt om mat*, *Reader's Digest*, some Christian magazine, and the newspapers *Dagens Nyheter* and *Svenska Dagbladet*. To the right, on its own table, was an aquarium with two kinds of fish, some black fish and some see-through fish. Hans Peter imagined that the black ones were called Black Mollies. The cleaning lady had told him once, but she spoke Swedish poorly and he didn't really understand what she had said.

The cleaning lady was responsible for the aquarium. She made sure that they received their food and once a week she cleaned their home with a big plastic scoop. She was a Greek immigrant and her name was Ariadne.

Of course, Hans Peter thought when he first met her. A Greek woman named Ariadne! He tried to talk to her about the Labyrinth at Knossos, but she had just covered her mouth with her hands and laughed. She had noticeable gums.

At times when she didn't have a babysitter, she brought her daughter with her. Her daughter was blind. She would stay on the cot behind the curtain. Hans Peter knew at once when she had been there. The pillow smelled and the pillowcase was wet and a bit sticky. The girl usually lay there sucking on raspberry candy ropes.

Next to the cot was a door that led to the small kitchen. For the guests who wanted it, Hans Peter could make sandwiches with shrimp or cheddar cheese and olives, which he would cut in half and fasten with toothpicks. Part of his job was to make the rounds at two in the morning and pick up all the shoes that had been left out for cleaning. This service from days gone by was something that Ulf chose to preserve. He was careful with his services and Hans Peter didn't care one way or the other. This way he got a break from the night's monotony. He went around with a big basket on his arm and collected the shoes, writing the room number on their soles with chalk. The first night he was on the job, he thought that he would be able to remember which shoes went where, but it was much more difficult than he imagined. He had to take a chance on guessing right. Two pairs of men's shoes landed up at the wrong door, but the guests didn't get upset. They thought it was a funny episode that they could tell when they returned home.

Tonight the rooms were all booked. Hans Peter had made himself comfortable on his chair and had put aside the newspaper. He was about to read the seventh song in *Don Juan* when the outer door opened and a swirl of snow came in. A man stood in front of the registration desk. He had wet hair which clung to his forehead.

"May I help you with something?" asked Hans Peter.

The man closed the door and stamped his feet.

Hans Peter asked again if he could be of service somehow.

"I want to see one of your guests," said the man, and Hans Peter could tell that he was drunk.

"Yes, which guest would you like to see?"

"Agneta Lind."

Hans Peter flipped through the register. He didn't recognize the name, but he recognized the situation, married men looking for their unfaithful wives.

"I'm sorry, but we don't have any guest by that name here."

"Don't mess with me. I know she's here."

Hans Peter shook his head. Now he had to be tactful. The man was large and strong, and he wore a buttoned, somewhat worn coat, and around his neck he wore a gold chain with an amulet.

"She must have registered under a different name."

"That would be hard to know."

"Don't you have to require someone to show their ID?"

"Actually, no."

The man had tried to look as intimidating as possible, but now he took a few steps back and sank into the sofa. He hid his face in the elbow of his coat. It sounded like he was crying.

"Damn it all to hell. If you knew how degrading this is. . . ."

These were always difficult situations. What was a person to say? Whatever he said could be the wrong thing. He waited.

"If I describe her . . . would you recognize her?"

"Please understand . . . we can't do that. We have to protect our guests."

The man wasn't listening.

"She's . . . thirty-eight, but you'd never know. Everyone thinks she looks younger. She has short hair, dyed red, but it's not red everywhere . . . and now that bastard . . ."

"Why do you want to find her?"

"She's my wife, dammit! She's here with her lover, and I don't give a damn that she is here. I've tracked her down. Tre Rosor was written in her planner. She's never been too clever. Tre Rosor, that's the name of this place, right? Isn't that the name of this fucking hotel?"

"Yes, but this is not that kind of a hotel."

"What do you mean, that kind?"

"We don't have a . . . bad reputation."

"That's not the point here."

"All right . . . but . . . there's no person by that name here."

"Her lover . . . I know who he is. I've seen him. He has glasses and funny outfits, some kind of fucking lawyer who is upstairs screwing her, I'll kill them both."

He really ought to throw the man out or call the police. That would be the right thing to do.

Instead he said, "Would you like a cup of coffee?"

He made a shrimp sandwich for the man and put on a large pot of coffee. Suspiciously, the man bit into the sandwich, and a few shrimp fell off onto his knee. He chewed loudly and looked around with quick glances. *I hope Ulf doesn't show up now*, thought Hans Peter. Ulf wouldn't be so thrilled with this. It didn't look right to have someone come and make themselves at home in the middle of the hotel's foyer.

Once the man drank a cup of coffee, he started to calm down. Hans Peter hoped he would go away soon.

"That was great!" said the man and swallowed the last bite of the sandwich. "An unexpectedly warm welcome, I'd call it."

"Thanks."

"I'm Björn. Björn Lind."

Hans Peter did not want to know the man's name. He didn't want the man to get to know him better either. But against his will, he began to chat, just like him to land in situations that he really ought to know how to ward off.

"Have you two been married long?"

"A couple of years at least."

"But it's not been going so well for a while, right?"

"I certainly don't think so."

"What about her?"

"Hell if I know. Never heard her complain."

"Have you talked about a divorce?"

"Not at all. But I know that she has others on the side. I can feel it. She says she's going to the movies with a friend but in reality. . . ."

"Maybe she really went to the movies."

"Fuck that idea."

"What's your line of work?"

"I own my own business. I have a message delivery service and a couple of cars. She was one of the drivers. That's how we got together."

A fish came to the surface and snapped some air. The fish did that at times, when they needed extra oxygen. Hans

Peter wondered if they knew that they were captive. At any rate, they could see out through the water and the glass. Whenever Ariadne approached, they all swam up to the surface at once; they knew she was bringing food; they recognized her.

"If your wife is seeing other guys, maybe she has a reason," he said carefully.

"What do you mean, a reason?"

"Well, maybe she's not so happy with how you two are doing. For me that's what happened."

"Well, life's not always a bouquet of roses!"

"Of course not."

"But maybe it is here at the Tre Rosor, ha, ha?"

Hans Peter laughed.

"What about you?" the man said. "You married?"

"Have been."

"There you see how easy it is."

"Yep," sighed Hans Peter.

"Did she take off? Or did you?"

"Well, neither of us took off exactly. We just . . . drifted apart."

"But Agneta and I . . . we. . . ."

"Can you two still talk with each other?"

"Talk this, talk that."

The man grew quiet. He took up one of the newspapers and flipped through it, mostly to have something to do with his hands. Someone was walking along the hallway upstairs. Just think if there really were an Agneta Lind among the other guests? Think if she came down dragging her lover behind her. Hans Peter tried to remember who had checked in during the evening, what they looked like, had there been a woman with short red hair? He didn't remember one.

"Hey," said Björn Lind, as he with great effort got to his feet. He now appeared completely sober. "I'm going now. Thank you. I mean it. Not sure for what. Maybe the food, if nothing else."

Hans Peter couldn't read any longer. He couldn't comprehend the words. He washed up the cup and the small plate, rinsed the coffee pot. A feeling of depression was settling into him without his really knowing why. He wished that the night would go by quickly. He wanted to go home and lie down. His legs were aching, as if he were coming down with a fever.

Chapter NINE

After a long break, the girl began to visit her again. The girl had changed. There was something unfamiliar about her, something in her bearing. As if all the knots in her spine had been smoothed out and she had returned to being that Justine she had been when she was little. And she held that persona up like a shield whenever she stepped into the room.

Yes, even that, her way of walking was different, no longer that careful pattering that relatives of sick people got into the habit of doing, but she would open the door and walk right in. With a terrible screech, she would pull a chair to the bedside and sit there without moving, straight and cool. Sit there and stare directly at her with that same crafty look that she had had enough of long ago.

A creepy feeling came over Flora as she lay there in the bed. The blanket felt heavy on her ribcage. Yes, it was like she was again able to feel her own body with all its fragility, down to the smallest cell, as it had been before the stroke. She tried to close her eyes and pretend to be sleeping, but time and again she had to open her eyes slightly to see if the girl was still there, if the girl had changed her position. It became a compulsion.

She found herself listening for the girl's footsteps, even in the middle of the night. If she could only get those damned white uniforms to understand that she didn't want visitors any longer. Not by anyone. Not even closest relatives.

At first Flora had been unconscious and didn't know whether she had visitors or not. When she slowly began to come to, the girl was standing next to her bed. And that feeble voice, that pleading: "Can you see me, Flora? Can you hear me?"

Flora's tongue felt like dry tree bark.

There was light in the room; a nurse came in.

"Does she understand what I'm saying?"

That look the nurse gave before the two of them left together. Flora tried to lift her hand to move the blanket. She wanted to get out of bed, find a mirror, see what had happened to her. They had given her drugs; she had forgotten how she had come there.

But she could not get her hand to lift.

Could not even move it.

During that first period, they had subjected her to a great number of tests. Every day, they had rolled her away to lab-test rooms and X-ray rooms. They had stuck needles into her arms; they had tested her foot with instruments and asked, do you feel this, Mrs. Dalvik? Do you feel this at all?

After a while, they'd given up.

They had tied her to a stretcher and two young ambulance workers had rolled her out. It was the first time in ages that she had breathed outdoor air and it sunk in that as far as she was concerned, her life was over. When the ambulance turned out of the driveway, she saw a glimpse of the emergency hospital and remembered the sound of sirens.

At the nursing home there was no such hurry.

Sometimes during the night, she felt a certain closeness, as if Sven was back with her. He was strong and young, just as he had been in the beginning. She wanted to cover her head with the sheets; he shouldn't see her like this, so old and humiliated. Go, she wanted to scream at him, go back to your French wife.

That woman had died at the height of her greatest beauty. She was the one he had chosen; she was the one who had given him a child. Flora had never been more than a surrogate, however much he had tried to deny this.

If he had only agreed to sell the house, that would have been the ultimate proof that he meant the things he said. That he wanted to start a new life. But he refused. She could get him to do many things, but not this. The house was holy to him. His French wife had chosen it, and she had placed her weed of a child in it as a continual reminder.

Her own womb was barren.

Now it was morning again. There was sound in the hallways, light, curtains being drawn back. She looked toward the window, black and shiny, but the uniforms had still turned on all the lights.

A chipper voice from a white uniform: "Good morning, Flora. Did you sleep well?"

What right did they have to use my first name?

The blanket taken away, hands on her hips and rear. At least she could still pee.

She avoided looking at her skinny limbs and the black hair which had faded to gray.

The white uniform sang; she was just a child with golden locks.

"Now we have real winter Flora. Isn't it wonderful! A great deal of snow fell last night. And it was cold, below zero. I had to get a ride here from my boyfriend and we almost didn't make it up the hill. Although he has summer tires still on and they're really worn out."

Yes that was it. Snow. The dull scraping of snowplows; that was the sound this morning.

"I'm going to come back soon and wash you up, and then a bit of food would be good, wouldn't it?"

That chirpy, naive optimism. As if food would taste good in her situation.

Snow. . . . Snow was on the ground when he first took her to the house. She slipped on the slope, and almost fell. He took hold of her arm, but not hard, not as if he wanted to own her.

There was a woman in the house. A housekeeper. She had made dinner and set the table in the room that Flora would later make into her blue room. There was a draft between the front door and the door to the basement. Something was wrong with the heater, even though it was new. He was so touchingly impractical.

Flora's feet were freezing. She hadn't taken any indoor shoes with her. Sven found a pair of woolen socks and they were much too big, so she continued to freeze until she drank a glass of wine. Then she became hot and in the mood to laugh.

The housekeeper had come in with the girl. She resembled her father, the same light skin and chin.

"This is my daughter Justine," said Sven and lifted the girl into his arms. She hugged his neck strongly and refused to shake Flora's hand. She had to take it back and she felt humiliated.

They finished eating and they were sitting at a smaller table for coffee. The child clung to Sven and would not look up. Finally he carried her from the room.

"You must excuse her," he said when he returned. "You know what happened. She is at a difficult stage."

A few weeks later, Flora invited him to her place. She had recently moved into a two-room apartment on Odenplan, next to Gustav Vasa Church but facing the courtyard garden. She had gone home right after lunch, and she still remembered what she had served him for dinner. Baked ox fillets with sautéed chanterelles and fresh strawberries for dessert. Her parents had helped her to find the strawberries, which were out of season, as well as the chanterelles. He was thoroughly impressed.

That evening they slept together. He had been alone for so long that he came right away. They remained in bed and she cupped her hands around his thin buttocks and felt an increasing tenderness.

"Sven," she whispered.

Yes, she whispered his first name, and he was no longer her boss but a man who had been inside her, and she took his fingers and placed them between her thighs. Then he hardened, grew, and she laid on him and led him into her in a way she had never done before with anyone.

He liked her. Yes, almost loved her. Every evening he returned. She lay in his arms and she told him about Hässelby and about herself.

"I love your name," he said. "Flowery."

"It's not for nothing that I'm the daughter of a master gardener."

He laughed and tickled her with the tip of his tongue. She turned, mouth next to his knee.

She continued her story from this position.

"My parents owned a garden supply store for over thirty years. They took it over from my paternal grandfather. They intended to keep it in the family, but . . . well, it didn't happen like that. We were four sisters with flower names, but it didn't help; none of us had the desire to grow plants. I'm the youngest. Rosa is the oldest, and then this is Viola and this one is Reseda."

"Reseda?"

"Yep. That's her name."

"And if you were boys?"

"Then we wouldn't be sleeping together."

She turned again and followed his hairline with her index finger. His glasses were on the table; his eyebrows were light, almost invisible.

"I mean, what kind of names would they have?"

"I got it the first time. Maybe Root and Branch. Like the Root and Branch of Jesse. . . . My parents really wanted boys. None of us girls wanted the garden store. We had had enough."

"Were you able to help out?"

"Able? Forced more like it."

Her father had beaten them with flower supports if they did not obey him. He hit Flora the least, but he was always beating Rosa, the oldest sister. She should have known better. Rosa had no patience and she hated getting her fingers coarsened and cracked. She hated dirt and especially its smell. She would sneak away from the weeding and go to the beach to swim. She ought to have learned what would happen when she returned. It was as if she forgot from one time to the next.

Flora could still remember her crying when her father took Rosa into the tool shed. Afterwards she was striped and swollen over her entire back. The sisters had to fan her with rhubarb leaves and clean her with water.

Life had since gone well for all four girls. Rosa had married a ship owner and moved to Göteborg. Viola had gotten a job at NK, and Reseda became the principal of a school for girls.

None of them were living any more. Only Flora herself.

Creamed wheat. What else was she ever going to have? Who would have time to sit and wait until she had swallowed something that she would have had to chew. The slimy, salty taste triggered her gag reflex. She started gagging, but took hold of herself and swallowed.

The white uniform was talking to an older one.

"Think if we could get them into snowsuits and put them on snow boards out there. Or sleds. We could pull them all around Råcksta. They'd like that, don't you think?"

"We wouldn't like it."

"Oh, Ing-Marie, don't be such a spoilsport. You have to keep the child in you alive."

"You keep your child and don't show it to us!"

The younger one was drying Flora's chin.

"Flora, wouldn't that be a lot of fun? Of course you went sledding when you were a child? Wasn't that a lot of fun? You remember, don't you? Oh, Ing-Marie, you can enliven them by helping them remember the good things from their youth. I've read up on it, and it's true."

Flora wanted to cough, so that the creamed wheat would fall into her airway and force her to cough up both the creamed wheat and all the slime, too, and make an end to this ridiculous breakfast. But she didn't. She had always been such a good and dutiful girl.

The day before Midsummer, Sven asked her if she would consider moving back to Hässelby to his house, and to be a mother to his daughter as well as his wife. He had said it in that order. Mother to my daughter and my wife.

The evening was beautiful and mild. They had eaten dinner at a restaurant and were wandering down Saint Eriksgatan with the breeze brushing softly against her neck and arms. She was so happy. She stopped in the middle of the street and embraced him.

She thought about the child.

"She'll get used to it," said Sven. "Finally there will be some stability in her life. Give her a little time. She'll come to love you, just as much as I do."

They got married a short time later. Flora had always dreamed about a big church wedding, but it was so soon after the French wife's death that she thought it would be too scandalous. Everything had to be kept simple. On the other hand, she was able to convince Sven that they take a honeymoon in London. She had always wanted to go there.

The hotel was close to Oxford Street, but she had forgotten its name. He took her to the theater. He had been in London many times before. One of the Sandy business's daughter's concerns was located here. They visited it together and were guided around the most modern plant. Flora was able to try out her English. Everything was still there, just waiting to be used. She noticed that he was impressed.

She was getting dressed, as they were going to Albert Hall. She wanted to experience everything, everything that she had only read about.

It was late afternoon of their third day. A knock on the door.

A man stood there with a telegram from Sweden. It was urgent. The girl was ill.

They traveled home early the next morning. Sven wanted to travel that very night, but there were no seats on the plane. During the whole trip, he was silent and thoughtful. She saw that he was suffering, that he blamed himself for leaving the girl behind, that he was reliving the death of the girl's mother.

Of course there was nothing really wrong with Justine. She had just had a bit of fever. The temperature had been over one hundred and four, so Sven's mother had thought it best to send for him.

Don't children often get high fevers? Wasn't that part of being a child?

She quit working for the company. During the night, she lay beside Sven. She lay there and listened to his light snoring and tried to forget that the child was on the other side of the wall. She wanted her own child, so that she could become a real mother.

He would never regret that he had taken her to be his wife. She would be his beautiful representative, who made fine dinners for all his business acquaintances. She would converse in English and they would be impressed: What a beautiful and talented young wife you have there, Mr. Dalvik.

She and the girl. They were alone in the house. Sven had gone to work. Justine had left the breakfast table without eating as much as a bread crumb.

"She has to eat," she whispered to Sven. "You see how thin and undernourished she is. Children need food in order to grow."

"It'll come. Give her some time; have a little patience."
She stood at the kitchen window and saw him get into the
car. She waved and he threw her a kiss. The classical tableau.
She was taken by the desire to call him back, take me with
you. I want to be with *you*, not this child.

She was in the house. She cleaned up after breakfast and
went upstairs to make the beds. The girl was in Sven's bed. She
had rolled herself into the blanket with her head in the pillow.

Flora sat next to her.

"Justine," she said softly. "We ought to be friends, you and
me. I want to be your friend. Don't you want to be mine?"

The child did not answer. Flora then realized that the
child hardly ever spoke.

She laid her hand on the blanket. The tense body jerked
away.

"I've come here to be your mother," said Flora, and she
raised her voice a bit. "You must stop ignoring me. I am asking
you nicely to be friends, you and me. You are to look at me
and answer."

The girl leapt out of the bed, slid past Flora down to the
floor like a hurt, furious animal. She stood in the doorway and
her face was direct.

"You are not my mother. You're a fucking whore."

She had not gotten angry. She had gone to the bathroom
and locked herself in. She stood in front of the mirror and
cried. That child had made her cry. Sven's child. But he was
never going to know.

"Wake up, it's daytime. We can't have you sleeping. Why
don't we get you into a chair instead? Won't that be nice?"

The white uniforms. While sitting in the orange-yellowish
chair, she saw how they made her bed and mopped under it.
The dust tended to collect there, making dust bunnies.

Then she looked at the other bed and saw that it was
empty. Yes. The woman had died. Was it last night or a different night? Anyway, people always died at night.

They had dressed her in a pink housecoat with big white buttons. She used to look good in pink. She had colored her long eyelashes, and the pink evening dress rustled when she would slip it over her ears. Sound of spray, sound of music, he dances like a god, my husband. And she flowed through mirrored ballrooms, down stairs as wide as avenues.

"This is Märta. She will be your new roommate."

A winkled old-lady face, suspicious.

"We hope that you will be comfortable together."

"If only one person can speak, at least we'll never have arguments."

Now they sat across the table from each other.

How many roommates had they introduced? Was she supposed to outlive them all? That was just not right!

She bought the girl a doll. It was a very nice doll, one that she herself would have wanted when she was a girl. It had real hair, a bow, and eyes that could open and shut. She had it wrapped up nicely.

The next day, when Sven had left, she went to the girl's room and laid the package on the bed. Justine sat all curled up on the window sill, her hair unwashed and her mouth in a grimace.

"You shouldn't sit in the window, you could fall!"

Justine turned away her head.

"Go and wash up, and we can see what clothes we can find for you. And when you are ready, you can open your present."

The girl went stiffly. She went into the bathroom, locked the door, and refused to open up again.

Flora pretended to leave the house. She crept behind a desk and was completely quiet.

Trench warfare was what it had become, pure trench warfare. That kid in there, prepping the cannons; she in the trenches.

What happened then?

The heat from the child's skin, her hands hitting blow after blow. The naked body creeping into a corner.

Part 1: Chapter Nine

"You are going to do as I say, you little brat! Are you a human or an animal? I'll kill you if you don't obey me, if you continue to humiliate me and treat me like I am invisible. Listen to me and don't look away. From now on there are new rules in this house, and from now on I no longer want to be your mother!"

"What have you done with her?" asked Sven, but there was no reproach in his voice, just wonderment.

The girl sat between them, clean hair, scrubbed pink.

Chapter TEN

Carl Lüding called a meeting at nine Monday morning. He had sent his assistant, Jenny, to buy coffee cake. Now it lay there in the middle of the table, sticky and cut into pieces that were much too large.

"Please help yourselves," he coaxed.

His long, well-kept fingers flipped a pen nervously. The name *Norrbottenskuriren* was inscribed on it, Berit noted. Well, why not. He was from Norrbotten Province.

No one was eating the coffee cake, not even Curt Lüding. He sat at the short end of the table. He brought his coffee mug to his lips, over and over, taking very small sips. He didn't ask anyone how their weekend had been. No small talk this Monday. He was dressed in his dark suit, which he began to use during the winter. Earlier he had usually dressed in sweaters and corduroys. Something had happened to change him, Berit thought. He's turning so—respectable.

They waited. Annie stared into her coffee cup. Lotta cleared her throat and coughed, as if she were coming down with a cold. From Lillian one could hear a kind of humming which was hardly audible; she always did that when she was angry or worried. Instead of saying something, she would walk around and hum.

An ambulance went by, sirens blasting.

The telephone rang.

"Is the answering machine on?" asked Carl Lüding.

"Of course," said Jenny.

"All right then, let's begin. Yes, well, as you know, there's a reason that I've called all of you together for a meeting so early on a Monday morning. As you all know, I started this publishing house a while ago, and then I pumped a lot of capital into it and took it over when the others weren't interested any longer. Yes, you all know the story. And the years have gone by. Sometimes it was difficult; I won't sweep that under the rug. But you've all done a wonderful job. It never would have come together without you. Many of you have been here for a long time, you Berit, for example, and you Margit. . . . I imagine that you have feelings that are just as strong as mine for this place."

He was quiet and looked out the window.

Snow was still on the ground. The thermometer showed minus seven degrees, and for the first time this winter, Berit had worn her fur.

Get to the point, you old hypocrite, she thought.

She craved a cigarette. She was trying to cut down and had begun chewing nicotine gum instead.

This was probably not the right time to quit.

"As you know," her boss continued, "I was born and raised in Norrbotten, in a little village named Sangis. My father was a logger. My mother was a nurse for the district. I grew up among the spruce trees. You all know me so long that you've heard me talk in my wild dialect as soon as I loosen up, especially at our parties. . . ."

Yes, that was right. Up to a few years ago he had thought it was great fun to have parties for the employees. He would even help organize them, and taught them all how to eat almond potatoes and *surströmming* when he had them over to his country house. He would sing for them, sad songs from the North. His wife Maud had been with him in those days, a glad and exuberant woman who was also from Norrland.

His change had come with the divorce. Maud fell in love with someone else and left him, moved abroad, to Maastricht, in Holland; there was something to do about the parliament of the European Union. Carl Lüding hadn't been himself after that event.

"Now, my dear friends, let me tell you what this is all about. This is the deal. Hold on to your seats, because great changes lie in store for us. I am planning to move our publishing house to Luleå in Norrland!" He became silent and looked at each of them. The crows' feet next to his eyes lifted.

"You're surprised. I can tell."

Somewhere in the building, a drill started up. There was always some kind of repair or renovation going on. It seemed the landlord sent out a notice every month: "Please excuse our dust. We are going to repair this and that during such and so week."

"Why Luleå, you may ask? Let me explain. Running a publishing house up there is much more cost effective. Parliament has promised subsidies. It seems that a renowned publishing house is sorely needed up there. The entire Northern region is filled with amazing authors who are just waiting for us."

He drank more of his coffee, his eyes shining, and he smiled slightly; he was relaxing.

He's lost it, thought Berit. She bit her tongue, but didn't feel it. The Northern region! Sweden's very own Siberia!

"And us?" someone asked. It was Annie. "What will happen to us? Have you thought about that?"

Curt Lüding placed his pen on the table, and started it spinning with his finger. It spun around and fell to the floor with a clang.

"Here's what I have to say about that," he said, and he was still smiling. "Every organization needs to go through a reduction in order to reach its optimum efficiency. This can be painful, I am aware of that."

"Curt, you didn't answer my question!" Annie said shrilly. She was beginning to turn red all the way down to her neck.

"Yes!" Berit agreed. "What will happen with us?"

"But . . . you can come, too, of course. Everyone. I'm counting on taking care of the move during the summer, and then we'll go full throttle from August onwards. And friends, Luleå is a wonderful city, believe me."

"He's gone absolutely fucking crazy!"
Berit and Annie were in the sushi restaurant on Upplandsgatan. The sushi didn't taste the same today, as if it wasn't properly fresh. They'd probably all get food poisoning that evening. But who the hell cared?
"The goddamned Northern region! Who the hell would want to move there?"
"Well," said Annie. "This is even worse than we had imagined. We could handle moving to Bonniers. But that mosquito-infested hell-hole! He's been plotting this for quite a while, the bastard. And not even hinted one damn thing about it."
"He's gotten so strange and weird. He's undergone a complete personality change. If only Maud had stayed put! She never should have let this happen! Why'd she have to run off with that EU-guy!"
"What are you going to do, Berit? Are you going to move up there?"
"I'm not single. That's a problem. Tor is never going to agree to leave Stockholm."
"If you were on your own, then?"
"No, not a chance. This is my home. I was born here; my roots are here."
"Fuck it all. Up there it's winter all year round. The snow comes in September and stays till Midsummer. I couldn't stand it. The darkness unbroken for months! And those damned mosquitoes!"
"That bastard knows that we aren't all going to move. He won't have a snowball's chance in hell to get us all move up there together. A couple of us would move there, maybe Jenny, maybe Ann-Sofi. She's from there herself; at least, that's what I've heard."
"The question is, what are the rest of us to do?"

"Oh, you'll land on your feet just fine. You'll be offered another job. You're capable; people know that you've been editing that old witch Karlberg. That alone will get you an offer."

"Oh there's a real silver lining. I'll be rid of her!"

What a strange weekend it had been. The worry about Curt Lüding's plans had been pushed away by that strange visit in Hässelby.

It was true, as Justine had said, that she had felt drawn to her former classmate's house to see if anything had changed. If that poor girl had survived. She was practically filled with fear at the thought of running into Justine, but she had secretly hoped that Justine would be standing at the top of her stairs, thirty years older and strong at last. That she would be standing there in her wide, flowery pants and say: "Come on in."

And then there she was! And did just that!

Berit had repressed all those events during her entire adult life. She had put it aside into her subconscious, but as she walked closer to the house, the whole thing returned to her like a tidal wave. She wanted to fall into the snow and scream, "Forgive me, Justine! We were just kids! Forgive us!"

They sat in the upstairs room with the view and drank *glögg*. They watched the sky change color and turn red and sparkle as if it were burning on the other side of Lake Mälar. It was a cold, formal winter day and perhaps she blabbered on too much, revealed more than she ought to have. She was not used to talking to anyone for such a long time.

Justine. Just as she had always felt her to be.

But neither of them mentioned their childhood.

The great bird scared her from her senses. Berit was not afraid of birds; the boys had had parakeets, and she had enjoyed them, even though they always messed up the place. But this enormous being that suddenly just appeared. It surprised her; it set its claws deep into her hair and pulled.

"Just be still," Justine soothed. "Just sit down and be still."

Berit had become hysterical.

Justine had taken her by the shoulders and forced her back into the chair.

"He's frightened, you see. With you screaming and thrashing about like that."

Slowly, Justine worked the sharp, black claws from her head; she trembled from discomfort. She saw his sharp beak and she began to cry.

It was not like Berit Asarsson to cry.

"He was just a little curious. . . ."

"He scared me half to death! Why do you keep a bird like that in the house!"

She pulled herself together and went out on the balcony to smoke. When she returned, the bird was sitting on top of the bookcase.

"What's the deal with you? Are you pretending to be an Asa goddess? Is he like Odin's birds Hugin and Munin?"

"An Asa goddess? Oh no, this isn't a raven like them."

"It sure looks like one."

"Ravens are larger."

Justine had warmed up the *glögg* again, filled Berit's mug.

"How's your clothes? Any bird poop?"

"It doesn't matter."

"I'm ashamed of myself, but that's another story from our childhood, damn it all."

She was able to go to the bathroom and clean off the worst of it. When she returned, Justine had lit a fire in the fireplace. "You must dry off before you go back out. It's cold, well below zero."

And Justine had patted her on the cheek and helped her sit down in the chair, wrapped a throw around her and gave her more to drink.

"Justine, I'm going to be totally smashed from all this."

"Would it matter?"

"Fuck it all. I want to get plastered."

They had sat there for a long time, and the fire was warming and she thought that it had been a very long time since she had felt so relaxed—and all this in spite of Curt Lüding's meeting for the beginning of next week. She felt as if she were dozing off and wished that someone would massage the soles of her feet while she was sitting there, and just as she felt the longing for it, Justine slid down to the floor and drew off her socks.

Justine's hands were quick and warm; they kneaded and pressed.

"Oh how nice you are, Justine; what a great talent. Where did you learn massage?"

"I don't know what to say. I didn't study massage. . . ."

"But you can really . . . oh, sweet Jesus, that feels wonderful."

Justine kneaded up her calves, massaged and pulled.

"You are tense, Berit. What's the matter? Things not going well for you?"

"Oh, I'm just fine, this, this is fantastic. . . ."

"I don't mean right now. Otherwise. With your life."

Her face fell, forced back tears, sniffled.

"Some days it feels like everything is coming to an end," she said huskily. "Don't you sometimes feel like that?"

Her hands pushed down and worked in.

"You have a knot here, Berit, right in the middle of your footpad."

"I know. I think that I'm always giving and giving and giving but never . . . anything in return. The boys, they're not boys any longer, they're all grown up, young men, handsome, devilishly handsome. They did their army stint and came back wearing the uniform of the crown. When I see them, whenever one of those few occasions occur where I see them, I can't imagine that I really carried them, that they were growing in me and I gave birth to them during the pain of childbirth, that they nursed at my breast, that I've changed their diapers, and watched them grow. . . . We can't even talk to each other any more, Justine. Well, maybe we could if we had some time, if I were alone with them on a desert island and there were no other distractions, no one livelier than their old mom."

"And your husband?"

"Oh, well . . . since it's now just me and him again . . . it's difficult. If you had been married and had children, you'd understand what I'm getting at. For many, many years, everything has been centered on the kids. You do your best to keep them safe from danger and temptation; your whole life revolves around being a good parent; you don't have enough in you to be a good partner, too . . . not enough energy . . . too much work all day long . . . and then one day it's all gone. The birds have flown the nest. So you sit there and stare at each other, man and woman, and have no idea how you're supposed to act any longer."

"What about taking a trip? Doing something fun?"

"We did that. Went around the world last year."

"And?"

"I don't know. Not the same guy I got engaged to, the one who admired me and wanted to make love over and over again on the very same day."

"Well . . . what were you expecting?"

"Not this alienation at any rate. This alienation frightens me, scares me shitless."

She was half-lying in the chair, sliding toward the floor. There was an ache behind her eyes from too much *glögg*, too much crying.

"Don't you ever feel alienated, Justine? Are you content with your life?"

"I'm starting to be."

"Starting to be? What do you mean, starting? In fact, you haven't said anything about yourself. You just let me ramble on and on."

"Not much to say."

"Of course there is."

"Maybe. What's your line of work?"

"I'm in the publishing business. Or was, I have to soon say. He's going to fire us all. I'm dead certain about that."

"Any hints about it?"

"Hard times, you know. I'm not worth much on the job market nowadays. Too old."

"Naaah."

"Seriously, I'm forty-five, Justine. So are you for that matter. I don't know anything else except working with manuscripts. What am I supposed to do if I can't do it any longer?"

"Can't you start your own publishing company? People always like books?"

"Yeah, right, do you know how easy that is?"

"Your husband?"

"I don't want to live off his income. No, no. Freedom is the most important thing that a person owns. You know that yourself. Maybe that's why you didn't get married."

"You don't have to be married to feel imprisoned."

"Hmmm."

The bird cawed up on the bookcase, and then flew down like a big black veil. He landed on the floor and hopped over to Justine. Berit screamed and pulled her feet back on the chair.

"Oh yes, he loves to eat the toes of former classmates."

Justine tickled him on his neck; he fluffed himself up and looked thick.

"I'm sorry . . . but aren't they a bit disgusting?"

"Different tastes."

"He's like your child, isn't he."

"Probably even more than that."

"Animals never let you down. Isn't that true, Justine? People always say so, is it true?"

"It depends on what one expects from one's pet."

"Once . . . the boys . . . they're practically the same age. Jörgen and Jens. The police called . . . we had to go get them at the hospital. They had drunk so much that they couldn't make it home. You can die of it, you know, alcohol poisoning. It was worse for Jens, he was so small; he was lying in the embryo position when I arrived. I wanted to just scream, Justine, my little baby. Why can't they stay with you forever?"

Chapter ELEVEN

She bought herself a car, a Volvo. It was so new that no one had owned it before, but it didn't lack personality. It stood, red and elegant, in the dealership window, and Justine stepped inside and opened the front door. Even the smell was new. It was warm, comfortable, and had automatic transmission. Of course she could bargain, but she didn't feel like it.

She took out the money and returned the following day. The salesman said, "This is one great car. It has a lot of power. You're not going to regret it."

"I know."

"Fast as a silver bullet. If you're going to drive in old Deutschland, you're even going to pass the Porches."

"I'm not planning to drive there," she said. "But thanks for the tip."

It was snowing. Thin, light flakes which swirled in the wind and made it difficult to see. The snow tires were in the trunk. The salesman said that he could put them on for her, but she would have to wait one more day.

"But you can feel safe on these tires. They are stable, year-round tires, made for the Scandinavian climate."

In the Vällingby roundabout she skidded. She corrected the skid without any difficulty.

A strange, funny name came to her mind.

The High-Wire-Artist. Well, why not?

Flora sat in the armchair next to the window. They had supported her with pillows and tied her to the back with a restraint.

Justine had run up the stairs. Now she was standing in the room and clumps of snow were melting next to her boots.

"Great! You're awake," she said. "I'm going to take you out."

The woman's lip moved, a string of thin saliva.

The door slid open, a nurse pushing a wheelchair. A strange woman sitting in it, her long veined hands picking at something on her knee.

The nurse said, "Look Flora! You have a visitor. Isn't it wonderful that your daughter has come."

"I've bought a new car," said Justine.

The radio was on; someone was crying in the hallway.

"I can only dream of that!"

"Why do you say so?"

"Me, buy a car! How much do you think nurses earn?"

"Take my old one then. It's all right, for the most part. If it's acting up, just spray it with some 5-56. Then it works like a dream. I don't need it. An Opel Rekord, take it and say it's a long-term loan, drive it till it falls apart."

The nurse turned red.

"I didn't mean to. . . ."

"Well, I'm not going to use it any longer. One car is good enough for me. It's at my place; you can pick it up whenever you get around to it. It's just in the way."

"I couldn't really. . . ."

"Otherwise it goes to the junkyard."

"It runs?"

"Certainly it runs."

"I don't get it. . . . Why did you buy a new one then?"

"You only live once. I can so I did."

"Well, that's one way to look at things."

"Or how you see yourself."

"Excuse me?"

"Oh, nothing."

Justine gestured.

"How's she doing?"

"Same as usual."

"I'm thinking of taking her for a test drive."

"Isn't it a bit cold?"

"And what of it?"

"Well . . . well, why not? Didn't you say if you can do something, you should?"

"Exactly."

"It's just. . . . Can you get her dressed yourself? We are a little short today. I have to take care of Märta here. She is Flora's new roommate, by the way."

She was as thin as a paper doll, no control over her arms and legs. If you bent them back and forth, they'd break at the fold.

Justine carried her to the bed. She hardly weighed more than the bird. She put on socks, flannel pants, a cardigan and a jacket. Also plaid cloth slippers and a shawl for her head.

She called to the nurse.

"Is this enough, do you think?"

"Sure. But it's easier to get them dressed when they're sitting."

Justine took her step-mother in her arms. She could tell how the emaciated body trembled. She got a strange taste in her mouth.

"Use the wheelchair to get her downstairs."

"I can do it. She doesn't weigh more than a four-page letter."

"A wheelchair is more appropriate."

The nurse adjusted the knot under Flora's chin.

"Flora," she laughed. "You look just like an Easter witch."

She took the elevator down with the wheelchair.

Two women in white dresses stepped in at the same time.

"Oh, how nice it will be to get outside for a little while. Don't you think that will be nice?"

"She can't speak," said Justine.

A sound came from Flora's throat, a gurgling noise.

But the women were already talking about something else. They stepped out now, and one helped maneuver the wheelchair out of the elevator.

She left the wheelchair in the foyer while she went to get the car. She drove right up to the glass doors. She placed her hands under Flora's body and lifted her into the passenger seat. She fastened the seatbelt around her. Flora's eyes wandered randomly; her shawl slipped down on her forehead.

"It's been a long time since you were outside, right? Have you ever been outside since you . . ."

She stepped on the gas and skidded immediately.

"Whoopsie! This can be a little risky. Where do you want to go? Not home, though, you've been there too much. No, let's go on the highway instead. I have to check how fast this baby can go."

On the curve entering E-18, right past IKEA, she had such a major slide that the car turned and stopped facing backwards. There was a hiccoughing sound from Flora. Flora's hands were lying like wilted leaves in her lap. Justine touched them; they were ice-cold. She hit some buttons; the heat came on. Then she turned the car and swung out onto the highway.

She turned on the radio, same channel as at the nursing home, Megapol. She recognized the melody, something from the time she had been together with Nathan, and a blow hit her in the stomach. She turned up the volume and he was with her now. He sat in the back seat and he leaned over towards her; his hands caressed her breasts. Everything was like it had been before they got on that airplane; he was good to her, and kind.

No. Flora was here. . . . Justine had zoomed into the left lane and she whooped as if she had to override the sound of the motor. As if the snow and wind could have made her weaker.

"It's the first time that I'm driving it. Really driving it. I wanted you to be here, too."

Pedal to the metal, all these lousy small cars, she was on the Autobahn now, why not. She signaled them, but they stayed where they were like stoppers; she swung to the right and passed them. Stepped on the gas some more, felt how the car took over.

"My High-Wire-Artist!" she yelled.

The salesman explained that it was called turbo-power. He had a special kind of voice which he used just for women. She noticed he was married, imagined him throwing himself on his wife, driving his turbo in.

"Power," he said and opened the hood. Everything was new and clean in there. He stroked the motor; his hand was pink and common.

When he handed over the keys, he took her wrist and held tight.

"Here's my business card," he said. "If you need anything, just call."

The woman beside her had bowed her head, as if she was sleeping. A weak odor was streaming from her pores, melting into the new car smell.

"How fast do you think we can go?" yelled Justine.

The speedometer was trembling at 180 now, zigzagging. It was before noon; there was a great deal of traffic. Exit signs, fields. She stayed in the left lane, no one was ahead of her any longer. But someone was behind her. The police? No. A white Mercedes, driven by one lone man. He hugged her tail, wasn't letting go. She hit the gas pedal again, noticed his round mouth in her rearview mirror.

He was tough, swung to the right, ready to pass.

No way. The High-Wire-Artist could not be passed.

She sped up, he gave her the finger. Then she saw his car careen off the road right into a barbed-wire fence.

She loosened her grip on the wheel.

She moved into the right lane, and stayed there until they got to Enköping; turned into an OK gas station. Parked.

She heard Nathan's wild laugh behind her: my dearest, my Amazon.

I'd cut off my breasts for your sake, you know that.

She lifted Flora's head, stroked her cheeks with her sleeve. The deep holes of her eyes, as if they had flooded.

"Don't worry," she said. "It's just the speed and the wind."

When she let go, Flora's head fell back to her chest.

"Do you want anything? Coffee or something? We are on a day out. Think about what you want, Flora. I'm going in to use the bathroom for a minute."

As soon as she entered the gas station, her legs started trembling.

No! Nathan was not supposed to see that!

She found the restroom and went in, locking the door. Someone had scrawled graffiti over the walls, threatening words.

She took some headache medicine, drank water straight from the tap. She stood there for a minute and pulled herself together.

She saw her own eyes in the mirror, her face rigid and terse. She looked like herself, but then again not.

"You bitch," she said, and the woman in the mirror began to laugh.

Chapter TWELVE

Berit filled the tub and took a long warm bath. She was freezing from the inside out. She lay in the bathtub and thought that every small bone in her body had turned completely to ice.

They had eaten supper, she and Tor, one small take-out pizza per person. She was not hungry, ate just a bit from the center. He noticed her plate when she cleared the table, but he didn't say anything.

She said, "We should have gotten a dog, don't you think?"

He shrugged his shoulders.

Then he went to his little room on the second floor which he liked to call his office; the room had been the boys' playroom. A car track had run from one side of the room to the other, and the boys and their playmates had sat in there and built Lego sets. They managed to build an entire city. Now everything was packed into boxes and stored in the garage or in the basement. She couldn't remember. One of these days they'd be taken out again, she surmised, when the grandchildren started coming.

Tor had made the room into his own and she had nothing against it. There were always papers he had to deal with, or phone calls he had to make. They had driven out to IKEA and gotten the Kavaljer desk, the Kristofer desk chair, and the computer table Jerker. They spent one Easter vacation painting the room white and nailing plasterboard to the ceiling. Berit found a remnant of cloth that was just big enough to serve as a length of curtain. Then it was finished, the little home office.

After dinner, he usually went there. He was able to ignore all kinds of discussions that way. He couldn't deal with problems; she'd learned that during all their years together. Everything was supposed to flow easily and smoothly, and if it didn't, he made a face and complained that a migraine was coming on.

Berit's mother insisted that she had noticed this trait early on.

"I don't want to make you upset, sweetheart, but I think you have to get used to the idea that you will be the strong partner in this marriage."

"But Mamma, how can you say that?"

"Mothers see these things," she answered cryptically.

Mothers see these things. Berit was also a mother, and what did she see in Jörgen and Jens and their girlfriends? Who was weakest there?

In many respects, Berit's mother was right. Like the time that she was in labor with the boys. Tor had come with her to the hospital, but couldn't stand sitting and waiting; the hospital smells went into his sinuses and made him pale and nauseous. So she had to lie there by herself and fight through the long painful hours and, once it was over, the midwife couldn't reach him at home.

Afterwards he said that he had wandered about the whole night and thought of her. He had sent strong and intensive thoughts her way, in order to give her strength. She must have felt them, right?

And later, when the kids got chicken pox and all those other childhood illnesses— Jörgen kept getting ear infections—who had to take the blows? Of course, Berit was home those first few years, but she still could have used a bit of a break. But no. He hated illness of any kind and probably would have rather moved to a hotel for the duration, if it wasn't for the fact that it would look bad.

"Those analytical types," her mother used to say with a special look in her eyes.

Berit's father raised cucumbers.

She got out of the bathtub and dried herself off carefully. It was nine at night. Might as well get into a nightgown right away and get to bed. She was a bit warmer now, and it was best to go straight under the covers before she chilled off again.

"Tor, I'm going to bed now," she called. "You're going to be up for a while, I take it?"

"Yes, the evening has just begun!"

He stood in the doorway; she pulled the towel up to her chin, shyly.

"Are you coming down with something?"

"No, not at all," she said. "Just tired. Today was a hell of a day."

He surprised her by going into the bathroom and slowly and carefully loosening the towel. He looked at her, took off his glasses.

"What's up?" she asked peevishly.

"Well, after some thought, I decided that I should go to bed, too."

Was he intending to make love? She couldn't deal with that either. She realized that she didn't remember the last time that they had made love.

She lay on her back in the bed while he went around the house turning off all the lights. The dishwasher started. Yes of course, it was totally full. She was wearing her knitted pajamas and thick gray socks. Then he came in and she closed her eyes and pretended that she was sleeping.

First he lay down in his own bed, but after a while, he lifted her blanket and got in.

"Tor . . . I don't want to," she said.

"Not that," he said.

He appeared hurt. Was she supposed to make it up to him now, make everything all right?

"Sorry," she said, and turned toward him.

A few seconds later, she said, "Tor?"

"Yes?"

"Can you imagine moving to Luleå?"

He chuckled dryly.

"I'm serious. Can you see yourself moving?"

"To Luleå of all places? No way."

"Well, then I guess I have to move by myself. That is, if I want to keep working. Curt is going to move the whole publishing business there."

His arm came out of the blanket. He scratched the wall searching for the light, found it. He sat up in the bed and looked at her, without really seeing her of course, because his glasses were on the dresser.

"To Luleå?" he asked and in that moment she was so tired of him that she had to hold herself in check to keep from screaming.

"Yes, Luleå! He's getting a hell of a lot of subsidies, and he has his damned roots in that little corner of hell."

"Berit . . ."

"That's what's happening! Shit!"

"When did you find this out?"

"He announced it on Monday. But you weren't home, of course. I didn't have a chance to tell you."

"Are all of you going to be fired?"

"Oh no, not fired. And that is what is so devious about the whole thing, because only one or two of us are going to be able to move there. No one wants to go voluntarily."

"But doesn't he need you all?"

"Need, right. He is certainly going to downsize. And of course there's lots of Norrlanders who'd want the job. If he wants to expand, that is."

"You should get in touch with the union, Berit. He can't do this, not without following all the proper procedures and rules."

She snorted and put her feet on the floor.

"The union! We're not unionized. It's not customary in this field, you understand."

He said, "Let's go downstairs and talk for a while. Let's go and have a cognac while we're at it."

He lit a fire in the fireplace and wrapped a blanket around her. Gave her the glass of cognac.

"Well, that's a blow," he said. "Luleå!"

"I'm going to be unemployed, Tor. At the age of forty-five, almost forty-six."

"You can be a housewife again."

"I'd rather die."

"We wouldn't have to eat take-out pizza."

"Something wrong with the pizza?"

"Don't ask me."

"I really wasn't hungry," she said and sipped the cognac. "Maybe you can understand the reason now."

"Berit," he said softly. "Don't throw in the towel! You're still young. You should start looking for a new job now. It'll work out."

"With the high unemployment these days? Don't you ever read the paper? Today there was an article about this twenty-five-year-old guy who hadn't found a job since he finished his engineering degree at The Royal Technical College. A fine, well-educated kid, highly qualified, who was looking for any job at all. He had a folder filled with rejection letters. More than forty of them from the whole country. Even Luleå, by the way."

"Hey, Sweetie, don't make a mountain out of a molehill. At least not until you've looked around and seen whether the job situation really is all that bad."

They emptied their glasses and went back to bed. They didn't have much more to say.

He lay down in his bed, but reached to stroke her cheek.

"There's one more thing," she said. "And I am terrified about it."

He mumbled a little; he was already falling asleep.

"In Hässelby, last Saturday, when I came home so late. That old classmate of mine . . . the one with the French name . . ."

Why was she the way she was? Why did things happen the way they did? What made a child into a victim?

And what was it about me? Where did that cruelty come from?

Children noticed differences, and what happened to her mother made her different from us. She didn't have a real mother. Her mother died in that mysterious way in their house. When Justine was little. Then her father had married his secretary; there was a lot of gossip. We must have heard some of it when the adults were sitting down to coffee. It happened during grade school, first grade; we went to the stone building then. . . . Justine had her place next to me, I wanted to sit next to Jill, but there was a misunderstanding. Our teacher said, that's fine girls, sit there. Justine was ugly and spindly, like a fish. But weren't we all . . .? She clung to me; just because we happened to be next to each other, we were supposed to be best friends. I believe I told her right away that we were not going to be friends, but she was somewhat slow on the uptake; she didn't get it. All normal people would have understood, but not her. During recess, she would follow Jill and me: what should we play now, can I play, too. We were forced to hit her to get away from her. She had money; her dad was rich as Midas. She went to the store and bought candy during recesses, a huge pile of candy. She would hide it in different places for us to find, and we crept around and looked for it. It also made me mad, I remember that. Miss Messer discovered her, and then it was forbidden to leave school grounds and forbidden to have candy at school. She had to stay after school, I believe; our teacher didn't dare hit her, but made her sit and feel ashamed of herself.

She made us crazy. It was her fault. We were kids; we didn't know better. . . .

She tried to buy me. And the person who has to bribe is always lower down the ladder.

"Come home with me after school, Berit. I have a whole box full of Sandy Candy."

"What about Jill?"

"Jill can come, too."

It was that very house, the one down by the lake, and they had a dock that jutted straight out, and a large, fine boat. Her dad owned the whole Sandy concern.

"Flora's not home," she said.

"Flora . . . is she your mom?"

She shrugged.

"You're mom's dead, right?"

"Yeah."

"Is she in the graveyard?"

"Yeah."

"She was foreign, right?"

"She was from France. And when I am grown up, I'm moving there."

"Could she speak Swedish, your mom?"

"Of course."

"Can you speak French?"

"Pappa's going to teach me. When he has time. But he has too much work nowadays. With the factory."

When we got closer to the house, she told us to sneak in.

"In case Flora hasn't left yet."

She hadn't left. We lay behind the big stone and saw her come down the stairs. She didn't look like our mothers. My mom was old; I could tell when I saw Flora. She was nearly as thin as we were. She was made up like a film star. She had trouble walking on the gravel with her high heels; they sunk in. A car was waiting for her at the road. We saw her get into the back seat; the chauffeur held the door open for her and shut it again.

She didn't notice us.

"She's going shopping," said Justine. "She loves going shopping."

She had a key in a string around her neck. She had to stand on her toes in order to open the door. It seemed sort of disgusting to sneak into Justine's house, as if we were doing something forbidden. As if she herself were doing something forbidden.

Her room was on the second floor. It looked like mine. Bed, desk, books. Some dolls and stuffed animals. She went down onto her knees and pulled a box from under the bed.

"Ta-da!" she said, and took off the lid.

The whole box was filled with small boxes of Sandy Candy.

"Go ahead. Help yourself," she said.

We took four boxes apiece, Jill and me; that was all we could hold.

"OK. We're going now," said Jill.

Justine jumped up and blocked the door.

"Do you want to see the place my mom died?"

We looked at each other.

"OK," I said.

"Follow me!"

It was next to the big window on the second floor.

"Here on the floor was where my mom died."

"Why'd she do that?"

"Something broke in her brain."

"Was your mom crazy?" Jill asked and giggled.

"No. . . ."

"You're crazy; maybe you got it from her," said Jill.

"I'm not at all crazy!"

I glanced at the shining brown floor and tried to imagine how the woman who had been Justine's real mother had lain there and breathed her last.

"Did you cry?" I asked.

"What do you mean, cry?"

"When your mom laid here and died."

"Probably."

She ran in front of us down the stairs.

"Want to see something else?"

"No."

"Come on. Don't you want to see something else?"

"What?"

"In the basement."

"What in the basement?"

She had already opened the door to the basement and started down the stairs.

Jill looked at me. "You go ahead."

There was nothing special about the basement. A big oil heater, a clothes rack with sheets hung up to dry. A mangle by the window and a pile of square stones with empty flowerpots on it.

"What's so big about the basement?" I asked.

She looked secretive. Her beret had gotten loose and was hanging by a few hairs. She opened the door to a smaller room.

"There!" she said and pointed.

There was a big washtub in the room, one that people used to boil laundry in. Nothing else.

"What about it? My grandparents had one of those."

"Flora puts me in it sometimes."

"Huh?"

"When she's angry with me."

"She puts you in that?"

"Yeah."

"Why's she do that?"

"She puts water in it and says she will boil away my stubbornness."

Prickles went up and down my spine, but it wasn't sympathy or fear; it was something else, and it felt kind of good.

I've been thinking about this the last few days. Children seem to lack empathy. But do all children lack empathy? Or was it just me . . . or my home? I had nice, kind parents who treated me well. Maybe even spoiled me a little; they were very old when I was born. I was the only child; no other children to rub against. Of course you get a little spoiled in such a situation.

But even a child can choose her friends. She should have bothered someone else, not just Jill and me the whole time. She carried Sandy Candy boxes in her school bag; we could choose menthol or honey, and if we couldn't choose, we got both. Oh, how we wanted to be rid of her!

I believe it was my suggestion that we go to the cemetery. It was a long way, the whole length of Sandviksvägen, if you went there directly and didn't run through side streets.

She stuck to us like a leach. Jill and I talked to each other and pretended that she wasn't there, but I knew that she was going to follow us and, in fact, I was counting on it.

It must have been late September or early October because the leaves were still green, but there was a snap in the air. We were wearing jackets and long pants and we had our school bags, which we always took with us. We were still very proud of them, and of being old enough to go to school.

The boxes of candy lasted until we reached the cemetery.

"What are we going to do?" asked Justine.

"We're going to visit your mom."

With some effort, we managed to open the heavy iron gate, but then we couldn't figure out how to close it again. We left it open. Justine knew exactly where the grave was; she led us straight for a while, then to the right. The stone was tall and white and there was a name that I no longer remember.

"I wonder what she looks like now," I said. "Probably just bones left. And a lot of hair. They say that hair keeps growing on the dead when they're in the casket. Hair and nails, too."

"I don't want to be a skeleton!" shrieked Jill. "I don't want my fingernails to keep growing!"

"Nobody does," I said.

Justine said, "You have to have a skeleton inside yourself, or you'll fall into a heap."

We wandered toward the white building which was a bit farther in. An old man was right behind it, raking the pathway.

"That's the house of the dead," I said. "The bodies lie in there, the ones that need to be buried, and wait their turn." The old man stopped raking and yelled at us. We pretended not to hear. We hid behind a hedge. After a while, he hung up the rake and left. He went through the gate and shut it firmly behind him. Now we were alone in the cemetery. There was a rain barrel beside the house of the dead. There was a great deal of rain in the barrel, which I saw when I peered in, and the sides were slick with algae.

"Let's play fish," I said, because I noticed that Jill was going to say that she wanted to go home.

"What do you mean, play fish?" asked Justine.

"Aquarium," I said. "The rain barrel can be our aquarium."

Jill said, "We shouldn't be playing here."

"The old guy's gone."

It was totally quiet. The wind moved through the birch leaves, but no birds. They must have left for warmer climates already. I remember all this so well. It's strange. I was only seven years old.

"Justine's going to be the fish," I said, and noticed that she wanted to protest, but then pulled herself together as if she were gathering courage to say yes.

"Do I have to take my clothes off?" she asked.

"What do you think, Jill? Should she take off her clothes?"

Jill bit her lip and nodded. Then she began to giggle; she had this way of suddenly exploding into giggles. I was giggling, too. We told her to take off her clothes, and she did so. She didn't have to. Everyone has free will. She probably liked it somehow? Maybe she liked it when Flora put her in the washtub? Otherwise, why tell us about it?

There were pee marks in her underwear; I saw that when she put them aside. She had goose bumps. She couldn't climb in the rain barrel by herself, so we had to help her. There was a splash when she slid in. She screamed a bit; the water was cold against her naked tummy.

"Now you're our fish," I said.

She splashed a little, pretending to swim.

"We'll give you some food. What do fish eat?"

"They eat . . . worms."

Something happened with Justine, she stood straight up like a rod in the barrel and her eyes were wide open.

"No worms! I'm not that kind of fish! I only eat leaves!"

"Be quiet," I said. "Fish don't talk."

We pulled some leaves from the bushes and rained them down on Justine in the rain barrel. She calmed down. Her hair was wet, and her teeth were starting to chatter.

I don't know what came over me, what was going on with me; I was just a child, seven years old. I saw the hose hanging next to the wall of the house; I unrolled it and turned on the faucet.

"You're going to get more water in your aquarium," I said to Justine and she began to jump up and down and protest.

I've thought about it since then. I really wanted to see her with water up to her chin, yes even to her mouth and nose. I knew she could drown, but that was something that didn't affect me. Or rather, it would be interesting to see how that could happen. When people drowned. I pulled the hose to the edge of the rain barrel and began to spray water into it.

First she screamed and flailed around wildly. I couldn't stop myself from spraying her right on the head. Water streamed down her face and into the edges of her mouth. Afterwards I thought it must have been really cold. Now the water was up to her chin.

Jill said, "You should turn off the water."

It was almost as if I couldn't help myself.

"Turn it off, Berit! Turn it off!"

When I didn't react, she went and turned it off herself. Justine was so cold she was shivering violently.

I walked around a while, thinking. Then I took a stick from the ground.

I held it a bit over the edge.

"Look! I'm fishing!"

Jill ran and got a stick, too.

"Who'll get a bite?" I called out. "Who will get a bite first?"

Maybe I thought that she would grab the sticks and we could pull her out and she could get her clothes back on. But she didn't do it. She stood there in the barrel and howled. I hit her with the stick, right over one of her ears. Jill looked at me, and then she did the same thing.

If she only would have cried.

Then I remember that we heard footsteps on the gravel, and Jill and I threw away the sticks and ran. Good Lord, how we ran, down the hill which is now the meadow of remembrance for those who have been cremated, out the gate and into the forest to the right, and then we threw ourselves into the moss. I don't think we thought so much about Justine, how she was doing, if we had hurt her. The only thing we were worried about was that she might tattle, that we would get caught.

She couldn't sleep. The lit clock on the wall showed it was twelve-thirty. Tor was lying with his face toward her; he was snoring slightly and audibly. She got up. There must be some sleeping pills in the cabinet, once she had received a prescription for Sobril when her nerves were acting up, but she'd never opened the package. Yes, there it was. Maybe the medicine was too old; she couldn't read the date without her glasses. She popped a few of the small white tablets into her mouth and swallowed them with a bit of water she poured into her toothbrush mug.

Chapter THIRTEEN

Hans Peter's apartment was on Fyrspannsgatan with a view over the cemetery. On All Saints Day, he usually lit two candles and placed them in the living room window. He would stand still for a minute. Outside, the grave votives shone their solemn light. It was the only time of the year that the cemetery parking lot was full. Cars were even parked along Sandviksvägen.

At that time, with darkness like a cape over city and countryside, it was natural that he thought about his sister. She would have been thirty-eight years old now, probably a happy mother of two children and maybe a preschool teacher or the owner of an organic food store. This was how he imagined her. She and her husband would most likely have a single family house in Stuvsta, near their parents. Oh, his mother would have been happy.

This morning he woke from the light and the sound of a snowplow driving back and forth, clearing the sidewalks. An ache, almost a real pain, was situated behind his temples. He hadn't been able to sleep when he came home at five in the morning; he dozed a bit, dreamed strange and sick dreams. What was the time now? Ten-thirty. Might as well get dressed.

Snow lay over the cemetery like a thick layer of whipped cream. Hans Peter prepared some coffee and made some sandwiches with ham and sliced tomatoes sprinkled with salt and black pepper. Sat at the kitchen table, flipped through the newspaper, *Dagens Nyheter*.

Today there was quite a bit about a woman who was going to be executed in Texas. She was called Karla Faye Tucker and she was condemned to death. She was just as old as his sister would have been. Karla Faye Tucker had thick hair and beautiful calm eyes. The article stated that she had been saved and converted. Even the Pope had asked for clemency, but that probably wouldn't happen. Probably she'd be tied to the stretcher in the death chamber at one in the morning, right when he was sitting behind the reception desk. An executioner would search for the vein in her arm and then, once he found it, inject the deadly liquid.

You only have one life, and you do with it what you will, he thought. Karla Faye Tucker didn't understand that until it was too late.

He still felt down. This happened a few times a year, not a real depression. He imagined that a real depression would be heavier, deeper, more difficult. No, it was a certain kind of weariness. Weary of the rhythm of the days, the standardization of everything.

Maybe a long walk would help him get into a better mood. He put on his lined winter boots and his parka, which he once received as a birthday present from Liv. It was still around even though the birthday had been a long time ago. It wasn't all that warm, but it kept out the wind, and if you put on a sweater underneath it, you didn't freeze at all. He usually sprayed waterproofing on it each time he washed it, and he imagined that it helped.

Right when he was about to leave, the phone rang.

It was his mother. He said that he was about to go, anything important, could he call back?

"It's your father's birthday today, Hans Peter."

"Oh hell. Of course!"

"You hadn't forgotten it?"

"There's been so much going on at work. Yes, I totally forgot."

"You don't have all that many relatives to forget."

That burned him.

"I know! I just forgot! It was unforgivable."

"He went out early to look for the mail."

"Stop it now, Mamma."

"Are you coming by for a visit this weekend? We can have a birthday dinner then. If you have time, that is."

"Yes, yes, yes, of course. I'll come."

He walked between the bus stops on Sandviksvägen and turned to the left at the gold kiosk. The snow made it difficult to get by in certain places. The cars crept along. The snowplows were out in force, pushing away the snow and sanding the street. He saw a young mail carrier fly past on his heavily burdened bicycle and remembered when he himself had worked delivering mail. Nice that job was over. He was too old for that kind of thing now.

He would soon be too old for everything.

He passed by the hill toward the General Bathhouse, which today looked nothing at all like a bathhouse. The snow covered the sand and the piers and lay over the ice so thickly that you could not even see the edge of the beach. It was still snowing, but not too much; it didn't have the small white flakes that whirled into your eyes and gave you a headache. At least, they didn't make his headache worse. He pulled his cap further down and followed the beach path toward Riddersvik.

It would be nice to live here, in one of the row houses with their fantastic views of the lake. But of course, they cost an arm and a leg. And he was a single man. Sometimes he thought about finding an apartment in the middle of Stockholm instead, but he liked nature; he was not really a city person. This was a combination which suited him fine.

A few years ago, a boardwalk was built along the side of the hill and out over the water like a balcony. It made a short cut to Riddersvik and Tempeludden. He felt closer to nature out here, close to the large willows. When the lake froze, large groups of long-distance skaters came gliding all the way from Enköping or places even farther away. He wondered whether the ice was strong enough to hold, but didn't see any human tracks, just light paw prints from smaller animals. The bushes had frozen; drowned in snow and ice, they looked like large coral chunks. He leaned out above the edge and observed them. He should have brought his little camera. Why did he never think of taking photos in the middle of winter?

He heard a sound and saw a woman coming with a large black dog, walking over the bridge path. The dog was strong and she had great difficulty holding on to it. Its shaggy nose was speckled with snow, and the sight was so funny, he couldn't help smiling.

Then she stopped, pushed some hair back under her hat. Her face was red and she didn't wear make-up; her jacket was bright yellow.

"Nice dog," he said, but he didn't know whether he should dare pet it.

"Yeah," she said. "It's my daughter's."

"You going out with him, or is he going out with you?"

"You could wonder which," she laughed.

She pulled the leash and said something which sounded like Freya.

"Is she named Freya? Like the radio program?"

"No, her name is Feja. And usually she's not so stubborn. Just with me . . . my daughter and her husband are teaching it to be a rescue dog."

"Rescuing what, then?"

"Well . . .," she said evasively, "people who've gone missing or gotten trapped in a fallen house. Things like that."

"Sounds interesting."

"But she's still fairly young, three years old."

"Is she a Schnauzer?"

"Yeah, a Great Schnauzer. She's in heat now; that's why she has difficulty listening. But we have to go now. Come, Feya!"

He stood there and watched them disappear over the hill.

For the umpteenth time, he thought he should have had a dog.

If only he had one. Then the two hounds would sniff each other for a while, in the butt, as dogs do; and then he would have continued his walk, just as he was doing now. Up on the right was Ridderviks garden and beneath the hill were all the garden plots; he would have let Bella run loose precisely here. She would have rushed up and down the hill like crazy and rolled around in the snow. Maybe he would have had a stick to throw for her.

He trudged up the hill where the unusual pavilion stood with its pillars like a temple from a story in *Arabian Nights*. Black iron railings closed it to pedestrians; they sang like an orchestra when the wind from Lake Mälar whipped through them. It sounded pretty and somewhat desolate. A heavy hook hung from the middle of the ceiling. He wondered if someone had hanged himself there, he could almost see a dangling, swinging body.

He found her a bit down the hill. She was half lying behind a large tree trunk, and afterwards he thought that if he had had a dog with him, the dog would have sniffed her out at once. As it was, he nearly overlooked her.

She lay against the trunk of the tree and snow was falling over her. She had brushed it away as long as she could, but now her arms were down on the ground and her head hung to the side.

His first thought was that she was dead. He stooped close to her and gently touched her chin. It was cold, but she was breathing. Then he placed her on the ground and lifted her legs, thinking this is what you do with people who have fainted.

A second later, she made a noise and opened her eyes. Her face was as white as the snow around her.

"Oh, you're alive, thank God!" he cried, and fell on his knees next to her. She smacked her lips, made some swallowing sounds.

"You must have fainted. I found you sitting here by the tree trunk."

"I was running . . .," she said roughly, and then he saw that she was wearing jogging shoes and some kind of jogging suit.

"What happened? You must have fallen."

Now she tried to sit up, and he took her arms and helped her.

"Take it easy so that you don't fall down again."

She yelped and grabbed her left foot. Lifted herself up with difficulty, holding on to his parka the whole time.

"It's my foot. . . . I remember now, it just gave out on me."

"Can it hold you?"

"No, not really. . . ."

"Maybe you sprained it."

"I have an old injury there. That foot often gives out; I should have thought of that."

"You'll have to go to the hospital."

"No, it's enough if you get me home."

She was his age, maybe somewhat older. Her voice was light and girlish. He thought that he really couldn't carry her.

"If you just let me lean on you . . .?" she said.

"Where do you live?"

"Not far from here. You see the house when you come out on the bridge."

She laid one arm around his neck and they started to shuffle and slide away from the tree. It was extremely uncomfortable.

"If it's broken, you'll need a cast."

"It's not broken."

"How can you be so sure?"

"I'm sure."

"Maybe I should . . . introduce myself. Hans Peter Bergman. I live in Hässelby Strand. I just thought I'd take a long walk."

"Well, that's the end of that."

"Not to worry."

"My name's Justine Dalvik."

"Kristin?"

"No. Justine."

They had come up to some buildings and a field with horses. The animals wore damp blankets; they pawed with their hooves in the snow and looked like they longed to be back inside.

"Shall we knock on the door and ask for help?"

"Oh God, no. That's just too dramatic."

Just then a man came out on the stairs. He looked at them indifferently, and then went to his car which was sloppily parked outside the gate.

"Hello?" called Hans Peter.

The man stopped.

"We need a little help here."

He came toward them, opening his hands.

"I speak badly Swedish."

"Not to worry, as long as you can drive."

"Can drive. You want drive you?"

"Thanks, that'd be great. The lady has hurt her foot. We just need a short ride; she lives fairly close to here."

They entered the house.

"Thanks, that was kind of you to help."

There was an undertone in her voice, as if she didn't want him to rush away immediately.

He said, "I can take a look at your foot for you. I learned some first aid in the army."

"Ok, if you want to. . . . Let's go to the kitchen."

There was a large bird on the kitchen counter. It was drinking water from a bowl.

"Hope you're not getting the wrong impression," she said quietly.

"About what?"

"Some people are afraid of birds."

"It's just an unusual one. Is it yours?"

She nodded. He untied her shoes, sitting right across from her, and lifted up her leg into his lap.

"Isn't it a bad idea to go running when it's so slippery out?"

Color was returning to her face.

"Obviously," she said dryly.

Her foot was strangely shaped with small, somewhat bent, toenails. He thought about something he read once. Women had bent toenails, men had straight ones. He wondered why.

There was a bit of swelling by the ankle. He held her foot and bent it back and forth a bit.

"Does that hurt?"

"A bit."

"Then it's probably not broken. I can wrap it for you, if you want."

"Thanks. In my bedroom there's a cabinet with a few medical items. There's an elastic bandage there, I think. Do you think you'll find it? It's the room with only one bed."

He went out into the hall and up the steep stairs. There were two framed posters on the walls from the forties. They were ads for candy. At the top, the hallway opened to a large room filled with books. He cast a glance at the titles, but didn't dare linger over them. The door to her room was slightly open. The bed was well made, but the floor was dirty with feathers and seeds. A large pine tree appeared to grow from the floor. Then he realized it was placed in Christmas tree stand. Obviously she kept the bird in the same room that she slept in herself.

"How's it going?" she called from the kitchen.

"Where's the cabinet again?"

"Left of the window. Do you see it?"

Yes, there it was. He squatted down and opened it. Lots of bottles and cans, and far to the back, an elastic bandage roll. When he took it out, the bird was behind him somewhere. It sat on its tree branch and made a rasping sound. Hans Peter didn't move.

"Don't be afraid," she called up. "He won't hurt you."

The bird glowered at him with one eye. It pulled up one leg underneath its belly and clicked with its beak. Hans Peter felt ill at ease. Would it leap at him if he moved? He put up his arm for protection and sidled out of the door. The bird flapped his wings, but stayed where it was.

"Why do you have that bird anyway?" he asked once afterwards, after he had taken care of binding her foot and warming milk for both of them. He hadn't had warm milk since he was small. They had moved to the large room upstairs, the one with the books. He had said he was going to leave; in fact, he'd said it a few times already.

"For company, among other things."

"Don't such large birds feel more at home outside?"

"Won't work. He's too imprinted by humans. If you let him outside, the other birds will attack him."

"Have you tried it?"

She nodded.

"He flew up to that oak out there. Suddenly the skies were filled with magpies. Some attacked him right away and actually that was lucky; he lost his grip and fell into my arms. Ever since then, he's been afraid the minute you open a window."

"Doesn't anyone else live with you?"

She shook her head.

Even up here there were framed posters of Sandy Candy. He pointed and asked why.

"Sven Dalvik was my father. The Sandy concern, you know."

He didn't know, and that seemed to make her happy.

He wandered to get a look at the books.

"You like reading, don't you?" she asked.

"Yes, in my next life, I'm going to be a seller of fine used books."

"What do you do in this life?"

"Oh, I'm the night clerk for a hotel."

"I thought rather that you were a doctor, the way you wrapped my foot like a real pro."

He looked at her seriously.

"You were sitting in the snow as if you were dead. As if you'd been murdered."

"Murdered! What made you think that?"

"It looked just like a murder in a movie."

"Ew . . ."

"If I hadn't come. . . ."

"I'd have woken up again after a minute. It's happened to me before. My foot gives out on me, it hurts like hell, and I faint from the pain."

"How come?"

"I broke it a long time ago. It's never been really all right since then. I've been trying to strengthen it by running. Now I'll have to give that up for a while."

"You certainly ought to!"

He kept looking at the bookshelves.

"Did you buy all these books yourself?"

She laughed, a short and somewhat spiteful laugh.

"Did you think I wouldn't be capable enough?"

"No, that's not what I meant."

"No, sorry, yes, of course they're mine. No one else in this house enjoyed reading, just me."

"Have you lived here a long time?"

"I grew up here."

"You did . . .? By the way, I see you have Bernard Malamud. Have you read much of him?"

"Well, I read him many years ago and I liked what he wrote. So I have three or four of his books."

"I like his style, too. But I've only read one of his. But it went right to my heart."

"You can borrow that one if you like."

He became oddly happy.

"Thanks, I'd like that," he said.

Chapter FOURTEEN

The light:

Which suddenly slid into a black and sweeping darkness. The glittering of a shard, an eye. Mother and sisters screaming, Flora, Flora, or the cry of seagulls far away. Did she remember this? She was a very small child and was sleeping in a basket under the tree.

No.

She had just heard it told.

Her eldest sister remembered:

How you lay there and how Mamma ran from us screaming.

Why was she screaming?

Well, there was a big bird on your chest.

It was pecking at your eye with its rough black beak.

Certainly this was in here somewhere. The smell of a wide open bird beak, the smell of its craw: voles, worms, mire. A drop of saliva falling on her cheek, and even though she was too small to feel afraid—she was afraid. She screamed with her mother's scream. And the bird's scream and how it flew off, because the sisters were coming; they took stones from the ground and threw them, but nevertheless it continued to circle above the tree for a long time afterwards.

"Flora, that is you, isn't it? You remember me, don't you?"

She turned her head. Morning.

The woman in the other bed had been lying there looking at her. For how long?

"I understand . . . that you can't talk. But you must remember me, Märta Bengtsson. Your father owned Klintgårdens Garden Supply; we used to go there and buy red beets."

The grey bloat under her chin, her turbid eyes, her veined arm which was pointing right at her.

"To think that we've ended up here . . . and in the same room to boot. The gorgeous Flora Dalvik and me."

Oh yes, she remembered that squabbling, clinging kid, who never was properly clean. Her sister's name was. . . .

"You and my sister used to go dancing. Oh, how I used to be so jealous. You were so pretty in your dresses . . . and you used to wear something pink. Yes, it was pink, though you called it apricot. Apricot! As if we were supposed to know more about apricots than that they were some kind of fruit."

Märta Bengtsson had managed to grip the railing above the bed and tried to raise herself up. Her flecked arms seized and she couldn't manage it. She fell back into the pillows while giving off a loud fart.

A chuckling laugh with no teeth.

"To think we'd end up like this, you and I! Who would ever have believed it?"

Flora closed her eyes. Siv was the name, Siv with the long toes. They learned to dance in her room, and one of Flora's sisters had been there, too. Which one of them? Rosa, the one who was most fond of dancing?

She got pregnant, Siv did, in the family way as they said. The taut skin over her belly, how she nevertheless didn't die, but smiled. Smiled and laughed the whole way through until one night the kid popped out and was born.

A family shame? Of course, it was always a scandal when something like that came to light. That someone had embraced a man without the blessing of the priest. She had embraced Sven Dalvik many a time with the priest's blessing, but still nothing.

"You heard Siv died, didn't you? It was quite a few years ago now, 1992. She just lay down on her pillow and died. Just like that. Why weren't we allowed to have a death like that? Just lie down on our pillows and die."

The white uniforms. Spray and stink of bedpans. Dampness between the legs, gone. She always froze when they took off her diapers, a wave of shivering went over her stomach and limbs. Just lying here giving off steam like a recently carved fish. Fixated on their young faces, would they be able to control themselves, would they be able to keep what they really thought under wraps. The sticky brown mess. Yes, her stomach was acting up, whether nightmares or in reality. She had heard the girl's steps during the night. They had come closer, like marching soldiers, and she had stared at the door, but it didn't open. It had been night.

"Have you eaten something unsuitable, Flora? I believe we'll give you tea today, no more coffee."

"For the love of God, how that stinks!"

"Don't worry, Märta, we'll open the window."

Now she was sitting in the reddish-yellow armchair, Märta Bengtsson was right across from her. Just like a pair of bosom buddies.

"But one thing doesn't make sense. Why are you in this kind of ward? Not that it's any of my business, but . . . you know, there are private nursing homes. I mean something really nice, almost like having your very own nurse. You must be able to afford it. Not that you really threw it around when you were living, I mean, when Sven Dalvik was living, of course. But then you lived a totally different kind of life. At least I . . . I mean, that's what we read in the papers. A real glittering gala life. You've lived a rich life, Flora. And so I'll say it again, to think that we ended up here."

A rich life? Yes, as far as money went. Yes, rich indeed.

And once she taught that kid some manners, things got much easier. She had offered love, ready to take the girl to her heart and love her. But that had been the wrong

method. Siege warfare was the name of the game. Siege
warfare and conquest.

She used to take Justine into the basement sometimes and
give her a round in the tub, sat her down and lit the fire. Never
hot enough to burn her, though, never anything like that.

A child has to learn boundaries.

Sven's kowtowing to the girl had gotten on her nerves.
The look in her eyes when he took her into his arms, and surprised her with kisses and cuddles. The girl's eyes never left
her for a second. They shone triumphantly in her direction.

There was something sick about that girl. Something akin
to mental illness.

She tried to talk to Sven about it, after the two of them had
made love. Then he was open and willing to listen to suggestions, even if he didn't agree with her.

"No!" he said. "The kid's all right. But you've got to try
and understand her, Flora. She is still grieving her mother."

"Sven, dearest, she can't possibly even remember her
mother."

"It's the feeling of loss. It's eating her from the inside,
tearing a hole inside her. We shouldn't let that happen. We
have to give her all our love."

All of it? *All* of our love?

And she opened her arms and legs. Come and have me
again, Dearest, sow me, make me bear fruit.

"She hears what we say, doesn't she, nurse?"

"One never knows. But it's best to choose one's words
carefully."

"Do you know that she was once best friends with my
sister Siv?"

Oh no, we weren't such close friends. Just on the surface,
if you could imagine that with your shrunken little brain. She
was coarse and clumsy, just like you. Your whole family was
like that, and now I'm thinking of your father, how he toddled
home on Saturday afternoon, that jerky, twitchy walk . . . and

how you all left home just like mice. He beat Siv sometimes; she ran over to our place and cried. How could she even tell us such a shameful thing? She was almost boastful, the way she showed us her bruises. But once that baby was on the way, he showed his other side. It was almost as if he had been converted at a tent meeting, how he became such a sweet grandfather to that boy.

But before then. Out into the cold with them, wife and children. Here I come, the master of the house. My mother would never ever have let herself be thrown out of her own house. If my father had even touched a drop of brandy in order to get drunk, I believe she would have buried him in the potato field.

Your mom had gypsy blood. That's why she couldn't resist. The guilt of having gypsy blood. He gave her one once on her mouth so that her lips burst open with blood. We saw that one through the window, Siv and I. "Gypsy whore!" he yelled at her, she was barefoot and half dressed. That she lets him get away with it, I said to Siv. And that's the day when our friendship ended.

"Then came the day you married that fine director and widower Dalvik. Snapped him up, just like that! You never came to visit once you married. My daughter Marie was in the same class as his daughter. We saw the two of you at parental meetings. You held his arm so properly. You pretended you didn't know me. But I wasn't the one who'd changed so much; that was you; but I had no problems at all recognizing you. You can't hide, no matter what the cloth you use for your clothes. Silk or velvet, hand-me-downs or rags."

They all resembled their father, his coarse build, his greasy, chapped skin. Flora was delicate.

"You are as small as a girl," said Sven Dalvik, and took her into his arms. Finally his daughter was sleeping; only then could he give himself fully to his woman. Gripped her narrow hips, were they large enough to hold a child? The small pink nipples, flat like a boy. She had short hair then; he called her his little guy.

The girl was sleeping, but you could never be too sure. She could wake up and stand there in the doorway with those glowering, wide-awake eyes, that what-are-you-doing-with-my-father look.

She no longer had orgasms.

He didn't seem worried about that. Did he actually even notice?

"I can't relax; everything's locked up; everything in me has locked up."

"Don't worry about it. It's because you're thinking about it too much that it's not working."

"Let's travel again. Our trip to London had to be cut short. Let's have a second honeymoon, but choose Paris this time."

He did not want to leave the girl. Not so quickly again. But he still traveled quite a bit for business. "Let's leave it for the future, Flora. Not right now."

But time went on and Justine began school.

"Who would take care of her?" he said. "If we both traveled, you and I? Who would get her dressed and send her off to school with her schoolbags?"

"You worked it out before."

"But it's different now. I don't want to disappoint her again."

And he went off by himself. Returned with expensive presents. A ring with diamonds to make it up to her and this trumpet thing for the girl.

"If you let her play that thing inside, I'm moving!"

Play, if you could call it that!

The girl would go to the beach and inhale so that her whole body bent double. The ducks would come, lured by the sound; they should have had better taste. But it seemed to make her happy.

"I'm playing for the birds, Pappa!"

"My fine, sweet girl. Soon you'll be able to start an orchestra."

The ducks climbed on the dock and got things messy with their excrement. Who did he think was going to scrub the dock clean! Did you think I moved here to be scrubbing filthy bird shit from an old dock!

No.

Impossible to argue with that man. He bit his lip and was silent. Until she had to come hat in hand, begging for forgiveness.

The kid. Everything was her fault. Overprotected and spoiled.

She had sunk into her chair. She was very tired. Märta Bengtsson had been staring at her, taking away her rest.

"Nurse! Please come here a moment! I think Mrs. Dalvik has fainted."

"No, no, she's fine. We just have to prop her up again, like this."

"Maybe she's tired and needs to rest?"

"No, it's good for you to be up as long as you can. It makes the day go faster."

A friendly thought, at least, from Märta Bengtsson. Flora looked at her and managed a nod. Märta nodded back.

"Whoever would have thought we would end up like this."

Every once in a while a fierce rage came upon her. Not at Märta, not at the caretakers. No, at Sven. Seventy years old and completely healthy up to that moment, one afternoon he clutched at his heart and fell down at the top of the stairs. She had been standing in the window and had seen him, and she had immediately called for an ambulance. She had to use all her strength to push him slowly away, so that a crack was open wide enough for her to get out the door. He lay there on the stairs and something frothy was running from one of the corners of his mouth.

He was dead the following morning.

She was sitting next to him, holding his hand. Justine was at his other side. He had them both, and still, he left them both.

Who will be sitting at my side, when the time comes?
I don't want to die.
I want to live.

Chapter FIFTEEN

Some days they all ganged up on her. Everyone in the whole class. They took each other's hands, mittened hands with wet thumbs, and made a circle. This is what the teacher saw: How the children were playing Christmas games with the memory of plundering the Christmas tree fresh in their minds. How the wind pulled at their scarves; their light voices. She then felt a warm flush in her chest and remembered her own innocent child self.

"Justine went in, Justine went out, when she went in, she pissed again."

For the fact of the matter with Justine was that she always had to go pee, but she forgot to go to the washroom, or dawdled on the way there. More likely the latter, actually. The girls had hindered her there and made her embarrassed.

Flora got angry of course. Held the piss-wet underwear under her nose.

Always being wet down there, she got chafing sores and red marks.

Now she was lying in the snow. No one had pushed her. She lay down willingly and the ring dance continued and their worn snow boots. Lay there like a sacrificial lamb.

Something hard at her side. The snow could be formed; it was a bit warmer now. They were building around her; they were building a well and she was at its bottom.

The bumpy white walls. Far up there the light, gray and whistling. The bell rang. Time to go in.

"We're going now," Berit called. She was the archangel, the one who decided everything. "Hurry up, so that teacher doesn't yell at you."

She could have gotten up. She could have braced herself against the walls and they would have crumbled; that wouldn't have been difficult at all.

She didn't.

The teacher and Flora and herself. The tick of the clock on the wall.

"Look at us when we're speaking to you!"

"Well, she has lost her mother. . . ."

"But that was many years ago and she has a new mother now. She can't profit from that old story for the rest of her life. We have to bring her away from that, help her. Otherwise, she is going to have a great deal of problems later on."

Flora wearing her white blouse.

"We only want the best for you, Justine; you know that."

The teacher with white chalk on her hands.

"She is not without talent. But she has to try harder. She can't sit there so quietly during the lessons. I know that she has inner resources. And she has a responsibility for her own life, just as all human beings do; even schoolchildren do."

"We will have to talk to your father about this, Justine, unless you change your ways. And you don't want to do that, do you?"

No, there she hit the nail on the head. Pappa had to be spared. He would never have to know. He had enough problems of his own with that witch woman in his house and in his bed.

Let's think about someone, Justine, someone only you and I know. Yes. Mamma.

Flora whipped her, but never when Pappa was home. She locked her in the basement with her school books, but she no longer had the strength to force her into the wash tub.

"I'll listen to you recite later, even though it won't make a difference. You're a real lost cause."

What does she mean, a "lost cause"?

Sometimes she fled from the schoolyard. But it would be more difficult later on, when they caught up to her. Berit grabbed her, pointing at her body.

"Look at Justine's French nose!"

"Yuck! What an ugly, disgusting nose!"

"Look at Justine's French chin!"

"Yuck! What an ugly, disgusting chin!"

"Look at Justine's French neck!"

"Yuck! What an ugly, disgusting neck!"

Hands pulling at her clothes, buttons, pulling down her zipper. Then she broke free and ran. They didn't expect her unpredictable movement. She usually played the role of the victim so well.

But now she was in flight, fleeing them.

Uprooted trees and brushwood. She had been there once with the Hunter. When she ran away from school, she would often meet him there. He wore a leather coat and smelled like leaves and earth.

The Hunter squatted and contemplated her.

No one else did that.

He brought her over to his place. There was a cat with white whiskers and an iron woodstove. Out in the back, he chopped wood to feed the stove. The kitchen roared with heat.

He did not say that she should not pay any attention to them. He didn't say anything at all.

But he stroked her lightly over the back.

They sat at his table and played solitaire. He had extremely small cards with Japanese flowers on the back. They competed to see who would first lay out all the cards. The cat walked on the table with delicate, soft steps. When the cat lay down, the Hunter scratched it under its paw pads with his fingernail. The whole cat body shook.

"Are you just as ticklish, Stina?"

He always called her Stina, not the French Justine.

What had the Hunter's name been?

She would never tell anyone about the Hunter. There was a witch woman in her house. The witch woman's evil eye could fall on the Hunter and no one could save himself from that look, not even with prayer.

Sometimes Pappa wanted to speak with her about serious things. She could tell by his way of lifting his shoulders. She could tell already at the dinner table and then she would lose her appetite.

In the evening, he would come to her room.

She quickly asked:

"Are you going on a trip again?"

"No, why would you think that?"

"If you're going on a trip, can I come, too?"

"I'm not leaving, Sweetie."

"But IF."

"Someday you can come with me."

"Where will we go?"

"Maybe to France."

She fingered the desk pad. She had drawn on it, flowers and sleeping animals. If only he would continue to talk, if he would add details, what we need to travel, passports and suitcases and we need to buy you some clothes to travel in.

But Pappa coughed as if he were catching a cold.

"Have you finished your homework properly?"

"Yes, I have."

"And you're doing fine in school, right, Justine?"

"Yes."

"You must tell me if something is going on. Promise me."

"Yes."

"The school years are so short, but so important. Take advantage of them. If you understand what I mean."

She didn't, but she nodded.

"You should also take advantage of your childhood. Unfortunately, you don't realize this until childhood is over. Childhood problems . . . they're small compared to the problems you will have once you are all grown up. Do you understand me, Justine?"

She nodded again.

Once he left the room, she would start to cry immediately. As long as he was in the room, she was filled with expectation, as if he would see right through her and with one movement rip her away from the chair and lift her straight to the light.

Everything was so heavy and soiled.

She lay on her stomach in the bed, and everything was warm and wet.

Justine ran to the forest to the uprooted tree. A swarm of shining threads. The snow had melted. Brown, damp grass. The sound of a woodpecker against a tree.

In the Hunter's room, the Christmas tree was still up with its soft light-green needles.

He called her Stina.

He once had a wife, a woman named Dora. Something happened. He mentioned it sometimes, and his face turned old. Then he was no longer just the Hunter but someone else, and she was disturbed by it but still had to listen, over and over.

They had had a small firm which sold gardening supplies. He operated it together with his best friend Jack. Dora took care of the books; she was very good at numbers.

"You didn't have any children?"

She had to ask, to draw out the story.

He made a wild grimace.

"No. We never had the chance."

He was getting closer to the difficult part, the inevitable part.

"One day when I entered the shed . . ."

She saw it. He had told the story so many times that she now could see the scene in front of her, the details, the colors, even the scent of Dora's lily-of-the-valley talcum powder which she put under her arms after washing up in the morning.

She saw the other man, the Hunter's friend, how he leaned over the woman. She saw it as if it were on a book, a Harlequin cover. The woman's hair in a page cut, black and slick; it fell down over the bench. The man's shirt of deer leather, somewhat unlaced. She saw their lips come closer. Shaking with lust, her fingers got cold and she had an unusual feeling of breathlessness.

"What happened then?" she whispered and the cat jumped to the floor and went to the door on its straggling legs.

"I don't know," he said with a gravelly voice. "I have no idea what happened to them."

Then she approached the Hunter and touched his cheek. And it was warm in the kitchen and the stove had begun to glow.

"When you're big, you're going to forget all about me," he said, and the cards disappeared into his huge hands.

"Never till the day I die!" she exclaimed, and then she cried, because she was starting to grow now, starting to be a grown person.

"I usually stand on the top of the bluff and scream," said the Hunter. "That usually helps. People think you're crazy, and one of these days I'll end up in the asylum. But it does help to stand on the top of the bluff and scream."

She went outside. There was a light in the window, but he didn't look out at her. He sat at the table with the flowery wax tablecloth and played one game of solitaire after another. She climbed all the way to the edge. Wind in her eyes, wind in her mouth when she opened it wide, like at the dentist's office.

But no scream came out.

"What do your parents say about you coming here?" he asked, and bent his head a little so that he could see her over his glasses.

She almost mentioned the witch woman. But she was older now, and the word was starting to fade.

"A single man has only one thing on his mind," he muttered.

"I did it! Look! I won!"

"I'm not talking about that now."

No, she knew that. He was having grown man thoughts which were filling his head and threatening to spill over.

She took her coat and left.

They hunted her down the cliff by the General Bathhouse, which was near her home. But she hadn't reached home yet. The blonde archangel Berit with her flowing curls; after her, Evy and Gerd, a girl from Stockholm. She had come as a foster child. Her parents had split up and disappeared like smoke in the wind. At least that's what Justine overheard Flora say to Pappa.

As smoke in the wind.

Gerd was tall, thin, and mouthy. She was drawn into Berit's radius from the very first day. And she learned the rhymes.

They had not yet managed the worst, to undress her and show her secret to the world and make fun of it. She knew they might succeed one day, and that gave her the strength to flee.

Gerd, with her long, strong legs. She got closer, caught up, knocked her over. She screamed and defended herself, substances dragged under her fingernails.

"Look how she scratched you!" screamed Berit. "You're bleeding all the way down your neck!"

Gerd sat on her stomach, keeping her arms under her back. She hit her face, one, two, one, two. Pulling her jacket over her head. They were doing something to her pants, roughly, and it was chilling.

It seemed like animal strength came over her and she threw herself to the side. When she tried to run and pull her clothes on at the same time, she sprained her ankle against the stones and fell off the cliff. As darkness came, she glimpsed their eyes, how they whitened and turned away.

Flora found her.

Two girls had gone to her house and had rung the doorbell. Justine has fallen off the cliff. Flora grabbed her coat and came.

"I grabbed my coat and came as soon as I could. Why were you girls running around near the cliff?"

Justine had come to. She was still lying on the ground and looked up in the mist; she couldn't walk.

What could a person like Flora do in this situation?

"We have to work together, girls. You carry her legs and I'll carry her shoulders."

"We were playing here and then Justine slipped and fell, and we got really scared because she was so strange, she, like, didn't answer us, and so we said, better run for her mom, and so we both ran and Evy was supposed to stay here."

"I don't know you," said Flora looking at Gerd.

"No, I'm the new foster child at the Östman's."

"So you're with them. What happened to your own parents?"

"They split up and no one wanted me."

"They didn't?" Flora sounded moved.

They carried her into the house, laid her on the blue rug. They didn't look at her. They said that they had to run home now; it was dinner time.

"Go on, then," said Flora.

When Pappa came home, he took Justine to the hospital in the car. She lay in the back seat, and Flora had turned to her, held her hand.

"They were playing like calves let loose in the meadow," said Flora. "Aren't they getting a bit big for that?"

Pappa kept quiet, driving like crazy over the Traneberg bridge. Once at the hospital, he lifted her up and carried her in.

The ankle was broken. Her leg was put in a cast that reached up to her knee. She felt heavy and happy.

"For six weeks, the girl needs to rest and not move around."

Pappa said, "I'll get a tutor for her. Summer vacation is almost here."

Flora said, "I can teach her, if that doesn't work out."

Pappa said, "I'm sure you can. But I know a young man who is free right now. My cousin Percy's son, Mark. I'll give him some cash if he comes to our place for a few hours a day."

Mark's parents were diplomats. They had lived in Washington, D.C., for many years, but had just returned to Stockholm. They did not yet know where they would be going next.

Mark appeared the next day with a bouquet of yellow tulips.

"To the little sickie," he said and stepped into the room carefully. He was slim and short; his hands were sweaty. His eyes were brown like nuts.

"What do you want to learn, cousin?" he asked with a grown man's voice.

"Cousin?"

"Your dad and my dad are cousins and that makes us cousins. First cousins once removed, actually."

She thought about that for a minute.

"All right," he said. "What do you want to learn, cuz?"

She became mischevious.

"Nothing. I already know everything."

"Really?"

"Nah. . . . Just joking. . . ."

Mark took out a book from his jacket pocket, thumbed through it, stopped at a page. The letters were tiny and practically jumbled together.

"Read this bit in English. Then I'll quiz you on the vocabulary."

She turned red, and couldn't pronounce anything, neither in Swedish nor in English.

He smiled, with a little bit of scoffing.

"OK, the rumors about Swedish schools are true. They're all shitty."

"My foot hurts," she whispered.

"I don't believe you," he said.

"It's true!"

"Where's it hurting, exactly?"

She pointed at the cast. Then he pushed her skirt up slightly, and held her leg right above the knee.

Once he left, she did the same thing as he had, placed her hand on the same place. Then she moved it slowly further upwards, and a hot and painful swelling appeared between her legs. A pain throbbing right to her brain.

Chapter SIXTEEN

That next Saturday, Berit returned to Hässelby. She bought a bottle of Gran Fuedo and a pot of tender crocus. She didn't call first; she just went. The day was foggy. She didn't bother with the bus. Instead she walked from the last station of the subway and took the road along the beach. She felt a growing anxiety, which she couldn't ignore, thinking that she was going to confront Justine again.

During the night, she had been dreaming. Tor had shaken her awake.

"Are you having a nightmare?" he said. "Or is the boss giving you a hard time?"

The dream had something to do with a company party. Everyone was there, and strangely, Justine was there, too. In the dream, Berit was wearing a dress that had been much too elegant for the situation, with décolletage and a deep back. Everything was wrong. She mingled and tried to talk with people, but they acted as if she were invisible.

Maybe it was the sleeping pills. She had continued to take them before bed. It was getting hard to go to sleep without them. Maybe it was all that old stuff from childhood.

Tor asked her to come with him to their summer house on Vät Island. He was planning to go there and stay overnight. It would be good for her, he thought, to get a little sea air.

"I can make blinies," he said. "I think we still have some caviar in the freezer."

"I don't want to," she said. "I just can't. I don't want to."

There was a thin layer of water on the ice. Some ducks came flying. They landed on the ice and went sliding before they could stop themselves. An old-fashioned boat, a *skuta*, was tied to the pier. The water wasn't frozen there because of the discharge from the thermal power station. Some men in dark clothes on the dock. She could barely make out the name of the boat, *Sir William Archibald* from Stockholm.

Then a distant sound that kept increasing. The clattering noise of a helicopter. The fog was too thick for her to see it, but it got closer and closer.

She never could listen to the sound of helicopters without thinking of the time she saw "Miss Saigon" in London with some friends. They had gotten good seats, but were practically scared to death of the sudden high roar of the helicopter in the introductory scene. And she remembered the ending, the curtain, the strong light right in their faces. Many people were crying. It was sentimental, all right, but also so unbelievably tragic.

Afterwards they had gone to a pub where Berit started some small talk with a handsome, unemployed young man who insisted on calling her "Mum." She enjoyed the pub's party atmosphere. She was amazed at her own command of English, but the next morning, she just wanted to go back home.

Now, a few meters up in the air, she felt two lights and the sound was very close. She felt a fluttering panic—what if it didn't see her, if it intended to land right there? She ran a few steps into the snow bank.

The helicopter glided past her so closely that raindrops shaken from the trees fell on her face. It belonged to the navy. It sniffed back and forth at the edge of the beach and she saw the pilot as a huddling silhouette. Did someone disappear under the ice? Someone who right now was fighting for life in chilly Lake Mälar?

Maybe Justine was not even home. She thought of that as she climbed up the stairs and rang the bell. No one opened up.

She waited for a minute and rang the bell again. Then she heard weak thumping inside the house, and stepped back a few steps.

It was Justine. She was home; her clothes were wrinkled as if she'd slept in them. On one foot she had a large woolen sock.

"Berit?" she asked.

"Yes . . . it's me. May I come in for a minute? Or are you busy?"

Justine stepped aside.

"No, come on in."

"I brought some flowers and also . . . this bottle of wine. I drank all your *glögg* the other day and I want to make up for it. . . . I thought . . . coming uninvited and all."

"Don't worry about it. Go ahead and hang up your coat."

When Justine went into the kitchen, Berit noticed that she was limping. She stopped, her arms hanging at her sides.

"What have you done to yourself?"

"Naah . . . it's nothing. I slipped when I was out running. It was a crazy thing to do, I know, go running in the middle of winter. But it'll go away soon; it's already feeling much better."

"You didn't break it, did you?"

"No. That foot's a little weak, that's all. It's always been weak. I keep spraining it all the time."

"You do?"

"Next time when you come by, it'll be all better, and we can take a walk and look at old familiar places. The old school. . . ."

"Maybe . . . what are you up to, by the way? Did I interrupt you with something important?"

"Not at all."

"Would you mind if I stayed for a bit?"

"No, not one bit. We can open up this bottle of wine and have a taste. What time is it anyway?"

Justine giggled.

"Always having that old Luther looking over our shoulders!"

"Of course, I thought you'd drink the wine yourself. I didn't intend to sit here and swig it down, too."

"Open the bottle, please. The corkscrew is in the top drawer in the kitchen. Then let's sit upstairs in the library, where we were sitting last time. It's so pleasant there."

They went up the stairs. Berit noticed the posters from Justine's father's candy factory. They were still hanging in the place they always had. The memories came back.

"Do you remember all those Sandy Candy boxes we used to get from you?" she asked hesitantly.

"Maybe you did get some."

"You always had a whole bunch of those boxes."

"Pappa brought them home. I got really sick of them after a while. Sometimes you want something else than that old Sandy taste in your mouth."

"But the kids were jealous of you! Your father owned a candy factory!"

"No big deal."

When they reached the library, the bird was sitting in the window. He turned his head toward them and squawked. Berit jumped so that she almost dropped the bottle of wine.

"Oh, did he scare you?"

"When he screamed like that. . . ."

"He's just making his presence known."

"Why would he do that?"

"So we don't forget that he exists."

"No risk of that! Does he ever attack you?"

"Attack me? Whatever for?"

"I don't know. I'd never trust a wild thing like him."

Justine took the bottle from her and poured. They lifted their glasses, said *skål*. They sipped the wine.

"Mmm," said Berit. "Not bad at all, if I may say so. I really don't drink wine often enough. But it's so good, so good for the soul."

The helicopter was there again; it seemed to be right outside the house. The bird flapped his wings, nodded his head.

"Someone has fallen through the ice," said Justine.

"How do you know that?"

"Heard it on the local radio."

"How awful."

Justine nodded.

"Happens every year. I live so close that I always notice, too."

"Isn't the ice a little too weak to walk on?"

"It holds at some places, and then suddenly it gets weak. People really ought to know better. But some people are just idiots."

Justine laughed and raised her glass.

"*Skål!*" she said. "*Skål* to those idiots!"

After a moment, she asked about Berit's job.

"Have you been fired yet, or what's up?"

"The business is moving to Luleå. My boss says we can all come, too. But no one wants to move to Luleå."

"Do you have a choice?"

"I don't know. . . . I don't know anything any more. . . . I can't sleep at night."

And tears welled up in her eyes, made her weak and exposed.

"I seem to come here and burst out . . . bawling."

"You are carrying so much confusion inside yourself. Just like the rest of us. . . ."

Justine stretched out one arm and made a clucking sound. The bird tramped around for a moment in the window and then flew to her with clumsy wing beats.

"Even this bird," she said. "He needs a female. He doesn't really understand that, but something is bubbling up inside him, making him weak. It's getting lighter; spring is coming. Then longing grows like a sorrow, just as it does in every living being."

"Justine . . . when we were little . . ."

Justine said quickly, "Tell me about your boys."

"My . . . boys?"

"Yeah, how they're living their lives, these young people with their whole lives ahead of them? Do they ever feel that sadness?"

Berit took some tissues from her bag, blew her nose; her head was throbbing.

"Sadness? No I really don't think so."

"Are they working?"

"They're . . . still both studying. But they don't know what they want to be yet. At any rate, they're not going into the publishing business. I scared them away from that."

"Do they have girlfriends?"

She nodded.

"They belong to another world. Young, thin, beautiful. Whenever I see them, I really understand more than ever that I am passé."

Justine placed the bird between them. He turned his beak toward Berit, and made a hissing sound.

"Yuck. Justine . . . can't you. . . ."

"You're afraid of him. He notices that right away. Try and be natural, relax."

Berit drank some wine and then carefully reached out her hand. The bird opened his beak and it was red and large in there.

"He sees through me," she whispered. "He doesn't like me."

"Don't worry, just ignore him. Well, whatever, I can move him."

She got up and limped toward the bookcase. The bird followed her, alighted on her hand. She lifted him to the topmost bookshelf and he took his spot there like a brooding animal from pagan times.

The cliffs, the round hill. Justine's body. The jacket up over her head. She had started to get breasts; they were already fairly large. That foster child, she was sitting on Justine's stomach and was starting to take off her pants. How suddenly everything changed, because Justine broke away and began to run, slipped and fell directly down on the stones below.

How they ran and ran.

"We've killed her!"

"Let's go!"

"Are you crazy? We have to get someone, her mom."

"No, no, let's run away!"

"No, we've got to get help!"

"Blame yourself then, if we get sent to jail!"

Gerd was her name, she suddenly remembered. Gerd was the one who forced them to run to the house.

"We'll just say she stumbled; we were playing and she just fell."

They rang the doorbell again and again. After a while, Flora stood there with her hair in curlers. She looked at them with mistrust and told them she was in a hurry.

They had to wait while she took care of her hair, stand in the hallway with the odor of shampoo and cigarette smoke. The woman grabbed her coat, looked down at her calf.

"Look at my stockings! Damn it!"

"Please hurry, ma'am." Gerd pulled at her coat. That she would dare.

"Where did it happen?"

"Over there by the cliffs."

"I have always said that you need to be careful. It appears that you are just as disobedient as she is."

That very word. Disobedient. She kept up her grumbling as she walked, rubber boots and coat. Justine spread out on the stones. Her clothes were on, but her jacket was to the side with arms still tied together. She looked to them like a sacrificial victim.

"Look. We've finished off this bottle in record time," said Berit. "I intended it for you; it was a gift for you."

"Doesn't it seem to you that they put less wine in the bottles nowadays?"

Berit rolled up the tissue and stuffed it in her bag.

"Yeah, I've noticed that."

"There's more wine in the basement."

"There is . . .?"

"You'll have to go get it. . . . It's in the same room with the old washtub. I know you'll see it."

She got up stiffly, afraid that the bird would notice and attack her. Justine laughed with a tone in her laugh that Berit had never heard before.

"You're walking like a spastic! Don't be such a bunny rabbit. It's just a goddamn bird."

It wasn't just the bird. She was back in the old days, these very steps, she and Jill, their strength from ganging up together, the smell of submission, of degradation. And she remembered what the child Justine had said about that washtub. Flora. That was the name of that woman with the painted eyes, the doll woman who was playing the role of mother.

She found the wine bottles right away. They were arranged on a shelf, just as Justine described. It was dark down here; she hadn't found the light switch. Shyly, she glanced at the washtub; saw it with the eyes of a little girl. The partition for the wood, did she really put a little girl in that and light a fire? To think she just sat there, waiting for the heat. The scalding heat.

She pressed the bottle to her chest and rushed upstairs.

"Justine . . . there's a lot that we need to work out."

Justine shook her head.

"Yes, we do! We really do! You have to listen to me, I can't get any peace."

There was an unusual expression that arose in Justine's eyes.

"You want me to cross out the past as if it never happened."

"Yes. . . ."

"Learn the great secret of life: love, forgive, and forget?"

"Well, something like that. Some kind of forgiveness . . . or . . . reconciliation. . . ."

Justine regarded her without saying anything. She drew her fingers through her hair, which then stood straight up. She broke out into a violent and jangling laugh.

"Just open the goddamn cork, why don't you!"

Chapter SEVENTEEN

Mark came during the day and they read together. He would touch her sometimes, but not much. To him, she was just a child.

This provoked her. Her breasts were changing and the skin over them was painful and tender. She took off her head-band, and she never put it back on again.

"Tell me about America," she asked.

Then he began to speak in English so fast that she didn't have a chance to keep up with him at all. She threw her pillow at him, right into his sneering face.

He lay down over her, pressing down her arms.

"You're just a little piece of shit, aren't you."

Enraged, she kicked him right in the crotch with her good leg. He turned white and fell off the bed.

He had a girlfriend in Washington.

"What looks she like?"

"What does she look like?" he corrected her.

"Yes, but what does she look like?"

"Brown eyes, big tits."

It sounded nasty.

"Her name's Cindy. She writes me every other week."

"Are you in love with her?"

He grinned.

"Tell me! Are you?"

He stood in front of the window and jerked his hand around his zipper.

"Start reading your book now. I'm not paid to answer your stupid questions."

"It's much too difficult. I can't."

"Read!"

"Da nyoo man shtands . . ."

"*The* not *da*! *New* not *nyoo*."

"The nyoo man. . . ."

"This is a fantastic book, Justine. Maybe you're just too little. Too bad. You miss a lot, being so little."

That put her off balance.

"What am I supposed to do then?"

"Nothing you can do. That's just the way it is."

"You're an idiot!"

"How's your foot doing? Getting any better?"

"Eventually."

"What really happened?"

"I fell off a cliff."

"You'll just have to learn to walk properly."

"I do walk properly. I just slipped, that's all!"

No, she wasn't too little. During the evenings, she lay turned to the wall and imagined how it would be. She and Mark in a whole different way. She felt her breasts, if they had grown, and her hand went down to that sinful place that was so wonderful to touch. A kind of restlessness came over her. She wanted to get away. But the cast was a ball and chain, it protected her from what was out there, but also transformed her into a prisoner.

Then the day came when winter had completely gone, when they took off her cast, sawing and cutting it away. A frail and shrunken leg appeared together with a sour smell.

But she was back to normal. And now school was over and the schoolyard had been filled with students in colorful clothes. All the teachers had been to the hairdresser; the flag had been taken out and raised.

She had been able to avoid all of that.

She imagined that it would be difficult to use that stick-like, narrow leg, but noticed that it was, deep inside, just as strong as before. In the evening it might swell and ache a bit, but she could walk and run, just like before.

She stood in the lee of the uprooted tree. There were candy wrappers on the ground.

She was alone.

She followed the forest path.

The Hunter was sitting on his front porch, whittling.

Shyly, she stepped into the garden.

He saw her. He didn't say anything.

She sat right next to him, his back was tense. His hands kept whittling.

She sat right next to him, and put her hand on his arm. His skin was brown and old.

No.

Not old.

She stepped into his sparkling clean kitchen. The wax tablecloth had been wiped; the dish rack was empty. The floor was white and swept.

He got up and followed her.

"What do you want here?"

"Sorry," she said. "It wasn't my fault."

"I want you to leave now."

"No. . . ."

"I want you to leave this very minute."

He stood against the wall. She went right up to him, her hips to his jeans.

"Stina!"

"Hold me. I've been so lonely."

She closed his door and locked it. She lay on his blanket. It was gray and warm from the cat. She drew her legs under her, round.

His body a template against the window.

"I broke my leg," she whispered, even though she hadn't intended to tell him.

"Stina. . . ."

"Come lie down next to me. Warm me up."

He did so while saying, "I told you to leave."

Her chin on his chest, the small curly strands. The smell of air and salt.

Her hands were so strong now. She was young; he was old. Oh, his tummy, so vulnerable and weak. She dipped her tongue, her lips, there.

Then.

The man.

She made him cry, and that made her afraid. When he saw her fear, he became strong again, and held her waist so that her legs could be like scissors around him.

"Stina," he whispered, "you know that this is wrong."

"Who decides what is right and what is wrong?"

And she sank over him and they did it again. He moved within her and she wriggled but let him remain there.

Afterwards he was full of regret.

She stroked him and tried to find words. She had to cry to get him to open up.

"I'm coming back to you. I will never leave you."

Day after day. The uprooted tree. The house.

Sometimes he locked the door and wasn't there. She waited in the yard. Then she learned how to break open the lock on his window. She lay in his sheets, his smell against her clothes.

A draft of chilly air. He stood in the light, a blanket in his hand. He turned his face from her.

His hand pounded the table.

"You can't," she said, and her mouth and jaws ached. "You can't drive me away."

Naked in his lap, the seams of his jeans.

"Don't you hear the blackbird out there?" she whispered.

"You're thinking of the thrushes."

"Do you hear their song?"

"Why are you doing this to me, making me weak . . .?"

The cloth was swelling against her groin.

"You're not that weak . . . see?"

Laughter, happiness. How he lifted her like a spread-out, fluttering butterfly. Opened her leaves.

Every time she was amazed. She was as thin as a reed and he. . . .

"I believe that you'll cleave me in half. . . ."

But at that white moment he was unable to hear her; he was a flailing fish, glitter on her stomach.

Then he stood up and shrank.

One day she was forced to tell him about the island.

"We're going out to the islands tomorrow. We're going to live there for a while in an old house that my grandparents owned. It's on one of the islands. We have to go there by boat. There's no other way there."

If she thought he was not going to say anything, she was wrong.

He wanted to know everything.

"Pappa has taken vacation. We're going to live there for a while. There're not many houses on this island, just a few; food comes by boat. Still, there are some people who live there all year round. Do you think they go fishing, or else how do they live through the winter? I get to decorate my own room; it will be my very own. I'm going to help paint it. Pappa has brought home some wallpaper designs, and I've already picked one out."

He looked at her sternly.

"Now I want you to listen to me. I will be gone when you return, and you're the one forcing me to do this; but I'm not blaming you, not at all."

She was too filled with her future plans to listen. She sat in his arms, stroked his soft eyes.

"When the apples ripen, we'll pick them, and I am going to bake you into an apple pie and cut you all up into pieces. And then I'll eat you up with vanilla sauce and ice cream. But now I have to go home."

Chapter EIGHTEEN

Sven's parents had always surprised Flora. They had a vulgar aspect to them which did not fit either their position or their class. Both of them were large and had loud voices, and her father-in-law had lost some of his hearing so that her mother-in-law had to raise her voice even more so that he could hear her. They used coarse words and language in their speech and they seemed to enjoy shocking others by it. They approached their environment with childish expectation, waiting for reactions.

Sven had prepared her.

"They're a little different. I just want to let you know so that you're aware."

During a few occasions, while she was still working as a secretary, Ivar Dalvik had come to the office and they had been introduced. He shook her hand hard and asked for her name two times.

"Oh, Flora is it . . . can I open you up?" he joked. "If one wants to know more about a flower's innermost being?"

She always had trouble with that kind of humor.

She did not meet her future mother-in-law until she was Sven's fiancée.

She never felt really accepted by them. She and Sven discussed this from time to time. He didn't understand her. He thought she was taking things too seriously.

"They think that I am too lower class for their fine son; that's what it is."

"That's not true, Flora. They really don't care about what kind of person I've chosen to marry. I know it sounds strange, but that's the way they are. Let them be, two egocentric old people. Why would you ever worry what they think? We're living our lives and they're living theirs."

It didn't help. She always felt that she wasn't good enough for them. Maybe she should have been louder, used more gestures, like them.

When it came right down to it, she didn't have much contact with them, but that was a two-edged sword. On the one side, she despised them. On the other, she wished they would see her, acknowledge her, as the active and hard-working woman that she was.

They seemed fond of Justine and sent her small presents, but whenever they met her, they overwhelmed her with questions without the patience to wait for her answers. In a way, they were from a previous era. Girls were cute to look at, but you shouldn't invest in their future. For example, there was no talk about raising Justine to eventually take over the family firm. They would rather find someone else from outside. A man.

When they entered their seventies, they began to lose interest in the whole Sandy concern. They placed it in the hands of their only son. Now it was his business to nurture the company and make a profit. How he did so was no longer any of their business.

For all intents and purposes, they died at the same time. When it happened, she and Sven were somewhere in Italy. Ivar was still living when they returned home, but he died a few days later at Karolinska Hospital.

Flora remembered every detail—the telephone call, Sven answering, his sudden full attention. When he returned the receiver to its cradle, he turned to her and said with a neutral tone in his voice: "It's almost his time. We have to go home right away."

His mother was waiting for him before the entrance to the hospital, wearing an armless blue blouse which revealed her flabby underarms. She stood in front of the door and smoked.

When she preceded them into the elevator, she almost fell. She had difficulty speaking; her voice had shrunk, almost cut off.

Flora had never seen a person die. Not even that summer when she worked at the mental hospital. The women there were vicious and mean; every once in a while, she wished they'd die. They made fun of her and called her a whore. They didn't mean what they said; they were sick and they couldn't think straight, but it didn't help. No matter how much she reminded herself of this, she was filled with discomfort whenever she approached hospital buildings.

As soon as she stepped into her father-in-law's room, she remembered that unusual smell, the one that announced that a human being was in the process of dying. She knew it at once. She would never be able to describe it; it was just there.

The old man was on his back, coupled to tubes and apparatus. His nose hooked up from the withered face. For a few seconds, he opened his eyes, but he did not register their presence, his glance wandering toward the ceiling. He fumbled and scratched with his hands as if he were searching for something to hold him back.

Her mother-in-law broke down.

"Ivar!" she screamed. "You can't leave me like this, really, I forbid you . . .!"

His body shook; his jaw opened and shut. This made her cling to his sheets, hold on to the bed rail, howl.

Everyone was embarrassed. Two nurses led her out of the room and gave her an injection of a tranquilizer. Her husband lay there, dead and alone.

"We'll put him to rights and light a few candles," said a nurse. "Go out and take care of his wife for the time being."

Sven was obviously shaken.

He wanted to leave right away.

It only took a week and it was her mother-in-law's turn. A serious wave of influenza swept over the country. It set its claws into her, and, broken down by sorrow and shock, her body was not able to mount a real defense.

The double funeral was an orgy of music and roses. The deceased had planned it that way. Everything had been written in their papers, as if they had known that they would die at the same time.

They left behind quite a bit of real estate, which Sven began to sell off as soon as he could. There was a six-room apartment on the fashionable Karlavägen; there was a villa on the Spanish coast and a hunting cabin up in the Åre mountains. And last but not least the yellow house with the veranda and the bay out on the island.

Flora and Sven had been to the house on the island a few times. She had always felt a kind of happiness out there, a contentedness. She asked Sven to keep it. She caught the desire to make it her own, to put her stamp on it. Sven felt the same way. For a few light and heady weeks, they worked together on this idea, plans and fantasies.

They shipped out a few loads of the things they would need: timber, spackle, scrapers, paint. One man on the island, one of the permanent residents, offered to help them; Sven was the way he was when it came to practical things.

The February twilight entered the room. The smell of frying fish. Rattling in the hallway, time for dinner again.

"What are they going to treat us to today, I wonder," muttered Märta Bengtsson. The dinner hour was the highlight of the day for Flora's roommate. She seemed to have an enormous, almost grotesque appetite, to the point of grotesque. Something about her reminded Flora of her mother-in-law.

Märta sat in her wheelchair with her napkin tied under her chin and tried to stuff the food into her mouth with trembling, shaking hands. She ate fairly noisily.

A white uniform had pulled a chair over to Flora's bed and now began to feed her. She was in a bit of a hurry; one could tell because of her way of thrusting the spoon between Flora's lips and practically scrape off the potato blend against her tongue. She was very young. Had Flora really been so young?

She had a ring in her nose and a tattooed animal that crept along her underarm.

She talked the whole time, as if she had read in a practical handbook that this was the proper way to handle fellow human beings: one should speak to them, not about them. Märta Bengtsson tried to answer, but she had difficulty coordinating both eating and talking. Time and again she would choke on her food, and the white uniform would have to get up and help her.

"Today is Saturday; surely it is," she managed between bites. "Are you going out to have a good time, nurse?"

This white uniform was certainly not a nurse, just an assistant with barely any training.

The assistant giggled. "You could say that I'm going out for a good time tonight."

"Do you already have a close little friend?"

"Huh? 'Close little friend'?"

A new attack of coughing, Flora turned her head away, disgusted. She looked up at the shiny, empty ceiling.

It was there on the island that Flora realized that something was seriously going on with Justine. It began already on the trip out. She could not bear to be inside the cabin; she had to be outside with her head hanging over the railing, so that the spray made both her and her clothes wet. It was windy; white geese floated on the waves.

Flora looked at Sven.

"But she's just a little seasick," he said petulantly, as he went out to sit beside the girl. "She was never good at being at sea."

The house was waiting for them. It was a cool and cloudy day with rain in the air. In the yard, the wood was stacked under tarps where rainwater had collected into small pools.

Sven took out the key.

"OK, girls," he said, "now we've arrived at our own summer paradise."

Justine was able to choose her own room. She had chosen one that faced east, a room that was narrow and high, but not too big. Her grandmother had called it her writing room. She had pen pals throughout the entire world, but when she was on the island, she never got around to writing them because she was too restless to stay very long.

Her white writing table was still in the room. Flora had been tense going through all the drawers, as if she was expecting to find a note or two about Sven and herself. But there was nothing there besides her mother-in-law's rose stationery with her monogram in grey.

"Remember, Justine, that your grandmother wanted you to have that table," said Sven, as if he had known, as if he had ever talked to his mother about such things.

After dinner, the television was always turned on. Märta Bengtsson's two daughters had bought her a TV and set it up next to her bed. At this moment there was a program about winter sports, maybe some kind of competition; there was loud music. Young, strong people who flickered past from downhill ski jumps or on the ice. It hurt to look at them. She closed her eyes; they were aching as if she were becoming ill.

All of sudden it was silent. One of the white uniforms had come in and requested Märta Bengtsson to put on her headphones. Now there was just flickering light without sound.

Yes, it would be good if she became ill, had a fever. They would isolate her. That would keep Justine from visiting her. At any rate, it would prevent Justine from taking her on an outing. That terrorizing drive was still with her, a dizziness, a slowly growing premonition.

I want to die my own way.

But I don't want to die. . . . I want to live.

Justine grew even stranger while on the island. She would be sitting on a chair in the kitchen and she would suddenly fall asleep, her head thudding on the table. Snoring and sleeping.

"What's wrong with you that you can fall asleep like that?" Flora said. Then she stirred and her pupils floated around her eyes as if they were disconnected.

Flora thought about drugs. She went to the bent figure but did not smell anything unusual, just a distant strong electric field.

Justine was looking forward to putting up the wallpaper in her room, but suddenly she no longer had the energy. Right in the middle of a sunny afternoon, she would have to take a nap, snoring and sleeping just like an old person. Her skin became pale and doughy; she was getting blemishes on her shoulders and neck which itched. She scratched and ripped with her nails so that the skin came off.

"It's not so strange that she's tired," said Sven, which surprised Flora, because he usually went to fetch the doctor at the slightest sneeze.

"Why on earth would she be more tired than we are?"

"Hormones, you know. She's at a difficult stage."

As far as Sven was concerned, it seemed Justine was always at a difficult stage.

One morning she heard sound in the bathroom. Flora was alone with the girl. Sven had gone with the boat. She stood in the hallway; the bathroom door was ajar. The girl was squatting there, bent over the toilet.

When she came out, her face was very doughy and white. She was on the way back to her room when Flora grabbed her by the arm.

"Let me look at you! Let me look right into your eyes!"

The girl turned toward her like a sleepwalker. And there, deep in the shining green of her irises, Flora saw the flagrant answer. Just as she had suspected, the teenage girl was pregnant.

Flora bombarded her with questions and didn't leave Justine in peace for a minute. Who had done this to her? Who had raped her?

"No one," she said, crying so the snot pooled on her upper lip. "No one raped me."

"You stupid child. You're not much more than a child, dammit!"

Sven stood there among the paint cans, round-shouldered but tall.

"Leave her alone now," he said. "Leave her in peace."

"But don't you understand? She has to go to the hospital. They have to remove it!"

He had left off pleading long ago. He raised his voice to a rhythmic yell.

"I've decided—that you—leave—my daughter—alone!"

He had become so strange out on the island.

She just dropped all her plans at once and took the boat back to Stockholm.

She called her sister Viola who sold perfume at NK. She said that she and Sven had a serious disagreement, and that she had to get away for a while. She needed some time to think.

She was able to live in her sister's apartment, a three-room apartment on Östermalmgatan in the best part of town. She had the days all to herself, until that time in the evening when Viola came home; then they went out to eat at a restaurant.

It was as if she had a glass bell around her.

The days burned with sun, the asphalt hot and dusty. Nothing happened to her. She sat and listened to her sister's tales from her life at the perfumery.

"I'm going to dye your hair," said Viola and pulled out a heap of treatments. "You've always had great good looks. But just because you're married doesn't mean that you should let yourself go, you know. Do you think he's found someone else? What's his new secretary like? Have you checked up on her? You must be kind to him, tempt him a bit. Such a gold mine for a husband and always so nice!"

Part 1: Chapter Eighteen

At the end of August, she returned to the island. Sven was waiting on the dock; he was suntanned and healthy. He didn't mention what had happened. He took her around the waist, covered her lipsticked mouth with gentle kisses. "You are beautiful, Flora, you are my little doll. I've missed you. May I look? You've bought a new fine dress. Oh, do you look fine in it!"

All the work on the house had stopped; the rooms were half-finished. The girl was sleeping in the hammock.

When she woke up, you could tell.

But still, he refused to talk about it.

In the middle of September, they returned to their home in the city.

"What about school?" she asked. "Have you thought about that?"

"I've contacted the school."

"What did you say?"

"It doesn't matter what I said. She's gotten a leave of absence."

Justine stopped getting dressed, roamed around throughout the house in her burled robe. Soon no clothes would cover her growing stomach. Buying her maternity clothes would be capitulating.

But it didn't matter. She never left the house; she never showed herself to anyone.

It was expected around the time winter turned into spring. Who was the father? Was it Mark?

But she kept silent the whole time.

Such a silence, a dejection. It filled the entire house from the basement to the newly finished attic.

When snow started falling, she began to knit. She pulled out the yarn from an old sweater and knitted from this frizzy, gray-white ball of yarn. Knitting without a pattern and with sulky uneven lips.

Right around the first day of Advent, Sven had to go on a business trip to Barcelona. Flora remembered it very well. He didn't want to go, but he absolutely had to. He dithered about and let the taxi wait so long that he almost missed the plane.

When he left, Flora tried to resume some kind of contact.

"How are you? You can at least tell me how you're feeling."

Her light brown eyebrows came together.

"It's snowing over the lake; it looks like feathers. . . ."

"I didn't ask you about that!"

"I had an animal once, you didn't know about it."

"What are you talking about, animals and feathers? All this has gone to your brain."

"Brain? Flora, do you understand how roses can live within the brain?"

Flora took her by the shoulders, lifted her up. This smell of sweat and dirtiness. Hair like a mop, a bird's nest on her neck. She took her by the wrist and led her to the shower.

She expected a reaction of anxiety and fear. But there was none of that. The shiny round belly, the bellybutton poking out. Breasts like two bulging and explosive balls. Flora took some soap in her hand and began to soap up that nervous, pale gray body. Rinsed and shampooed the girl's hair.

Justine a pregnant statue. Now she clearly saw how the fetus moved around in there, his soft, round jumps. She laid her palm right against the girl's belly. The girl shook. But the child was there; she felt it.

A new nightgown, how it got stuck over her stomach on the way down. Flora had to take a scissors and cut it open completely on one of the side seams. The girl sat with an abstract smile, her mouth haughty and calm.

Then the comb. It was impossible to sort out the knots; she had to use the scissors.

She cut the hair short, not out of revenge, but for practical reasons. The girl's face round and swollen.

Part 1: Chapter Eighteen

"What are you crying for now?"

The girl moved her head stiffly.

"Save your tears, you'll have enough to cry about later."

One night it was time. Why do births always start in the middle of the night?

I should have been the one. I crept next to him. I opened myself in spasms.

The girl sat in her wrinkled nightgown. Her mouth was open; she had bit her tongue so that it was bleeding. She had cried out. We had woken up from her cries.

Sven said, no, he yelled to me: "Warm up some water and bring some towels, hurry up!"

It wasn't supposed to be like this.

It was already too late to leave for the hospital.

I said: "If we don't make it through this. . . ."

He lost his composure, hearing that.

I said again: "Such young girls . . . their pelvises."

Then he pulled me into the kitchen and his face was a like a mask.

She fought all the way until dawn, screaming and throwing her body around.

Flora heard Sven pray to God.

She had stopped approaching him, but she observed the girl's hips, so narrow and undeveloped.

If the baby becomes stuck, it will be our fault. If she dies while the child is still inside her, we are the ones who will be punished.

But she didn't die, she came through it.

The baby lay on the sheets, and it was an extremely tiny boy.

Sven took the scissors, cut the cord in the middle of membranes and blood. Gave that clump, that newborn baby to her.

I felt the warm body, it jerked; he was trying to get air, and then he wailed, his nose wide and flat. I set him into the hand basin, and the water turned bloody. I washed his hands; he held them in fists, I had to uncurl them and saw deep lines and marks. His penis swollen and large, his limbs like tentacles. His hair was dark, his eyes muddy. I cleaned him from her blood and fluids; I wrapped him in a cloth. He had stopped crying; his face was formed like a heart. His little exquisitely carved upper lip, how it turned against the tip of my finger. I sat down and opened my blouse, the hard greedy gums.

Sven was in the doorway. He saw me. He turned and left.

She reached her arms out to me to take him. I said, you're tired. You can fall asleep on him and he can suffocate. Look at him. Do you want to fall asleep on this beautiful little boy's face?

She was thin and had lost a lot of blood.

I lay him to her breast, but he screamed and beat with his little delicate arms. He was hungry. That was a good sign. But she was so young; she had no milk to give him. Sven had to go and get a bottle and some formula. The boy was heavy. He had lain in my lap. I was the one who taught him to suck. Every time she took the boy, he screamed. She was too young; she wasn't much more than a child herself.

They despaired because the boy stopped eating. What do you do with a child who doesn't eat? She sat with a spoon, opened his little mouth. What went in ran out again and behind his ears. She gave him to the girl. Warm him up if you can. But the girl was lethargic, no longer present.

The baby lived only four days. Then there was nothing more to do.

She wrapped him in a linen towel. Sven came with a box which had been used for shoes.

The child was too small and was born too early.

He never said what he had done with the box.

Chapter NINETEEN

His parents were standing at the window when he arrived. He glimpsed them behind the curtains, how they pulled back so that he would not see them. He was irritated; he couldn't help it.

He had bought tulips in the subway as well as a box of candy, *Romerska bågar*. What do you give a man who is that old? His father had never appreciated books.

His mother took off his coat.

"Go in to your pappa; the food will be ready in a minute."

It smelled wonderful throughout the whole house. She had made roulades; she knew that was his favorite dish. And large boiled potatoes. And peas and jelly.

His father dished up a portion.

"How are things going with you?" he asked. "Is there a lot going on at the hotel?"

"It's been a bit busy."

"But you are still just working the night shift?"

"Yes, but the night shift can be fairly difficult."

"I don't get it. Aren't the guests asleep then?"

"But Kjell, you'd understand if you thought about it for a second," his mother said and giggled.

"No, goddammit, I don't."

His mother looked at him and made a face.

"If there are a lot of guests . . . maybe even foreigners," Hans Peter said, "then there's a lot to do with their passports and such. And then you have to help them with information, and maybe call a taxi for them; sometimes they get lost."

"All right, so there's more involved."

"Take some more roulades," said his mother.

"Thanks, Mamma, this was great. You really know what I like."

She smiled tightly.

After dinner he helped her with the dishes. His father sat in front of the TV, something about skiing.

"He has become so touchy and brusque," his mother mumbled while she rinsed off a plate.

"Uh-huh."

"Nothing is ever good enough. I try and try."

"Is he healthy and all that?"

"Healthy? I think so. I haven't noticed anything wrong."

"What about you, Mamma? How are you doing?"

"What do you mean?"

"Are you doing all right?"

"Of course I am, healthy as can be. Well, sometimes I get a little dizzy, but that happens with age."

She went to the cupboard and took down a can of coffee.

"I've made him a *tårta*, one with chocolate, the kind he likes."

"You're always spoiling him."

She suddenly threw her hands in front of her face and burst into tears.

"But, Mamma, what's wrong?"

He tried to put an arm around her, but she pulled herself away.

"Mamma . . . are you thinking of Margareta?"

"Yes," she hiccupped.

That's the way it usually went. The memories became stronger around birthdays and holidays. She was always trying to talk about anything but that, but it was always there, ready to break out.

He didn't know what to say.

His mother stood there for a moment, turned toward the cupboard.

"Would you like me to make the coffee?" he asked.

She shook herself a little and turned on the faucet.

He felt impatient. He drank the coffee and took two helpings of cake. Every time he visited his parents, he stuffed himself with way too much food.

"Shall we have something with our coffee?" his father muttered.

"Kjell, we've had something with the coffee already. I made a *tårta!*"

"I mean something else than *tårta*, something stronger."

He smiled at Hans Peter, somewhat slyly.

"Or what do you say, H. P.? But maybe you're working tonight?"

"Yes, I am," he said hastily, "but I can have a little glass, anyway."

His father kept his liquor in an old cabinet with paintings of pumpkins on its doors and sides, which he had won at an auction. He found a bottle of whisky. He was wearing his old sweater with leather pads on the elbows. How long had he had it? His whole life?

"I won't have any," his mother said.

"Would you like something else? Some sherry?"

"Thank you, that'd be fine."

"Where are the glasses?"

"Where they've always been."

Hans Peter got up.

"I'll get them. I know where they are."

He wanted to leave. He was experiencing an unusual feeling, almost expectation, longing. The air here at home was suffocating him; he was having a great deal of trouble sitting still in the living room sofa.

After half a glass of whisky, his father became talkative. He started giving a lecture on golden parachutes, his own pet peeve.

"The newspapers are always talking about high directors who are fired because they can't do their jobs properly, but the strange thing is, they get fired with a hefty reward, millions of crowns for the rest of their lives. Isn't that crazy? I've done my job well for all those years and ruined my back to boot, just doing my job, and I don't get a damned million for that. What is a worker's back worth? Not one damn bit. But those high directors, they get to lounge around in their fine chairs and drive around in their fine, fancy automobiles."

"Kjell, we've heard that already; we know that."

"And even though I've paid my dues to the union, but even the union can't. . . ."

Hans Peter knew that the only thing to do was to nod along, so he did. He remained sitting for another hour, and then he got up and looked at the clock.

"Well, I've got to get rolling if I'm going to make it to work," he said. "Thanks so much for dinner. And many happy returns!"

He held out his hand to his father. His father took it and squeezed a bit. He made a grimace, as if he were about to say something. Then he cleared his throat and put his hands into the large pockets of his sweater.

"Take care of yourself, H. P.," he said. "Thanks for coming."

His mother came up to him and gave him a light hug. She was one foot shorter than he was. He looked at her. Her hair was thinning; he could discern her white scalp. He hugged her a bit tighter.

Hans Peter took the commuter train to T-Centralen, the central station, and walked from there to the hotel. It had stopped raining; he was longing for air.

In the entryway of the hotel, Ariadne was busy with the aquarium. She was running late today. She said that her girl was sick and she had to wait for her husband to return. She stood bent over the aquarium; she was wearing blue close-fitting jeans.

He took out the register and thumbed through it absentmindedly.

"What does your daughter have?" he asked.

"I think it's that influenza."

One of her arms was down in the aquarium; she moved the hose around the bottom and sucked up the small wormlike excrement.

"I've told Ulf to buy bigger fish," she said resentfully. "He says they wouldn't be happy. They would be happy; I know they would, I told Ulf that I was certain they would. But he said, no, the big ones wouldn't be happy."

All of a sudden he felt tired of her. He just wanted to be left alone. He wondered if she were finished with all the rooms. She probably was; she usually did the aquarium right before she went home.

"Are all the rooms finished?" he asked.

She turned and looked at him; her eyes were brown and questioning.

"The rooms?"

"Yes."

He thought that she should not be wearing such tight jeans. A fleeting thought flew through him, he wondered if her husband was good to her? Was he kind to her?

"Oh, don't worry about it. I was just thinking out loud," he said.

She went back to the aquarium. She'd spread out newspapers all around so that she wouldn't get the area wet. Hans Peter had the book in his briefcase, the book he'd borrowed from Justine. As soon as Ariadne left, he'd take a look at it. He longed to hold it. A strange feeling had come over him, a feeling of ceremony. He had placed the book in his briefcase with careful hands, as if it were something delicate and fragile. He had finished it after only a few days, and he thought about how he was going to take the book back to her. He wanted to lengthen the time that he had the book so that he could fantasize about how it would be when he brought it back.

The book had moved him in a special way. It was about a man in middle age, Dubin, who wrote biographies and one day began to look at his own life. There was a similarity he felt between Dubin and himself that made him uncomfortable. As if he had never really lived, as if his life was running out on him and he could do nothing to stop it. He longed to discuss the book with Justine. He didn't know her, but he had held her nude foot, held it in his lap and warmed it.

Ariadne placed the glass cover back in its spot and started to roll up the green rubber hose. She looked sad.

"I'll pick up the newspapers for you," said Hans Peter.

She made a hopeless gesture.

He squatted on the floor and started rolling up the newspapers. They were soggy, and a blackened and slimy water plant was lying on one of them. She was out in the kitchen, rinsing thoroughly at the faucet. He started feeling guilty. He squeezed behind her and threw the papers in the garbage.

"Is she very ill, your little daughter?" he asked gruffly.

"A fever."

"Say hi to her from me. Tell her to get better."

Ariadne nodded. He took her lightly on the shoulders.

"Have a good Saturday night, then," he said. "See you on Monday."

He dialed Justine's number. He almost thought that it wouldn't be in the telephone book, that she would prefer to keep it unlisted, but there it was. He recited it a few times to himself without noticing he did so, and then he had it memorized.

He signed in a few guests, gave them their keys. At around ten in the evening, he lifted the hand set and keyed in Justine's number. Five rings went through. Oh my God, maybe she was asleep at this hour? He was just about to hang up, when someone took the call, but the line was silent.

"Hello?" he said expectantly.

No one answered.

He said it again.

"Hello, may I speak with Justine Dalvik?"

A snap in his ear and the line went dead.

When he woke up late the next morning, he stayed in his bed for a very long time. In his sleep, he had seen her in front of him. She was balancing on a row of sharp stones; she was barefoot, slipping and sliding. The bird circled over her head; how it continually dove at her head. He saw himself in the dream, too. How he ran and waved his hands, trying to make the bird disappear. Instead, Justine was frightened by the noise and she fell onto the sharp stones and slit her throat. He stood and watched her, how her head was stuck in a little narrow heap of stones. He was gripped by deep despair and some of that was still with him when he woke up.

He got up. Outside, the temperature was milder, the shine of rain on the window. He stayed in the shower for a quarter of an hour. Then he called her number again.

This time she answered. When he heard her voice, he began to sweat under his armpits. Immediately he forgot the words he was going to say.

"Hello?" he said somewhat stupidly.

She seemed as if she had a cold.

"Who is it?"

"Oh, sorry, it's me, Hans Peter. Maybe you don't remember me."

"Of course I remember you."

"How's your foot?"

"Better. Not completely, though."

"Great. I mean, that it's better."

She laughed, but began to cough.

"Oh, have you also gotten the flu? The cleaner at the hotel, her daughter. . . ."

"Oh no, not at all. I'm just a little tired this morning."

"I thought . . . that book."

"Yes? Have you finished it?"

"Yes."

"What did you think?"

"I kind of wanted . . . to talk to you about it. With you most of all . . . so to speak . . . and eye to eye."

She laughed a low laugh. He saw her now, the round cheeks, the freckles on her nose. He wanted to ask what she was wearing, what she was doing the minute he phoned, what she wished for herself.

"Come on over, then," she said. "Let's talk."

She was wearing black tights and a sweater that went to her knees. Or maybe it was a thick, knit dress; he really didn't know for sure. Her fingertips were ice cold.

"It's so cold here in the house," she said. "I've been keeping the fire going in the fireplace, but it doesn't seem to help."

"I don't think it's cold."

"No?"

"No, pretty warm in fact. But I've been walking quickly, and so I'm, well, all heated up from inside."

"What may I offer you?"

They went into the kitchen. He noticed two glasses of red wine on the counter. He felt some of his energy slipping away.

"Right now I feel like having a large cup of strong coffee. I'll set the coffeepot on; would you like that?"

"Yes, thanks."

Justine had put a sock on the injured foot. He noticed she still had difficulty walking. Now she stood and measured the coffee into the filter. She rested her back against the counter and breathed heavily.

"Fact is, I have to have some coffee to turn into a human being," she said. "I had a late night. I'm a little hung over."

His palms tickled a bit. He turned away from the sight of the glasses.

"What? You've never been hung over, Hans Peter?"

"Of course, of course I have. But it's been awhile now."

"I don't like it, the whole day is lost."

"Well, if you had fun the night before . . ."

"I don't even like it then."

"Did you have a party, or something?"

"No, not really. A friend came here. A woman who'd been a classmate of mine in school."

He was filled with shimmering happiness. His midsection tightened; his face relaxed.

"Oh for crying out loud, sit down," he said. "I can look at your foot."

She let her arms hang down.

"Don't you want me to?"

"Sure. . . ."

"You have to be careful with a sprain."

"Can we go upstairs? If you take the tray with the coffee cups."

"What about the bird? Where is he?"

"Oh, he's sitting somewhere and stressing himself."

It was dusty and messy in the library. He saw signs of ice cream on the table. In the window there was a little pot of crocus. The bird was nowhere in sight.

"It's a bit of a mess here, as you can see," she said.

"It doesn't bother me. You should see my place."

He placed the tray on the table and pulled up the chairs so that they would be facing each other.

She had painted her toenails red. He saw that when he took off the sock and unwrapped the bandage. Her foot jerked; he could see that she was ticklish.

He saw the marks from the bandage on her skin. They looked like small valleys and he followed them with his fingertips, cupped his hand around her heel.

"It almost looks more swollen now than last time," he said.

"I didn't rest it enough. It's hard to stay still."

"Maybe you don't need to bind it so tightly."

"Maybe not."

"Justine, may I ask you something, apropos of nothing. Have you ever felt that life was slipping way from you?"

"Yes . . . sometimes."

"Once I'm gone . . . no damned soul is going to remember me or know who I was."

"The same with me, I fear."

"You don't have any children?"

She shook her head.

"People will remember you as the granddaughter of the man who founded the Sandy concern."

She smiled slightly, her upper lip was elegantly formed, her lower lip chapped.

"So what?" she said.

"Well, even if you've had children, it doesn't mean that someone will remember you. But you would be a kind of a creator, a part of you would in some way continue living . . . and into the next generation, too, but a bit more thinned out, of course."

"You can live a good life without being a creator."

"Of course, that's true."

"Why didn't you have children?"

"It just didn't happen that way."

"It didn't?"

"I was married for a long while, but no. Nothing happened. She got remarried later on and had a ton of children. Maybe there's something wrong with me; maybe I don't have what it takes."

His hand had begun to move along her foot. He made no move to pull her foot closer. His middle finger worked itself gently under the edge of her tights. He felt her calf, smooth against his finger.

"And you?" he said. "Why didn't you have any children?"

"I had a child once. It died after only a few days."

"Oh."

"It was a long time ago."

He took his hands away, but she left her foot there, with her toes pointing toward him.

"Your hands felt nice," she said. "I liked it."

Hans Peter smiled at her.

"By the way, I have to tell you something. I dreamed about you last night."

"You did?"

"Yes."

"Was it a nice dream?"

"Honestly? No. It was an evil dream, where you hurt yourself."

She stiffened.

"Yes? . . . And what I was doing?"

"Oh . . . you were walking on dangerous stones. You stumbled on them and fell."

"That's so odd . . . I've thought of you since you were here," she whispered. "I am so glad that you called. It was looking like it would be a tough day. But it doesn't feel like that any more."

"Justine," he said. "Do you have anyone now, any kind of relationship?"

"No. . . ."

"I've thought of you too . . . longed to come here again. But if you have someone, already. . . ."

"No," she interrupted him. "There's no one. The last one ended."

He got up and went around the back of her chair, stroked her shoulders. She reached up and took hold of him. He backed away; she held on, and the chair tilted until it was on two legs. He carefully got down on his knees and gently lowered the chair back until it reached the floor.

They lay next to each other on the floor. They looked each other in the eyes, no shyness, no strangeness.

"As long as the bird doesn't show up," he said in a low voice.

"Are you afraid of him?"

"Well, afraid, not really, but I get nervous when he's around."

"Don't be. He won't bother us."

"You sure?"

"I'm sure."

"I believe he was in the dream, too."

"He's my friend. Then he's your friend, too."

"I'm going to ask you something, but maybe you'll slap me; I hope not."

"I won't. Try and see."

"May I take off your clothes?"

Her eyes lit up. He drew the thick sweater over her head and made a pillow for her. Then he moved his hand behind her back and undid her bra. She had small breasts with nipples that turned in. He bent over them, touching them with his lips.

"They're shy . . .," he said. "They don't want to come out."

Then he saw her arms.

"My God, Justine! What happened to you! Have you battled a tiger?"

"Almost," she said. "A cat attacked me last night when I was taking out the garbage. Totally crazy cat."

"What happened? How did you get rid of it?"

"I had to actually tear it off of me. Maybe it was disturbed by the bird. I was afraid the bird would see it and be scared. As a tiny bird, he was almost eaten by a cat."

"Unusual that a cat would attack a person like that . . . what if it had rabies?"

"Nah, there's no rabies in Sweden."

"Well, what if you come down with cat-scratch fever or lockjaw?"

"I'm up-to-date on all my vaccinations."

She nestled into his underarm.

"Kiss my nipples again . . . bring them out into the light."

He bent over again and felt how they hardened and began to come out of their hiding places.

Then her fingers were there, agile and searching. They were warm now; they were around his waist, finding the buckle of his belt. The clicking sound when the belt opened. His penis rose into her underarm. He heard a noise around his ears; it seemed to come from inside him. Her hand went around him, held him, measured his strength.

"Wait," he whispered. "It's been such a long time, wait . . . I don't want to come too soon."

He drew down her tights and panties. She was strong and round; he gripped her waist and lifted her over himself. As she lay over him, she let her tongue run over his face.

"I like your taste," she said, and when she spoke, he felt the noise go from her ribcage into his. "I like your smell, and the softness on your chin . . . right before the stubble starts coming out."

He stroked her back and ass and the soft skin in the crack right where the legs meet.

"Know what?" he whispered.

"Mmmm."

"I want you to know that I didn't come here just to sleep with you."

"You didn't?"

"You shouldn't think that I came here for a quick fuck. . . ."

Justine giggled.

"You didn't?"

She rolled on her back and took his hand with her, moved it over her stomach. The hair down there was soft and curly. He desired to look at it; he sat up. It was blonde like the hair on her head. His fingers were in all that blondeness; she was wet. Those strong, substantial legs. She was big and swelling with the waving lines of a real woman. She looked like one of the models for one of the old master's paintings. Venus, the Sabine women, stolen and hanging from the horses, their veils and pale flesh. He drew off his clothes and lay naked beside her on the floor. Then she came up and he saw her stomach from underneath; sitting on both feet, she sank over him. He thought about her foot, he thought about HIV, he thought the hell with everything. She was warm and steaming. Her insides gripped his member, massaged it, those strong, joyful muscles; he saw the fleshy walls, how they embraced and sucked. He grabbed her hips and he came into a cramp that brought tears to his eyes. Somewhere far away, he heard her scream. She was riding him like an animal, pressing her heels into his sides, screaming right at the ceiling.

They were lying in her bed. She had covered them with her blanket; she held him in her embrace, stroked him closely over his head. The bird sat on his tree branch with one foot raised. He would sometimes make a little noise, but he wasn't paying any attention to them.

"Just hope he's not jealous," whispered Hans Peter.

"No, he wants me to be happy. If I like someone, so does he. He feels what my feelings radiate."

"And if you don't like someone?"

She chuckled.

"Well, then really bad things can happen."

"Justine," he said, and he realized that he wanted to say her name again and again, say her name to make it a part of himself.

Her lips against his neck, against his spine.

"Justine, you were so wonderful. . . . You made it so good for me."

"You, too."

"How much of your life do you want to keep for yourself?"

"What do you mean?"

"I want to get to know you. I long to find out about you. I am so light and happy. I can't remember ever feeling like this before."

"Sure you have," she said. "You certainly have."

Inside himself, he would have chosen that she would have answered differently, that she also had never felt like this for another man. He remembered what she said about a relationship that ended.

"To be here at the very beginning . . .," he whispered. "To have everything still in front of us . . . wishes, desires."

She didn't answer. He was lying in her arms, but she didn't change position. He got loose so that he could contemplate her. Those blonde eyebrows, the line of freckles over her cheeks and nose, those small, childlike breasts. His hand slid down her ribcage; her skin was damp with both his and her sweat.

"Justine, dearest . . . am I being too hasty? Taking things for granted?"

"No," she mumbled. "I don't think so."

He kept talking.

"This desire, this craving . . . not just that. There's something else, a sense of belonging that I never felt with anyone before, not even my ex . . . certainly not with her. From the minute I saw you in the snow, already then I knew that there was something about you that I couldn't let slip away from me. Could you let me into you, into that essence of you, and I don't mean just physically."

But even while he was speaking, he felt how his muscles were getting ready, how his flabby penis was now beginning to fill with blood again. She felt it too, and she looked down and smiled carefully. Her hand placed in the right spot, he grew against her palm. Do it like that, yes . . . do it . . . again.

She said that they had to eat. He borrowed her robe; she put on her long, green, knit dress and nothing else. In the kitchen, she fried some bacon and eggs.

"You get hungry after a hangover," she said. "Of course, I try and diet, but right now I am so hungry, I can't help myself."

"Don't diet," he said. "You are exactly how you need to be."

The bird flew down with them. She gave him the same food they were eating, and he swallowed it with greedy bites.

She poured some beer for them. They sat at the little kitchen table and looked out at the hill. It had stopped raining. He heard himself say something about the weather. It sounded so banal, but he couldn't help himself.

"It looks like winter is over for this year," he said. "Even though there's still some ice, it's going to break up soon. The papers said a man had drowned in Lake Mälar."

"They were looking for him yesterday. They must have found him."

"I don't get how people can take risks like that."

"Me neither."

"I'm just wondering . . . did you live here with that man? With the one that you've broken up with?"

"No," she said. "No, I didn't. He had an apartment in the city."

"Were you together long?"

"More than a year."

"Why did it end?"

She poked at some crumbs, drew them together into a small heap on the table.

"Hmmm . . . something happened to him . . . we went to the rainforest together, to the jungle. He had so many ideas, he wanted to start adventure trips for Europeans, you know, with long stays in the jungle. You were supposed to eat and live out there, great hardship. I went with him. He was going to create the trip route and make contact with the people living there who could be helpful and maybe work with the hikes and things. But then . . . something happened. . . . Actually, I don't really want to talk about it."

part two

Chapter ONE

A noise woke her. A knock. She was wide awake right away. She had slept stiffly and straightly, arms down her sides. Sweat covered her body, gave her goose bumps.

She looked around in the room. Nathan wasn't there. Another knock, then the door opened.

A woman stood next to her bed. She wore a scarf which covered her forehead and even her shoulders. She stared at Justine.

"Cleaning!" she said, loudly in English.

"Cleaning? No, you don't have to clean up; it is not necessary," Justine replied in English. She sat up, leaning against the wall, with the sheet up to her chin. The aroma of curry swept in through the doorway. From the street, she could hear the sound of motors, and a thumping sound, as if a huge jackhammer was attempting to beat something into the bedrock.

The woman grimaced, turned, and disappeared. The door shut.

Justine carefully got up. She felt dizzy. She went into the shower room. Her head felt like exploding. A piece of paper was on the floor and while she was sitting on the toilet, she saw a gecko creep in underneath it and hide itself. Something was written on the paper. She read while she was still sitting: *Out and about a few hours. See you this afternoon. Kisses.*

She didn't dare touch the paper. She took off her panties and laid them on the bed, afraid that the geckos would creep into them and make themselves at home. There was only one towel. Nathan had used it; it was hanging on the chair.

Between the walls and the ceiling, there was a gap. She heard shrieking female voices speaking a foreign language.

She washed herself carefully in the lukewarm shower water. She felt tender and aching all over. The trip had taken over thirty hours. In London, they had to wait in a crowded, smoke-filled lounge, whiny children, not enough seats. She had to go to the bathroom, but was afraid to leave the lounge, fearing that their flight would be called while she was gone. When she said this to Nathan, she noticed that he was irritable.

Then they had to run across the entire large terminal to find the right gate. Nathan did not like losing control of the situation. He didn't like asking directions.

Once in the airplane, their seats were far apart. Nathan ended up among the smokers. She ended up next to an elegant Belgian couple wearing fine clothes. She felt big and bloated. She turned and looked for Nathan, but couldn't see him. She stopped one of the young flight attendants, all of whom were gliding around in beautiful dresses. In halting English, she requested to change places. The flight attendant was named Hana; her name was on a small brass nameplate over her breast. Hana moved her lips; they had been carefully painted. Hana's lips told her that if she wanted to change places, sorry, she had to work that out for herself.

The Belgian man was listening in.

"Next to husband?" he asked, deciding to take part in the conversation.

"Yes," she said in English.

The man shook his head.

"Very long journey," he muttered.

She decided that she did not have the energy to confront all these foreigners, speak English, fall asleep next to them, long for Nathan. She stood in the aisle, and it was extremely narrow. She worked her way toward the back, looking for Nathan. Nathan was wedged into a middle seat. He gave her a pained smile.

Part 2: Chapter One

"Damned airline," he said.

"I asked them to help us, and they said we had to work it out ourselves."

"I've asked these people sitting next to me, but they won't move. They're smokers."

An attendant pushed past her, carrying some pillows.

"It's best you go sit down again," he said. "You're in the way."

They took a taxi to the hotel. The heat was oppressive and surprising. On the wall of a house, she saw an enormous thermometer; it showed 34 degrees Celsius in the shade. She looked in her backpack for her sunglasses but didn't find them. As they drove through the suburbs, she tried to think that the city was beautiful. She looked at the palms and the bushes with large red blossoms, which were growing along the median strips. She was so tired that she felt ill.

The radio was on in the taxi, music with loud talk in between. It seemed like a heated discussion. She didn't understand a word. Nathan sat in the front seat. The big backpacks were in the back seat with her. They had bought them at a supply store, Overstock, fifty crowns apiece. They had gotten most of their equipment there. That was part of Nathan's concept. Advice on where to get equipment for the people joining his groups. These were not supposed to be journeys for rich people.

He had taught her how to put on the backpack, helped her with the buckles, showed her how to fold in the ropes so they could be pulled out in one jerk. A name was written in ballpoint pen on the inside of the backpack's top: Bo Falk. He was the former owner, a short time in his care. She imagined him as a young man with peach fuzz, not yet had his growth spurt; wondered if he were content with his life, if he was happy.

The evening before they left, Nathan had given her a mascot. It was a shaggy, bear-like animal; she had tied it to one of the straps. The animal was supposed to be with her out in the jungle, and when they returned, she would put it on her bedpost as a constant reminder of what she had endured and successfully accomplished.

"It's going to be tough, Justine. Are you sure that you really want to come?"

She was sure.

Her eyes were blinded by the sharp white light. Looking like shadows in the front seat, she saw Nathan and the taxi driver, waving their arms around and gesturing. Nathan turned back toward her.

"How's it going?"

"Fine," she whispered. "But overwhelming."

"You know what the taxi guy's saying? That there's no such hotel. But I'm going to hold out until he gives in."

"Maybe it closed."

"The hell it did."

Building was going on everywhere. Half-finished skyscrapers pointing straight to the skies, shining windows of glass. Rows of cars and scooters, helmets on fluttering head scarves. Finally, the taxi pulled up to a bit of road between broken sidewalks and heaps of soil. The driver pointed.

"Hotel Explorer?" he said irritably.

That was it. Nathan had a look of triumph on his face; he patted the driver on the shoulder. The driver jumped back as if he'd been hit.

A teenage boy was lying on the sidewalk in front of the hotel. At first Justine was afraid that he was dead, but then she saw his ribcage rise and fall. His feet were naked and black. Justine wanted to say something to Nathan about the boy, but he was already carrying their stuff into the hotel. They were given their keys, Room Fifteen, top floor.

She was too tired to notice what the room looked like. It was somewhat dark and that felt nice. Nathan turned on the ceiling fan. It started up with a whine. He pointed to the bed nearest the wall.

Part 2: Chapter One

"You look like you're about to fall to pieces. Go lie down."

"Did you see the boy on the street? He was just lying there, what if he's sick?"

"Uh-huh."

"To think he's just lying there with people all around. And no one seems to care."

"The world is full of poor people."

She lay on her back, wearing nothing but her underwear; the fan whirled around. Nathan kissed her on the cheek. His forehead was thick with drops of sweat.

"I'm going to take a shower," he said. "Take a nap. I'm thinking of going out for a minute or two."

No, she thought. *Don't leave me. Stay next to me and be with me each and every second.*

Nathan had slept for most of the trip. He never had trouble sleeping no matter where. He explained that you learned to sleep standing up if you had to during his time in the military. It was important to save your energy. A few times she had gone past him as she walked up and down the aisle, keeping her blood circulation going. She saw he had his blanket drawn up over his head. Once he moved and she thought he would wake up and look at her. But he kept sleeping.

She wondered what the time was. Maybe the middle of the day, one or two in the afternoon. At home it was early in the morning. She thought of the bird with a tug of worry, but he had his entire attic filled with food; he was going to be all right.

Her long pants were hanging on a hook, wrinkled and somewhat damp. She smelled them. She was sweating again. Her skirt was in the suitcase; it was also wrinkled and it was tight around the waist. She chose to put on a T-shirt and when she saw herself in the mirror, she began to cry.

The hotel was built like a patio, with an inner courtyard covered by a ceiling. When she came out of her room, she could see all of the floors. Down on the stone floor, she could see heaps of laundry. A woman was standing on the stairs with a mop. When Justine walked past, she looked away.

She walked down the flights of stairs carefully. On one landing, she saw a little house altar with incense and candles. She drew in the sour aroma.

This is as far away from home as a person can get, she thought. She felt wiped out from exhaustion.

A large man, wearing a patterned short-sleeve shirt, sat in the hotel foyer. The shirt clung to his back. A fleck on the counter, a fleck on his shining forehead. Justine gave him the keys to her room and asked if he would be able to exchange some money for her.

"No, no," he answered in English. He pointed down the street.

She stepped into a burning wall of heat. She had to go through it. She had to get money and get something to eat, some water and food. The boy on the street was gone, and she felt relieved. She started to walk in the direction that the door-keeper had indicated. The traffic was lively, the air heavy. The direct light made her eyes hurt. It was one great dizziness, a whirling, smoking inferno with pieces of street all around, like a labyrinth. She followed what she believed was the main street, thought she saw a sign with the word "bank." She turned to the right, trying to imprint on her mind the look of the houses and the signs.

It wasn't a bank, but some kind of office. She saw how people milled about in there behind the shiny window panes. She grasped the door handle, but the door was locked.

She stood in the way of two women with colorful dresses and head scarves.

"Excuse me . . . but where can I exchange my money?"

They both stuck out their chins, the same confused gesture.

She had to turn back, but then realized that she didn't know where she was. Everything looked the same—same signs, same cars, same buildings. She felt faint; everything was going round and round, smells and sounds and thirst.

She heard someone call her name. She didn't know where she was. She looked around, but didn't see anything, blinded by the light and the sun. A taxi had stopped, the door opened.

"Justine, what are you up to?"

Nathan.

She grabbed the pocket of his shirt, heard a ripping sound from the seam loosening.

"Hey, relax!"

He led her to the taxi, helped her in.

Up in the room, he gave her water from a large plastic bottle.

"You better make damn sure that you don't go out there without having a lot of water in you," he admonished her.

"I didn't have any local currency," she said.

"You could have asked the guy at the desk. You could have gotten something in the room."

"And you, you could have stayed here with me and not taken off like that."

"I didn't want to wake you up. You said you hadn't slept a wink on the plane. It was out of consideration to you that I went out by myself."

She curled up in the bed and began to wail.

"But Justine . . . you should know that I would have to explore the area."

"You didn't have to start immediately."

"Yes, I did. I already had made some appointments. I'm here to work, you know. This is not a vacation if that's what you thought."

She lay there in her wrinkled dress and the elastic cut her waist. Her fingers were swollen from the heat.

She thought, maybe if we made love.

But when she touched him, he broke free.

She had met him at the dentist's. It was during a period of time when she was there fairly often; she had problems with a bridge. Every time she entered the waiting room, he was sitting there, and finally, they both broke into laughter.

"It seems our dentist is also a matchmaker," he said.

He was a few years older than she was. He had gray, tufty hair that would normally look ridiculous on a man of his age, but strangely did not on him. She heard someone call his name, Nathan Gendser.

Finally, they managed to come out into the waiting room at the same time. She was numb in her jaw from the Novocain. He was paying at the cashier.

"I'm finally done," he said. "Feels great."

She felt a twinge of disappointment.

"Lucky you!"

"Do you have much left?"

"Once or twice more. It wasn't just the bridge; there were some cavities, too."

"I have my car outside. Can I drive you somewhere?"

Her own car was around the corner. She thought a moment, then said, "Thanks."

It was summer. His plump, tanned hands; no ring.

"Dalvik . . .," he said. "I was wondering about that. Are you related to the Sandy Candy business?"

She nodded.

"Oh, I get it. That's why you have to go to the dentist's so often nowadays. Too much candy when you were a child!"

"I didn't eat too much of that candy. I didn't like it much. But I ate a lot of other kinds of candy."

"I'm not surprised."

He sat quietly for a minute. Then he asked her where she was going.

"Where are you going yourself?"

"Well, I can let you off at the subway station next to Odenplan? I live in the vicinity."

"That'd be perfect."

"Are you on vacation now?"

"No, I don't work."

"What! You don't work! Are you unemployed?"

"Not exactly."

She felt his look; she stared stubbornly straight ahead. People often were bothered when they found out that she didn't work. She had never really started a career. She had been sick most of her teenage life. Then she thought it was too late for anything. But you just couldn't say this to strangers. In order to avoid questions, she sometimes said that she'd worked for the family concern but was now thinking of trying something else. And then she would change the subject.

"I usually call myself an odd-job man," he said. "But the last few years, I've been working as a tour guide."

He let her out in front of the medical building on Odenplan. When he drove off, she went into the subway and rode back to the dentist's to get her car. Once she got home, she looked up his name in the telephone book. He lived on Norrtullsgatan. She got out the city map and found the exact place where he lived.

The next day, she did something unusual. She went there. This was unlike her. She talked to herself: what are you doing here, what are you expecting?

It was as if she were tipsy.

His car was parked next to the building. She glanced up at the façade, wondered which window was his. So that he wouldn't discover her, she went into a nearby bookstore and thumbed through some books, finally buying a paperback just for appearances. Then she walked along the sidewalk, up and down, in front of his building. As if she knew he was coming any minute, an intuition.

Her sixth sense was correct. He came out of the apartment building a half hour later. He was alone. She sped up, as if she were just walking along that minute, she said, "Hey, it's you. . . . I didn't expect to see someone I knew!"

His face: a look of surprised happiness!

"I was just going out to grab a bite to eat. Do you want to come, too?"

They took a boat out to the royal palace island of Drottningholm. He invited her to lunch at the exclusive restaurant. She felt she was waking up from a period of paralysis.

She had been silent for so many years. With him, the language began to return, one word at a time.

He stroked life into her body; he awakened her.

"You are so beautiful, I love women who are not anorexic. Like you, you're so alive."

She became violently jealous of all the women he had made love to.

"How do you know that I'm so alive?"

"I feel it, even though you're in your shell. I'm going to peel it from you, pluck your shell off, and show you to the world."

She thought it was just something that a man would say, but she gave herself to him, totally.

She had never made love as a grown woman. After her child, her life came to an end.

Fragments of discussions between her father and Flora. Flora like an attack terrier: "It's not just protecting her, you have to let her get well. We can't do this here at home. You can't, I can't. She has to go to a clinic."

She listened to her father's footsteps, how doors slammed, how it thundered and shook through the entire house.

Finally he allowed a psychiatrist come to the house to examine her. He spoke of what happened and called it a miscarriage.

"You have to go on," said the psychiatrist. "You have your whole life in front of you."

He did not realize that for her, the reverse was true.

Part 2: Chapter One

Yes, all the experts came to see her. He bought the best ones there were. Talk, talk, talk. He let her come with him on his trips, put her in the firm. Numbers and calculations, but nothing stayed in her mind. He brought home an electric typewriter, and Flora covered the keys so that she couldn't see them. She learned *a* and *ä*.

When Flora traveled to Maderia with her, her father set her up in his bedroom.

"Sleep in my room, so you can see when I fall asleep and when I wake up. If I have done you wrong in life, know that I didn't mean it, I've only wanted the best for you, Justine; you are all I have left of what was once my whole world. You are all I have left."

"What about Flora?" she whispered.

"Flora? Oh yes, of course, Flora, too."

She lay in Flora's bed, on Flora's pillow. She saw her father with new eyes. She saw that he had long ago passed his youth. His hair was no longer brown, but thinner and drab; his eyebrows shot out like bushes. He was sitting on the chair by Flora's vanity. He was looking in the mirror.

"What do you wish for in life, Justine?" he asked, and he had resignation in his bearing.

She had no answer.

He leaned forward over the table.

"That man who . . . came so close to you? You don't have to tell me who he was. But . . . was he important to you?"

She ran away from him wearing her nightgown.

Stood behind the door and refused to talk.

Her father had to coax and cajole. He handed her the horn, as if that would help, as if she still were a little girl that could be comforted with a musical instrument.

The horn's mouthpiece against her lips, the song of the horn.

She turned around, reflected in his eyes; his eyes were filled with pain. She wanted to cling to him and disappear into nothing. She was his only daughter, with great sorrow.

After some time, she began to stabilize. Flora had great patience. Whenever her sister came to visit, that was all they talked about, Flora's great, endless patience.

"You're certainly giving her just as good care as she would have gotten in a mental hospital," said Viola, smelling like perfume and flowers. "It must give her a sense of security to have you around her. And it gives him some peace of mind, too."

"It wouldn't make any difference whether she were here or in a hospital; she hardly makes a fuss these days. And Sven feels better, having her here at home. His little girl."

She said the last words with a bit of sarcasm.

Viola crossed her nylon-covered legs, and called Justine over.

"If I took you into the city, Justine, bought you a dress."

"Believe me," said Flora. "We've bought her so many clothes! I can't stop you, but it's a wasted effort. She never wears new things. At the very most, she will put it on for one day, and then she'll never wear it again. She says that it feels uncomfortable and affected. But it doesn't really matter. I mean, she hardly ever leaves the house."

"Don't give up, Flora. Clothes create grace and bearing. It could be a way to help return her to normal."

Flora lowered her voice.

"Normal! That child has never been normal! It's genetic, an inheritance from her mother. She has also been, let's just say, a little unusual, to put it mildly. Now I'm attempting to give her basic knowledge about running a house. That won't be wasted. And once Sven and I are old, she can care for herself and for us. Then she'll be of some use, both to her and to us. A human being has to have some value; that's among the most important things in life, to be useful."

Viola could not understand why Flora didn't hire help for the house or the garden. Married into wealth and still no additional household help.

Part 2: Chapter One

"You could sit here like a member of the nobility and just be waited on. And you would still be valuable as the wife of the well-known Sven Dalvik, just that alone."

Flora had her unusual reasons.

"I don't want strangers in my home. This is my territory."

The territory became Justine's as well. Slowly, she greased herself into it, although Flora didn't realize that. Wearing her father's cast-off overalls, she scrubbed the walls and the floors in the house. Spring and fall, year after year.

In the water were a few drops of blood from a cut on her finger.

Chapter TWO

The day her father died, she was working her hardest up in the attic. She usually began at the top and slowly worked her way down. She was on her knees, scrubbing and scrubbing. The floor boards cut into her knees and the pain felt good to her. The raw wood, the smell of well-scrubbed pine.

Then from far below a draft of cold air. She heard Flora call. Her father had collapsed on the outer stairs. He had lost a shoe. Mechanically, she took off his other shoe. Her hands were still damp from the cleaning water.

Together they managed to pull him into the blue room. Flora ran up and down the stairs, changing clothes, smoking.

"You should change clothes, too, if you're coming with us. You can't wear those overalls."

She sat with her father's head in her lap. It felt hard and little.

Only one of them could ride in the ambulance.

Justine took the Opel. She had gotten the Opel as a present for her thirty-fifth birthday. She followed closely behind the ambulance with its shrieking sirens.

As she already realized, there was nothing that could be done. A worn-out doctor took them aside to a room. She remembered a bandage over a cut on her father's throat. She sat and wondered what he'd done. Did he cut himself? Or was it a hickey? She thought of anything and everything in that room, just not her father.

"So here's what's going on. At the most, he'll manage to live through the night. I want you to be aware of this."

"We're aware," she said.

Flora became angry. She scratched her hands like paws. "How much do you want . . . to do your utmost?"

"My dear Mrs. Dalvik, there are some things that can't be bought. We have done our utmost."

They sat, one on each side.

"Poor Justine," said Flora. "I don't think you realize how serious this is."

Her cheeks were spotty with mascara. Justine had never seen her cry before. The sniffling bothered her; she wanted to be left alone with her father. She thought of death as a woman, maybe her mother, who had been sent to bring her husband home. She could imagine her coming through the window, big and tall, taking off his blanket, taking his hand, and leading him away from them. She would look at Flora with a spiteful little smile: "I'm taking him now, because he is mine."

Nathan took her to the biggest shopping center in Kuala Lumpur. It looked just like a large department store in Sweden, and she was amazed at the assortment of goods. She must have forgotten her sunglasses at home, or lost them on the plane. Finally, she would be able to buy a new pair.

Nathan made clear that she could not hold his hand or show any affection because that would be offensive. People just did not show public affection in this country.

"We'll resume all of this in the hotel room," he said. He was in a good mood again.

He also thought she should look at some clothes.

"It'll cheer you up. Women love to shop; just ask an expert like me!"

He had been married twice and had a live-in girlfriend once. There were photos of all his children in graduation outfits or wedding dresses on the living room shelf. He had six children. She asked about their mothers, punished herself with details.

"Ann-Marie is the mother of these two. They look like her, same blue eyes, but thank God not the same mental status, if I may say so. Nettan is the mother of the twin girls and Mikke, the boy. I was legally married to both Ann-Marie and Nettan, for five and seven years respectively. After that, I've been careful not to get married. When I met Barbro, we agreed to just live together. She also didn't want to get married. She had just gotten divorced from some crazy guy who used to beat her up. I lived with her for four or five years. Little Jenny is ours."

He was very proud of Jenny, who was a model. A thin girlish young woman with doe-eyes, a copy of her mother.

"And then, did you live by yourself?"

He waved his hand.

"In a matter of speaking."

"Why did it never work out? Are you so difficult to live with?"

"All three had one thing in common: they were a bit hysterical."

"What do you mean hysterical?"

"I don't want to go into that now."

"Am I also hysterical?"

"Not what I've seen so far. But if I notice it, I'll be sure to let you know."

"And which one was the best in bed?"

He pushed her into his bed, lay over her, put a hand over her mouth.

"The first one is you, the second one is you, the third one is you, Darling."

She looked through the clothes, but everything was too small. Malaysian women barely reached her shoulders. They appeared stamped from the same mold, and their waists were as narrow as one of her legs.

Let's go, she thought.

Nathan was speaking to a shop assistant; they were observing her. The assistant came up to her with a measuring tape around her neck.

"She's wondering about your size."

"Why? Nothing here I want."

Nathan held a dress up to her. It looked made for a pygmy. "I thought you might want something more elegant when we're out and about among people. This is still civilization, you know."

"Just look at that, Nathan, do you really think I can squeeze into that? Can you really believe that? It's made for a child!"

"Well, maybe not this exact one, but a larger size."

He turned toward the assistant; she had big, brown eyes.

"Bigger size?" he asked in English.

The assistant smiled crookedly, took the dress, and went away to search.

"Let's go," Justine whispered.

"Don't be such a troublemaker."

"But Nathan, you don't get it."

"The hell I don't. I want to give you a nice dress, and you're acting like a stubborn child."

He began to walk to the counter. Justine followed him. The assistant came. She looked at Nathan expectantly.

"Well?" he asked.

"Sorry, sir, not bigger size."

"As if I were an incompetent, stupid child!" Justine burst out once they returned to the street. "She ignored me completely!"

"Huh."

"She turned to you; she talked to you."

"She must have noticed how grumpy and unwilling you were."

Justine put on her sunglasses. She was crying again, and she had a headache.

Part 2: Chapter Two

That evening, her period started. She thought that was the explanation. She told Nathan, forgive me that I was so whiny."

"I pretty much thought that was the deal. I know women; they have their whiny phases."

She did not want to be one of those women he knew like that. She crept into the narrow bed. Just wanted him to hug her, nothing more.

He said, "Tomorrow afternoon, I'm going to meet Ben. He's coming with us on the expedition."

She took his arm, drew it over her, placed it on her tummy.

"Does it hurt?" he asked.

"Yes," she whispered.

He kissed her.

"Turn more to the side so I can hold you for a little while."

During the night, she bled horribly. She stained not only the sheets, but the mattress underneath. She didn't want the cleaning women to see it. She tried to clean the stains herself, but it didn't work.

She and Nathan ate breakfast at a restaurant which was next door to the hotel. They ordered juice and coffee with milk and there was a sweet, creamy mess at the bottom, which appeared to be some kind of sweetener. She stirred it suspiciously. Nathan was eating *roti*, a dish that looked like pancakes with meat sauce. Men and women were sitting around eating, all using their fingers.

"You might have noticed that they're using their right hands. Their left hands are unclean," Nathan explained.

"What do they do with their left?"

"Figure that one out for yourself."

Justine's stomach hurt, it cramped like tiny, digging nails. That's the way it always was, the first few days of her period. No pain medication in the world could help.

"Maybe you should just stay at the hotel," suggested Nathan. "You look a little ill."

She thought about the cleaning women.

"I'd rather die. Take me with you."

They took a taxi through the city. Nathan pointed out a few sights for her: the National Mosque, with its sun feather column and its minaret, which was over seventy meters high. For fun, he used a tour guide's voice.

"And here to the right, you will soon be able to see the famous twin towers. . . ."

He was acting like an eager boy.

"I love you," she said loudly. "Oh, Nathan, put me in your shirt pocket and take me with you wherever you go, and never ever take me out!"

The man called Ben was waiting for them in a room with air-conditioning. There was tea and juice on a table. Justine felt a spontaneous confidence in him. He was relaxed and had nothing of calculation or malevolence about him.

"So you're going out in the jungle to frolic with tigers and elephants," he joked, while handing her a glass of juice. He spoke excellent English.

"I hope I don't exactly frolic," she answered.

"You know that there are both tigers and wild elephants in the area we're going to," he said.

He observed her reaction; then he laughed.

"You don't see them very often. They keep away from humans; they're more afraid of us than we are of them."

"But they have attacked humans?" asked Nathan.

"Of course, but that hasn't happened in a while."

"Elephants scare me more than tigers," she mumbled. "Once a man let me ride an elephant. Pappa and I were at the circus. They didn't ask me; they just lifted me up and plopped me down right on that wrinkly skin. A few weeks later, Pappa told me that an elephant had gone crazy, managed to escape its chain, and ran amok."

Ben smiled at her. His brown chin was round, his nose wide and flat. He was born in the jungle, but he had received a decent education and even studied at the university in Kuala Lumpur.

"Elephants shouldn't be in a circus," he said. "No wonder they go crazy there."

They sat with Ben for a long time, talking and looking at maps, making long lists of the things that they would do and the things they had to purchase. In the evening, they went out to a restaurant. There was just one dish: fried rice with chicken. Justine was hungry. There wasn't much meat on the chicken; it was mostly bones. They each ordered a Coke.

Nathan said he longed for a cold beer.

"No beer here," he said. "I know another place; we can go there next time."

That night she slept soundly and didn't even wake up when the *muzzien* called to prayer at six in the morning.

She and Nathan took a shower together. She soaped up his big, light body; she could never get enough of touching him. Her hands could long for him, long to feel his skin, his warmth; he was so filled with life and strength. There in the shower, he had a strong erection, and she knelt and took him in her mouth.

Afterwards, he had tears in his eyes.

"Sometimes, I feel I need to rethink my idea of never getting married again," he said, stroking her cheek.

"Do you think it would work out? Or do you think that I'll also become hysterical?"

"You'll just have to refrain from it."

She had pulled up her underclothes, they were still a bit damp, but would dry on her body.

He said: "Today we're going to meet the others who are coming with on our excursion."

"Who are they?"

"Two Norwegians, I think; some Germans, a guy from Iceland and—believe it or not—a Swede. We're going to meet them at Ben's in about an hour."

Chapter THREE

Her father was not buried in what had been seen as the family grave, the grave where the French wife was at rest. Rather, he was buried on the other side of the cemetery, where the newer and smaller graves were.

Justine heard Flora say to Viola: "Should I let the two of them be together in death, and have all three of us there later? No! Once I die it will just be him and me, just him and me!"

"And little Justine?"

Flora began to laugh. "Don't you see that little Justine is not so little anymore? Soon, she's going to be past her best years, overripe."

Viola's tone changed, as if she'd been insulted herself. One could see her as "overripe," almost sixty. She had been bought out by NK and she had been recommended to start her own business. The truth was that the department store did not want old ladies at the perfume counters. They didn't have the same results in sales; in fact, they could have a frightening effect on the customers.

Viola had no choice but to take the money, and now she was renting an expensive little place near Hötorget. She started Viola's Body Shop, where she sold soaps, perfumes, and expensive lingerie. She had offered to take Justine as an apprentice; maybe she could be trained to take over the business. A few days later, Justine had indeed gone there. She stood behind the counter in a rose nylon skirt Viola had picked out, and Viola had also made her up and had taken her to a hair salon.

It didn't work.

"Quite frankly, she's rude to the customers," Viola reported later to her sister. "She pretended not to hear what they were asking her; just stood there drifting away in her own thoughts. Take her back."

"I didn't try to force her on you; it was completely your idea. I told you it wouldn't work out. I've always said there was something wrong with her mentally, but you never believed me."

After her father's death, they lived as usual in the house. Nothing had changed; all the routines remained the same. Flora continued to speak to her husband after she had closed the bedroom door; Justine could hear her voice through the wall which separated them. Flora talked loudly. She rebuked him for leaving her; she threatened to sell the house and buy an apartment in the city.

She also said this to Justine.

"Don't think that we are going to live here forever and ever. Anyway, it's not normal for two grown woman to share a house like this. Normal would be that you would have moved away from here many, many years ago; you have just been growing like an abscess on Sven and me during our entire life together. Your father has protected you and overprotected you, but he's not here anymore. Now I'm free to throw you out. He wouldn't be offended; he should have thanked me. He knows that everything I've done for you has been for your own good. Women understand these things better than men."

Justine would make herself scarce whenever Flora was in that mood. Sometimes she took the car and drove up to the cliffs near Lövista, wandered on old paths; never for long, though, anxiety drove her back home. What was Flora thinking of? Had she brought a real estate agent to the house, who was now wandering around figuring out how much it was worth?

All this remained unchanged for many years.

Part 2: Chapter Three

During the morning, they drank their coffee on their own side of the table, each fully dressed, neither wanting to appear in a robe in front of the other one. That would be a defeat. Flora was always made up, her eyelashes large and blue. These days they were a bit more uneven; her sight had started to weaken. When the warm days came, she would move to the balcony or into the garden. She had always loved the sun. She asked Justine for help with the lounger and had her also bring out a carafe with white wine and water. Wearing her strong glasses, she would paint her nails, layer after layer.

Her stroke came on such a day, while she was sitting in her lounger on the balcony. It was a fine, clear spring day, one of the first really warm ones. She was wearing a bikini and she told Justine she had the same bikini since she was a young woman; her body was as cute and small as a girl's. But now she had difficulty walking up and down the stairs.

Then she said that she had called a real estate agent.

"There is an apartment on Norr Mälarstrand which I am thinking of buying. One floor with a large terrace. I can sit there and sunbathe. You know how I love the heat."

"What about me?" asked Justine.

"You'll just have to find something for yourself. The house is definitely going to be sold. The real estate agent said that there were a number of interested buyers."

And she sank into the cushions and made herself comfortable. The sun shone on her knotty, hairless legs. She rubbed in lotion, stomach and arms; she raised her glass to her lips and drank.

Afterwards Justine told Nathan that she was extraordinarily angry at Flora that moment.

"So angry that I could have killed her. I thought I could put something into her drink, some poison or something. But where would you get that? Poison? Not like going to the drug store and asking to buy some strychnine. Don't they use that in the mystery stories? I went to the garden, got in the boat and roared off; Pappa never liked it when I would take off like that: you ought to be calm and careful, he always said. But I was angry, furious; I think he would have understood me; he also wanted to keep the house. Because of Mamma. I made a few rounds out there, because it was a normal workday and people were at work and I thought about what it would be like if we had to move and whether I would have the chance to stop her."

"But didn't you both own the house?"

"We probably did, but I never paid attention to that stuff."

"You never signed any papers?"

"Maybe I did. I don't know, I was really depressed after Pappa died."

He shook his head. "You need to remember those kinds of things, Justine."

"Need, whatever. Now I pay more attention. At any rate, when I returned to the house, the sun had disappeared, and I thought that Flora had gone in. I started making dinner right away; it was probably five in the evening. I had been out for an unusually long time, landed somewhere that was completely still all around me, only the birds. I stood there on the beach and wished she would die, Nathan. I really did."

"Did you ever give her a chance to be a mother to you?"

"Don't you get it? Flora isn't someone that you give something to. Flora is a taker."

"Maybe I should come with you when you visit her in the nursing home?"

"No," she said hastily, as if the old witch woman would arise from her sickbed, as if she would become strong again and begin to threaten them.

"Eventually I went upstairs. There was a draft from the upper level. I looked out and saw her sitting there in a somewhat distorted position. It looked so macabre, that dry old woman stomach and that bikini. . . . She'd had a stroke. I tried to get her going, but she was slurring her speech and was strange. Later, they found that she was completely paralyzed and couldn't even speak. Well, then I sent her off to the hospital and she never came back."

He took both of her hands.

"You seem to be a bit grim to me, my darling."

"She had me in her power for so many years."

"Please pardon me in advance, but it sounds a bit exaggerated when you say that."

"It's not exaggerated."

"It was surely not easy for her to become the step-mother of a spoiled child like you."

"If you had met her, you wouldn't think so."

"Oh yes, you probably deserved a whipping or two!"

"Nathan!"

But the conversation had turned into play. He had that ability, to get her to forget that evil and hurtful past; he loved wrestling with her and taking off her clothes piece by piece, as if they were trophies. Then he placed himself between her legs. He kissed her and manipulated her until she was taken over by spasm upon spasm of orgasms. He enjoyed her amazement and her gratitude. A woman of her age so completely without experience.

But still she had carried a child.

When she explained more about that to him, he said that he had already surmised it. She was wider, not closed in the same way much younger women were. He was careful to say that it didn't make her less attractive. It was one of the contrasts that made her so fascinating to him: so grown and wonderful but without any dissemblance.

He thought owning the bird was complete craziness. He came home with her once and the bird came flying, and he had to shout out in surprise. She had hoped that he would feel friendly. She had to close the door to the attic while Nathan was in the house. The bird did not like that. She heard him screech and fly around up there.

"I'm going to let him go into the wild," said Nathan. "This is animal cruelty."

"Do that and he'll die. The others will attack him out there; they'll hack him to death."

"Isn't it better to die a quick, albeit cruel, death rather than be forced to live in a house that was made for human beings?"

"You don't get it. He likes this house, and I am his friend."

"It can't be all that hygienic, either."

"People are always going on about cleanliness. Do you think that my house looks messy?"

"No, but. . . ."

"Let's forget about the bird. Come on, I'll show you something else."

She showed him photos of herself when she was little, pictures of her mother and the wedding photo of her father and Flora.

"Ah . . . so this is the notorious Flora."

"Yes."

"Such a skeleton."

"She has always been thin and beautiful."

"She probably rattled when she walked. No, Justine, you're the beautiful one; you're round and plump, something for a guy to sink his teeth into."

And he pressed his mouth against her underarm and gave her a large, dark-red hickey.

When he saw her post horn, he lifted it from its hook and tried to blow it. Not a single sound came from it. He blew until he turned red.

"It doesn't work, does it?" he said.

She took it from him. She had composed a few melodies when she was a child, but they were simple and easy to remember. Now she played them for him.

He wanted to try again. He blew and snorted, and finally managed a hoarse, deep sound.

"I've always been able to play it," she said quietly. "My Pappa gave it to me. He said it was made for me."

Even Nathan thought she should sell the house.

"Do it before the bird has destroyed it and left bird shit everywhere."

"You don't get it. I want to live here. My mother chose this house. I have lived here my entire life."

"That's why you should sell it. How many houses do you think I've lived in? I don't even know myself. You have to move around a bit, get a new perspective. You get stunted by the same damn view each and every day. Don't you get it? You have to keep growing, Justine. Try a little adventure."

They all got together at Ben's office. The two Norwegian men were already there when Justine and Nathan arrived. They were just under thirty; they were named Ole and Steinn. A little while later, the Icelander and the three Germans appeared: Heinrich, Stephan and Katrine. Heinrich was the oldest in the group, just over sixty. The Icelander's name was Gudmundur.

Then Martina arrived. She just opened the door and walked right in. Sat down as if she already knew them all, as if she'd just been gone a few minutes to run some errands.

"Hi, guys. Have you been waiting long?"

She was wearing thin cotton trousers, so thin than one could see her panties under the cloth. Her hair was knotted up, and she carried a camera on a wide strap, a large, advanced model.

One of the Norwegians whistled.

"A Nikon? Is it an F4?"

"Yeah," said Martina. "It's my work camera."

"You're a photographer?"

"No, a freelance journalist, actually. But then you have to do the photos yourself."

"That must weigh a ton. Are you really going to schlep it through the jungle?"

"I've schlepped it over half the world this past year, so I don't see why not."

She was going to be the youngest participant. She was twenty-five years old, and used to traveling by herself.

"Martina has promised to write up a piece about our excursion," said Nathan. "She is going to help with marketing for my new firm, and you all are the pioneer group. Everything will depend on you. . . ."

Everyone laughed.

Ben went through a few of the things that they had to know about. He was the one who decided that everyone should speak English at all times.

"That way, no one will feel like an outsider. You need to think about one thing, all of you in this room, and that is you belong to the few lucky people who will be able to visit one of the most beautiful places on the planet, the rain forest with all its animals and exotic plants. The rain forest, which presently still exists, but is shrinking greatly. I also want you to be ready for what this expedition will mean. . . . A few of you will think in the beginning that things are getting really heavy; we also have to carry our stuff. There are no roads or paths in the jungle. We will have to crawl, climb, and keep our balance. We will have to cut our way through with these *parangas*, these jungle knives that we are going to buy tomorrow as part of our equipment. We are going to be crossing land that no white man or woman has ever set foot on before. You still have the chance to back out. You have all night to think about it."

In the evening, Ben took them to a Chinese restaurant where there was beer. Justine would rather have had wine, but it appeared to be impossible to procure in this country. She ended up next to Heinrich, one of the Germans, with whom she felt an affinity right away. He and his wife had planned to start traveling once he had retired, but she got cancer and died less than a year ago.

"I stopped working when she died; now I travel for both her and me," he revealed to her. "Sometimes it feels as if she were with me the whole time. I talk to her in the evenings; I tell her what I've been up to. Having someone to share experiences with is half of the enjoyment."

The beer helped her relax.

"It's not easy to lose someone you love," she said.

"Elsie was so sweet. . . ." He took out his wallet and quickly showed her, somewhat embarrassed, a photo of his deceased wife. She looked rather plain. Justine didn't know what to say.

"We were married almost forty years. What about you? How long have you two been married?"

"We two? No, Nathan and I . . . we are, I don't know how to say it in English. We are together, but we are not married and we don't live in the same house."

"Lovers?"

"More than that. We will probably get married, we've talked about it."

Martina had changed into a dress; her hair was newly washed and shining. She kept silent for long stretches, observing them, one at a time. When she came to Justine, she said quickly in Swedish: "The first white women in this jungle. What do you think about that?"

The younger German man, Stephan, hollered and put his arm around Martina.

"Hey you! Only English, remember?"

"I just told Justine that she and I and your girl Katrine are going to have a great time out in the jungle with all these good-looking guys."

When they returned to their hotel room, they packed their things; they were going to leave early the next morning. They were going to travel into the countryside by bus until they reached a small town on the outskirts of the jungle. There they would stay overnight and finish up getting whatever else they might need.

Justine was done, she crept into bed. An unusual melancholy had come over her. She thought it was due to her period; her body felt swollen and heavy.

"Have you met any of these people before?" she asked.

"No."

"But Martina said she'd promised you an article."

"I met her yesterday while you had your beauty sleep."

"You didn't mention that."

"Do I have to account for everything I do?"

"I didn't mean it to sound like that. . . ."

"You didn't?"

"I think it's a bit reckless, a young Swedish girl heading out all by herself like that."

"You do? Girls are tough, nowadays."

She couldn't stop herself:

"Nathan?"

"Yes?"

"Do you think she's sexy?"

"Don't be silly. No one can compare with you."

"You sure?"

"She could be my daughter, for God's sake."

The fever and shakes came that night. She woke up right in the middle of a dream. A body in the leaves, herself. Thirst was eating her from the inside, unquenchable, plowed her tongue full of furrows. She felt around in the dark; everything was pitch-black. She lay on her side, one leg weighing down the other, knees and joints.

She cried without making noise.

"Nathan. . . ."

When he came up out of sleep, he was angry.

"For Christ's sake, we've got to sleep; we have a rough day tomorrow."

It was five past two in the morning.

His fingertips.

"Dammit, you're burning up."

He got some Alvedon, a fever medication, and water.

"Get better, my darling, it will be extremely difficult tomorrow otherwise."

"I know, Nathan, I know."

The call to prayer. That hard, echoing voice. She froze more than she ever had in her life.

"I have to go to the bathroom. . . ."

He helped her out; he cleaned her face. She saw something move in the corner. She screamed and hit around wildly.

"It's nothing, just a cockroach. Take it easy, Darling, take it easy. . . ."

Then back to bed.

"I can't, I just can't. . . ."

"Shall I get a doctor?"

"No, just let me be. . . ."

He went down to the registration desk and came back with two blankets. It didn't help. She grabbed his arm tightly.

"I can't go with the bus. . . ."

"I understand, Sweetheart."

He had to go out. She hallucinated due to the fever. She was in the jungle and she was sinking; Martina stood wide-legged in the river. Then it seemed she was lifted from the lumpy mattress, a shimmering flood of cockroaches; she hung down. Someone was holding her. Someone was rubbing ointment into her back. She was freezing between her shoulder blades. A glass came to her lips. Someone said, drink. She drank and fell back into the rising shadows.

In the evening, he was with her again.

"Nathan, I was calling for you so. . . ."

He said, "I was sitting here pretty much the whole time. I've been keeping watch over you; you have been very sick."

"What day is it?"

"It's Wednesday."

"Tuesday was yesterday already?"

"Yes, it was Tuesday; you've been very sick . . . but now you're better; the crisis has passed. I got some medicine from Ben. We can take the bus tomorrow."

As soon as she thought of that, she wanted to close her eyes again; she tried to get more air.

"Ben said that you'd be much better tomorrow. You've gotten a fantastic medicine. But now you have to drink a lot. Drink both of these bottles."

He did not let her sleep. If her eyes were closed for too long, he woke her up again and forced her to drink more water. She was no longer freezing. The aches in her legs were beginning to lessen. He was sitting next to her; he didn't go out.

"Forgive me . . .," she whispered. "Forgive me for hindering you . . . us."

"You don't need to ask for forgiveness; you couldn't help it. On a trip like this, you have to expect that anything can happen."

"What about the others?"

"It's better it happened now than in the jungle. Right?"

"Ew," she complained. "Do you think I'll be able to go?"

The next day it was over. She was feeble and exhausted, but the fever had left her. Nathan helped her take a shower. She was still bleeding from her period. He wasn't irritated. He was singing as he kneaded her dry.

They took a taxi to the train station. She had her backpack between her knees. She was very weak; she couldn't handle the weight on her shoulders.

The bus was old and worn out and was quickly filled with people. Ben had made sure that they all had places together. The seats were jammed tight; there weren't enough for all the passengers. Some young boys had to sit on folding chairs. She felt immense sympathy for them.

The group received her with great warmth.

"You really need to forgive me," she said.

"Well, our turn next time," said the Icelander.

She liked his accent.

Heinrich had bought her a small bag of rock candy.

Part 2: Chapter Three

"You need a little sugar," he said, as he gave her a friendly nudge. "At home in Hannover, we always used to get a little sugar when we were small and sick."

"Thanks," she said. "You're all being so kind."

Martina had gotten the seat in front of Justine.

"Feeling better?" she asked.

Justine nodded.

"I had something similar in Peru. It hung on in my eyes afterwards. I was afraid that I was going to go blind. Imagine trying to fumble your way around a foreign country without anything but darkness in front of you."

"How did you manage?"

"A man I got to know found me some kind of powder, something the Indians used. It stung like hell, but the next day, everything was all right."

"To think you'd dare try it! You could have really been blinded!"

"Yeah, you could say that after the fact. But sometimes, you have to take a risk."

"I got a fantastic medicine from Ben."

Martina snorted.

"Our Swedish social system would shit on themselves if they saw the stuff you get here."

"That's true."

"Try and rest during the drive. It'll probably take all day."

A fat, temperamental Chinese man drove the bus. He stopped twice, once for a quick lunch and the second time for an eight-minute bathroom break. He held up his sausage-like fingers with thumbs folded in: "And I tell you! Only eight minutes! After that! Bus is gone!"

The toilet was unbelievably dirty and consisted of a hole in the floor. Justine barely kept her balance in there, and her shoes got wet.

There was no such thing as toilet paper.

She said so to Nathan.

"Do they have to have such dirty toilets? It smelled disgusting in there; how can they not notice that?"

"Do your best to put up with it," laughed Nathan. "It'll be better in the jungle. At least there you get fresh air and leaves."

"Also leeches!" Martina added.

Justine didn't understand the English word *leeches*. She waited a minute and then asked Nathan. He glanced at Martina and smiled conspiratorially.

"Oh, you'll find out soon enough."

In the bus, Martina sat turned toward them with her legs in the aisle. The arm rest of her seat was long gone. She had a fine little face with dark eyebrows. A vague smell of soap surrounded her. She took some photos of them.

Suddenly the bus lurched so strongly that she almost dropped the camera.

"Damn idiot!" she cussed.

Nathan had caught her.

"You okay?"

"Oh, yeah. But that asshole up there has certainly not gone to driving school."

"That's for sure, but you have to realize that we still have a lot of miles to go and he probably doesn't want to drive in the dark. God knows if there's any headlights on this monstrosity."

"In Guatemala, I rode the whole night long in a vehicle that makes this one seem like a luxury bus. We rode from Tikal to Guatemala City, and the bus had stone-hard seats without any cushioning . . . talk about a sore butt when we finally arrived at the crack of dawn."

"Were you reporting?" asked Nathan.

"Yeah, I sold a piece to the travel magazine *Res*. They gave me a number of pages and even the cover."

He ruffled her hair.

"Well done, Martina. Do the same here."

"How much are you offering?"

"How about, you know, *in natura*? We'll come to some kind of agreement, you and me."

She gave him a shrewd look.

"There's an old English saying, old but true: Don't screw the crew!"

The Icelander said, "Martina, weren't you nervous in Guatemala?"

"Oh yes, the soldiers stopped me a few times."

"I think that's unwise, even stupid, to tempt fate like that, going out into the world as a young woman on her own."

"Why not? Shouldn't a gal have the same freedom of movement as a guy?"

"You understand what I mean."

"Well, no one ever tried to rape me, if that's what you mean. The worst thing that ever happened was once I lost my passport. But the embassy fixed that up."

"Have you seen the whole world?" asked Justine.

"Never been to Iceland, but I don't really have any desire to go there, either."

They arrived late in the evening. It was still very hot. The air was filled with birds; they looked like swallows. Their shining silver bodies filled the telephone wires, which ran back and forth over the streets. Ben was thrilled.

"Oh, I'm so glad that you get to see this. They're migratory; they're only here a few times a year."

"But I don't think you're supposed to walk under them," said Nathan. "I hear that's unlucky."

Everyone laughed.

They were quartered in a bare and simple guest room. Justine was very tired; she stretched out on the bed. The room was as hot as a Swedish drying cabinet. She would need to wash up a bit; she smelled funky; her whole body was itching.

"How are you feeling now?" asked Nathan. He had already taken a shower; he was standing with his feet wide apart, under the ceiling fan to dry off. The golden hair on his legs. He was handsome. She longed for him, that he would embrace her and kiss her, reassure her that nothing dangerous was going to happen, and that they always, always would be together.

"Fine," she whispered.

"You seem down."

"Nothing, I'm just tired."

"Let's go downstairs and eat something."

She shook her head.

"Not me."

"Well, I have to get something to eat."

He left. There were no sheets on the bed, just a thin, flowery spread over the mattress. It felt like she was lying on sand, but when she tried to brush it off, she saw that it was smooth. She wanted to wrap something around herself, not because she was freezing, but because she was used to it. She felt naked and unprotected.

She heard the others getting together downstairs. The room was square; the floor was cement. The bed was the only piece of furniture. On the other side of the window lathes, a growing chorus of cicadas and frogs.

She sat up; she itched and burned in all the places where skin rubbed against skin. She got on her clothes and went into the hallway. At the end of the hallway, there was a laundry room painted an unfortunate color. To the right, there was a shower and an Asian toilet. She went into the shower room and took off her clothes. There were no hooks for them. She hung them over the door, but while she showered, they managed to get wet.

She rinsed her bra and panties. Covered just in her bath towel, she ran back to the room. What if someone saw her like this? It certainly would not be acceptable to appear in a Muslim guest house, wearing nothing but a bath towel. Maybe she'd be whipped or stoned to death? She put on a T-shirt and long pants, spreading out the wet clothes on the floor. Her wet hair felt good against her head. She felt a pang of hunger. She was returning to health.

She carefully walked down the steep, dark stairs. A TV was on; some young boys were sitting in front of it. They didn't notice her. A woman looked out from behind a veil.

"Have you seen my friends?" she asked in English.

Then she found them. They had taken a few tables, which stood on the street. She stood in the doorway. They didn't notice her. Martina was sitting in the center. She was in the middle of telling them a story.

Nathan sat next to her, so close that his hand was resting on her leg.

She stood there for a long time, watching them, their shining faces, their intensive listening. Something inside her closed down. She couldn't bring herself to go to them, nor could she face returning upstairs. All the sounds of the day were still in her head: motors, voices, cicadas. She stood there as if she had turned into a statue—of a middle-aged, charm-less, pale, fat, female tourist.

Ben saw her first. He got up and approached her.

"Sit over here, Justine. I'll get you something to eat."

"What are you guys doing?"

"Nothing. We've eaten and now we're just sitting around, relaxing."

She slipped in between the chairs.

"I thought you were sleeping," said Nathan.

"Uh-huh," Justine said, feeling stupid.

Heinrich patted her on the cheek.

"It's good that you've rested. You'll have strength for tomorrow."

She nodded. She felt about to cry, so she hastily put on her sunglasses.

"Now you look like Greta Garbo," said Stephan. He had a fairly thick German accent. Katrine imitated him unmerci-fully, and then she repeated the phrase again, very clearly. Stephan and Katrine were engaged. They were well-trained; she noted the muscles on their calves. They were certainly not going to have trouble keeping up in the jungle.

She forced herself to say something.

"What have you eaten?" she asked.

"Guess!"

"I have no idea. . . ."

"Fried rice and chicken."

"It's the national dish of Malaysia," said one of the Norwegians.

Justine had difficulty telling the Norwegians apart.

"Are you Stein or Ole?" she asked.

"Ole, of course. Maybe we should wear name tags."

"Well, you guys look identical."

They both burst out laughing; they had the same clucking, well-meaning laugh.

"Are we? That wasn't very nice!"

"Maybe because you're both Norwegian."

"So you think we Norwegians all look alike? I don't think you Swedes look alike."

He looked over at Martina.

"She's dark-haired, for example, and you are blonde."

Ben arrived with a plate of food and an ice cold Coke. She drank eagerly.

Ben said, "We talked about packing yesterday. Nathan will show you. Take the least amount of things necessary. Remember that you have to carry everything that you pack. And think that wet clothes are heavier than dry clothes. All the stuff that you're not going to take with you, we can store here at the house until we return."

"OK."

"You're going to get another pill from me. Tomorrow you'll be stronger than ever."

She couldn't sleep. Nathan lay beside her; he snored slightly. In spite of the heat, she wished she had something to wrap herself in. She also had to go to the bathroom, but she didn't want to put on all her clothes, and she didn't have the energy.

Martina had said, "Good night, everyone! And remember that tonight is the last time we get to sleep in a bed for a long, long time!"

Justine thought that she was going to be longing for a bed, even this one.

She must have fallen asleep after all, because when she woke up, Nathan was already up and busy packing all his things. The aroma of food drifted into the room. The chorus of frogs was intense.

"Good morning, Sweetheart," said Nathan. "How do we feel today?"

She stretched.

"Fine."

He was sitting on his haunches, pressing his stuff into the backpack.

"Nathan. . . ."

"Hmmm?"

"No, nothing."

"Well, get up then. I just heard someone leave the shower."

"Can you help me pack?"

"Nah. You can manage yourself. I have to talk to Ben a little bit. Take a change of clothes and something to sleep in when we make camp. Don't forget the malaria pills! OK, I have to go now. Come down as soon as you can."

Chapter FOUR

A truck covered with a tarp took them away from the town. Out of consideration, perhaps because she was the oldest woman in the group or because she had been sick, Justine was allowed to sit up front with the driver. The others crowded into the flatbed with the equipment.

Once she turned. Nathan sat with his legs pulled up. Leaning against them was Martina.

She drank some of the lukewarm water from the bottle. The man next to her drove jerkily; he seemed not used to this truck. Every time he changed gears, he tore the gear control so that the small cogs squeaked and howled. This appeared to make him nervous. The windows were rolled down; dust was sucked into the driver's cab. He took a peek at her from time to time but he couldn't speak English. He had very dark skin. The jungle was right next to them on each side of the road.

Once, he called out something and pointed at a place on the road. A python, many meters long, was lying there. It was dead; it had been run over. She heard the others asking about it; she didn't hear the words, just the excitement in their voices. She thought about nighttime. She shuddered.

After a few hours, the truck turned onto a sandy road, heading right into the jungle. The tires slid a bit; they almost got stuck. Then the man turned off the engine, and the jungle noises began to come toward them like a great and growing orchestra.

Justine was sore over her entire body. She jumped down onto the red sand; she massaged her legs.

Nathan stood next to her.

"Here's your backpack. And I bought this for you."

He gave her a knife in its sheath; it was wide and black and a half meter long.

"A knife?"

"A *parang*," he said.

"It's unlucky to give something sharp."

"Whatever. But you're probably going to need it."

Justine pulled on the backpack. She let her water bottle hang from one of the metal hooks on the side. She had her fanny pack around her stomach, and she attached the knife there. The heat radiated, pressing sweat drops from her hair fastener. She thought . . . no she didn't want to think. If she began thinking, she would lose all her energy; she wouldn't be able to make it through.

They started off slowly. The first leg was a steep, sandy hill; then the primal forest took over. Ben and Nathan went first. After some time, she noticed that some native men had joined them. She hadn't noticed them at first. Immediately she thought they had evil intentions, but then she understood that they were going to accompany them on the journey. Ben explained to her that they were members of the Orang-asli, the original people.

They climbed up a slick and slippery slope. Her backpack kept pulling her off balance. She held tight to roots and branches, trudging upwards with difficulty. Heinrich was right behind her, a whistling sound when he breathed.

"How're you doing?" she panted.

"I hate to complain when we've just started," he said. "But this goddamn heat."

Yes, the heat was enervating; it made movement slow and breathing heavy. It forced out sweat so that their clothes became wet, made the cloth from their pants cling to their legs making their steps even more difficult.

Once at the top, the plant growth stood like a great green wall. The native men began to clear a path. Justine tried to use her knife, but it was hard to grasp, she needed both hands to hold on to it. One of the men took the knife from her and showed her how to hack. It seemed so easy when he did it.

They cut their way through up there, and then there was a sharp drop, a ravine full of mud and slippery leaves.

"Do we have to go down right here?" said Gudmundur.

"That's right, they really didn't give a damn about informing us how the jungle is constructed," said Heinrich. "They should have told us all the way to the very last vein in the very last leaf."

Ben came up to them.

"Having a rough time?"

"If only it weren't so damn hot. We're not used to it."

"Drink a lot of water. Don't forget to drink."

One of the native men started the descent. He was wearing a shirt with "Pepsi" written on it, and dark blue shorts. His legs were skinny and scratched. She thought she might slip and roll all the way down to the ravine's stony bottom. Her muscles shook from the strain; she climbed down extraordinarily slowly, holding tightly to vines and branches. Fell on her butt and slid down quite a ways until a tree stump stopped her. She sat for a moment, hugging it like a lifesaver. Once she let go, she managed to set her hand right into a thorny bush. She swore to herself.

Nathan was quite a bit ahead of her. "Aren't you coming?" he called.

Martina had already reached the bottom.

"We can take a short rest," Ben said.

The yellow river ran rapidly; from a distance came the thunder of a waterfall.

"Take off your backpack," said Nathan, but she was too tired; her hands were shaking. He helped her, lifted it off; the straps had cut into her shoulders. Her arms had swollen so that her watch was too tight. She had to loosen it a few holes. She looked at her fingers; they were swollen like small sausages, and she could hardly bend them.

Heinrich was the last one down. His eyes wandered; his clothes were soaked and dirty.

Ben looked at them all.

"You'll get used to it. It's hardest at the beginning."

"I wonder," said Heinrich. "I'm not sure you can teach an old dog new tricks."

They had stopped at a beautiful place. Large white flowers were blooming at the river's edge; higher up they saw grottos, and a group of bats came out into the light, frightened by their closeness. Justine fell to her knees by the river. She let the water run over her hands and face. An enormous butterfly was sitting on a twig which was sticking out over the water. She noticed more of them all at once; they circled around her and she held out her hands. One of them landed on her thumb. She felt its small cool feet and its antennae as it slid across her skin.

"Don't move!" said Martina. "I want to get a close-up."

But when she approached with her camera lens, the butterfly became scared and flew off. She sighed with disappointment.

"Damn! That would have been the best picture!"

"They're looking for salt," said Ben.

"They are? I thought butterflies looked for sweet."

"Well, that's why they're landing on Justine," said Heinrich. He had taken off his shoes and dropped his feet into the water. He grimaced strongly.

"*Usch*. Have any of you gotten blisters?"

"I don't know," said Justine. Her gym shoes were soaked through and muddy. "I don't dare take them off. I doubt I'll ever get them back on."

One of the native men came up to Ben. He was somewhat younger; he had a scar running across one of his cheeks. He was holding a blow pipe in his hand. A quiver hung on his hip.

He appeared excited. He kept repeating the same word again and again.

"What's he saying?" asked Nathan.

"Tiger tracks."

"Where?" Martina forced herself forward. "Let me see so I can take some pictures."

About ten meters away they saw the prints of large paws in the sand.

"Ben, you did say that they are more afraid of us than we are of them," mumbled Katrine. "I really hope that's true."

"Oh yes, of course it's true. He certainly heard us and ran away. He's far away by now."

They started off again. They were going to follow the edge of the river. The mountain stood straight up on their left side. They had to balance on slippery roots and cliffs right where the mountain met the water. One of the men had tied a rope of rattan between the twigs and branches. They held to the rope and slowly moved forward.

Eventually, the mountain leveled out, and they turned into the forest.

She and Heinrich were always coming last. She was stressed by the pace the others kept. She managed as best she could. She struggled with breathing and she lost her rhythm. In the beginning, Nathan waited for her and helped her over the most difficult passages. In the beginning, he also exhorted her.

"Try and go a bit faster, Justine; you're holding up the whole group."

Later, Ben let one of the native men go with Justine and Heinrich. Every time they caught up to the others, they had already rested for a while and were ready to keep going. This kept increasing her stress and her feeling of incompetence. Heinrich noticed this and he tried to comfort her.

"Not everyone has the same ability; that's just the way it is. And if Nathan wants to arrange jungle adventures in the future, he should inform his customers that you have to be a marathoner and an elite gymnast in order to go."

She was noticing so clearly how her body had become more limited. She wasn't young any longer.

They sat on some stones and rested. Justine kneaded one of her ankles and felt something warm in her hand. It was blood. Her socks had large red stains. She touched one of the stains and felt something rubbery. She screamed aloud.

The native men laughed.

Four leeches had attached themselves through her socks. Their bodies were swelling and thickening. She had drawn up her socks over her pant leg, but they had sucked their way through.

"There's leeches for you," said Nathan.

"Take them off!" she screamed.

Martina came near with the camera.

"Hold still. This will take only a few seconds."

Justine screamed in Swedish, "Go to hell!"

She threw herself on the ground, shook her leg against the ground, kicked, howled.

Nathan gripped her shoulders.

"Don't get hysterical, Justine. Dammit, don't make an idiot of yourself."

She froze, sniffled.

"Take them off, then! Take them off!"

"You take them off! We've all gotten leeches on us."

She forced herself, fingers on slimy, soft bodies, fingers that trolled, her eyes closed; in with her fingernail next to the sticky, rubbery mouths: there! They twisted in her grip, black and aggressive rings. With a grimace of disgust, she struck them against a stone.

Her wounds wouldn't stop bleeding, but there wasn't any pain.

"They spray in something that kills the pain and prevents the blood from coagulating," Ben said. "They figure they can suck out quite a lot before they're noticed. They're not dangerous, even if they're not all that pleasant."

"If they're in the river, we don't have to walk right there," suggested Katrine.

"They're everywhere. They wait for their victim. They have an incredible sense of smell. When an animal or a person comes by, they get ready to jump, and they almost never miss."

Gudmundur said, "All living beings have their place in the circle of life, but leeches? What is their function? I think they don't have the right to live."

And he pulled a mightily swollen leech from his ankle and mushed it to pieces under his heel.

Later in the afternoon, they reached the river again. They were going to camp on the other side. One of the native men, who barely seemed older than a boy, took Justine's hand and led her carefully into the water. The bottom was slippery and full of stones. She held onto the boy tightly. When she was almost on the other side, she lost her balance and fell head first into the water. The boy lost hold of her; she came up sputtering.

Two hands gripped her from behind. Nathan.

"You clumsy little thing!" he said. "Now you've gotten your whole backpack soaked."

Martina behind her, Martina's ringing laughter.

"Sorry, Justine. It's just looked so hysterically funny!"

She lay on a large, fallen tree trunk. A group of small flies swarmed around her. Everywhere there was rustling, buzzing, chirping.

She heard how the others were setting up camp. She lay unmoving on the trunk. The flies crept into the corners of her eyes; she was too tired to sweep them away. Martina's clucking small sounds, content and mocking, soft as the sound of the gibbons high in the treetops.

She could discern hands and arms through her eyelashes; she heard voices and their calls.

In the distance, thunderclouds rumbled. When she opened her eyes, the first raindrops began to fall. She had never experienced rain from this perspective, from beneath. The white drops like pearls, she lay there and let them come, let them soak and be sucked up by her skin and clothes, let them clean her and bring her body back to life.

Ben was squatting under a shelter. He had changed into a sarong. He was stirring a tin pan.

"Justine?" he called.

"Yes."

"Everything OK?"

"Yeah . . . I guess."

"Go and change into something dry."

She looked at her fingertips. They were wrinkled, as if she'd spent a long time in a bathtub. Her hands were full of pricks.

She said to Ben, "My fingertips are blue."

She wanted to say bruises, but didn't know the word in English.

He nodded without listening.

A plastic covering had been set up between some sticks. She bent over, ran there. Heinrich and the German couple were already sitting there. She put down her backpack. Lightning flashed among the trees. Thunder followed immediately.

"Where's everyone else?" she asked.

"They went to look at the waterfall."

She sat down and tried to untie the damp gym shoes. There was a hole in her pants; she was bleeding from a scrape on her knee. Everything in the backpack had been wrapped in plastic bags. That had worked to keep out the water. Everything in the belly pack was ruined: headache medicine, three tampons, a notebook and paper tissues had all turned into one big glob.

She got out a towel and began to rub herself dry. Out in the river, the man wearing the Pepsi shirt was walking around with a large fishnet. He pulled it up occasionally and picked out the fish, stuffing them into his pockets. After a while, he waded back and gave his catch to Ben.

Justine put on her shorts and a dry shirt. It wasn't cold. The thunderstorm increased its intensity; it thundered both at a distance and directly over them. The rain came down in sheets now, making the ground even muddier.

"They didn't have to go to the waterfall," said Stephan. "There's just as much water here."

"Why didn't they say anything?" asked Justine.

"They did, but we'd had enough of climbing for one day; we had no desire to go with them."

"I was lying right there on the tree trunk."

"They probably thought you were sleeping."

She saw Nathan's backpack and moved it next to her own. The forest seethed and hissed; the lightning flashed. Katrine crept closer between them.

"It looks so dramatic," said Heinrich. "You can feel how small we human beings really are."

"Just so long as the lightning doesn't strike the ground."

"But it does, all the time. Look around and you'll see trees split in two."

"No, I mean strike here, on us!"

"It's worse for the others out there."

"What if they don't find their way back?"

"They've got the Orang-asli guy, the one with the scar; I forget his name. He's certainly going to find his way around. People who live in the jungle have an inborn radar system."

"What do you think, Justine?"

She didn't answer. The night was coming; the jungle increased its power. A cutting sound like sawing very close by.

"What the hell is that?" asked Heinrich.

Stephan looked up.

"It's an insect, I think."

"Has to be one big fucking insect, in that case."

"Maybe it's a frog, though. Anyway, one of the night creatures."

"How are we supposed to sleep in this noise?" said Katrine.

"Maybe it'll stop soon. I hope so."

They saw the roving light of a flashlight.

"Thank God, they're coming back," Katrine said enthusiastically.

The thunderstorm seemed to be retreating against its will, but it was still raining. Nathan peered in under the plastic sheeting. He touched one of Justine's feet.

"So, here you are, enjoying yourselves."

She couldn't meet his glance.

"You should have seen the waterfall! What a high!"

"You could have told me," she said. "Suddenly, you were just gone."

"Yes but you were so tired. You wouldn't have made it. It was almost impossible to get there."

"You still could have said something."

He crept inside; his forehead was wide and dripping wet. He looked at the backpacks.

"We'll have to spread out a plastic ground cloth, you know. We can't just sleep in the middle of the mud."

He carried in her dinner: hot tea in a plastic mug, fish and rice.

"No need to get your dry clothes wet."

"Thanks," she whispered.

A moment later.

"Is it going to stop raining soon?"

"It rains almost every night at this time of year."

She spread out their sleeping bags, made them up nicely. The rain had slowed somewhat.

One of the men went around the camp carrying a bag and spreading out a powder. It shone with a weak golden-white gleam.

"Snake powder," he grinned.

Inside the circle was a protected zone.

They had eaten. They were full. The orange plastic plates were heaped together out in the rain. Martina was wearing a head lamp and sat fussing with her camera. Nathan took it from her. He held it against his eye and photographed her where she sat. The flash lit up her face.

"The photographer almost never makes it into a picture," he said.

"I had a press photographer as a boyfriend once."

"Had?"

"Yep. Had."

"Shouldn't we clean up and brush our teeth and stuff?" asked Katrine.

"We've already taken a shower," said Martina. "In the waterfall. It was so unbelievably wonderful. Soft and warm water, clear as crystal."

Justine put on her raincoat and her wet gym shoes.

"Where are you going?" asked Nathan.

"Behind a bush," she said.

"Watch out for snakes!"

She walked out right into the mud and almost slipped. Had to turn around, ask for a flashlight. Lit up the slimy, dark leaves. Stepped over the line of phosphorus and went a few steps beyond it. Sat in the dark.

It rustled. She saw a flecked branch that resembled a snake; her heart was pounding, a scream in her throat.

"Shut up!" she whispered. "Don't be hysterical!"

She saw the camp down there, the flickering light of the fire and some paraffin candles. Ben and the men lying down under their own plastic covers. One of them was sitting and stirring the fire; he appeared to be a hunched shadow to her eyes.

When she came back, the others had already crept into their sleeping bags. Martina was lying next to Nathan's right side. She was turned away from him. Next to her was Ole, and out on the edge was Steinn.

"Everything all right?" mumbled Nathan.

She didn't answer. She kicked off her shoes outside the cover and pulled down the zipper on her sleeping bag. The ground underneath her was cold and lumpy. She longed for a pillow.

Nathan leaned over her and gave her a hard, silent kiss.

"You're ice cold," he said.

"Yeah."

"Are you afraid?"

"Afraid of what?"

"Of the night. Of the jungle. Of the fact we're lying direct on the ground with all the snakes and tigers and elephants."

"I'm not afraid."

"Great. Good night, then."

"Good night."

They fell asleep, one at a time; she heard how their breathing got heavier. She lay on her back; there was no other way to sleep. Her knee was throbbing. The sound of the forest came at her from all directions, shrill and piercing. She thought she saw two eyes. She turned on the flashlight, and they were gone. As soon as it was dark again, they reappeared.

A tiger? she thought. *Well, come on then. Come here and rip out our lives with your strong jaws, kill us all!*

The eyes stayed where they were. Nervously watching her.

She turned toward Nathan. He lay with his face away from her, bent like an embryo. She reached out and touched his lips while she whispered, "Nathan?"

He was sleeping.

"Good night," she whispered. "Good night, then, my darling."

The rain stopped at dawn. Instead there were layers of fog. As it lifted, the tree trunks slowly took shape. A new kind of noise took over, the sounds of dawn. The apes woke up, as well as the small swift birds.

Had she slept? Had she slept at all? She sat up in her sleeping bag; the others were sleeping with hidden heads. She massaged her sore fingers.

The sun broke through like a warm and bright curtain.

Justine took her towel and swimsuit and sneaked away to the river. In the cover of some bushes, she changed clothes and then stepped into the yellow, warm water. She was wearing her gym shoes. Who knows what lurked in the water, but she had to get clean; she felt the smell of her own stale, sour sweat.

She washed herself with sand, scrubbed the marks left by the leeches. They started bleeding again.

She stayed in the water for a long time. She thought that Nathan might come, that they would hold each other, that he would embrace her there in the water and reassure her that everything was still the way it was, that nothing had changed between them.

But he didn't come.

At camp, Ben was busy making breakfast. The sun warmed them; they hung up their wet clothes to dry on branches and bushes. She saw two pale mushrooms. They were the eyes that were shining in the night. She would have to tell Nathan how they fooled her. Nathan would laugh and think it was a funny story.

But Nathan wasn't there.

She asked Ben.

"They're out to get some roots. I'm going to boil them for our breakfast."

One of the Orang-asli men squatted and smoked. It was the same man who had accompanied her and Heinrich. They were always smoking, these men. They learned how to roll their cigarettes when they were only a few years old. It could take some time until the hunters returned to the village. Smoking held the hunger pangs at bay.

Justine tried to shape her tangled wet hair. The man gave her a quick look, smiling shyly, before he glanced away.

"Mahd is going out hunting," said Ben.

"Hunt what?"

"Whatever we can eat. A monkey or a small pig."

"Can people eat monkeys?"

"Sure they can."

Mahd's blow pipe was leaning up against a tree. When she touched it, it fell over. She hurried to set it right again.

The man named Mahd plucked a dart from his wooden quiver.

"Is it poisonous?" she asked.

"Yes," said Ben.

She scratched her arm strongly. During the night, she had gotten a number of itchy small bites. She thought they might be ants. When she got up from the sleeping bag, she saw many of them scurrying about where they were resting.

"Would you like to go hunting with him?"

"Would he mind?"

Ben said something to Madh. Madh grinned. His teeth were long and uneven.

"He says it's fine."

He ran like a ferret through the bushes. Even though she had hardly slept, she felt strong. She followed him, tried to move as noiselessly as he did. At times he turned around to see if she was keeping up. They went along the river for a while. The heat was beginning to return; the sun glittered in the dark green leaves. The fog was almost gone.

He chose paths where she could walk. He held branches back for her. Once he took her wrist and pulled her up a hill. He was short, but very strong. She wanted to say something to him, but he couldn't speak English. She was wondering about figuring out some sign language when the man suddenly stopped. Justine halted in the middle of a step. She could smell his odor—tobacco and something vaguely like vanilla.

He slowly lifted his hand and pointed through the bushes. She didn't see anything. He placed the blow pipe to his lips; she held her breath. She saw his ribcage flatten. At that moment, there was a shrill shriek, which cut off. It seemed as if it came from a child. The whites of the man's eyes were bloodshot. He made a quick grimace, then relaxed. There was a body in the water. The body of an animal. When she came closer, she saw that it was a small wild pig. The dart had pierced its throat. Madh said something to her, which she didn't understand. Then he imitated the sound of a pig. She reached out her hand and stroked the pig's rough, muddy fur. The animal's eyes were wipe open and appeared to look at her.

She felt something hard against her arm. The blow pipe. Madh gestured at her to try it out. He looked enthusiastic. She looked around, shrugged her shoulders.

He pointed to a tree hanging over the water. He walked over to the tree and put one of his long brown rubber shoes on a broken branch. He then returned to her and showed her how to hold the blow pipe. Pointed to his shoe and laughed, took hold of his knees and laughed again.

The blow pipe was long, but lighter than she thought. In one end, the end for blowing, there was a dry piece of resin. A simple design was carved into the bark right below it. The air was thick with sound; the heat pounded against her head.

She lifted the blow pipe to her lips. It smelled rancid next to the hole. She concentrated, took a deep breath, blew with her diaphragm the same way she had done at home with her horn. She noticed the dull thump of a dart that hit something. She heard Madh take a sharp breath.

The dart had gone into the tree, a few millimeters from his shoe. It sat so deep that he almost didn't get it out again.

Their clothes did not dry during the night. There was the stench of them beginning to rot, but they still had to put them on.

They had struck camp and gotten ready to go further. Justine stuck her feet into her socks the stains had gotten stiff and brown.

Ben stood before them, looking worried.

"You think you're wet now, but I'm afraid you're soon going to be even wetter."

Heinrich grimaced.

"We will, huh!"

"I'd hoped that we could avoid it, but it seems that we will have to cross the river again, close to the waterfall, and it's fairly deep there."

She had a panic fear of water . . . how it forced its way into you, filled you up, weighed you down, took away your air; how you fought and hit wildly, forgetting that you'd learned to swim. She really did not want to be here anymore; she didn't want to go along . . .

She looked at Nathan.

No, she thought. You will never see me hysterical again.

They didn't say anything. They hiked in silence. Then they arrived at the spot where they were going to cross the river. The water rushed and whirled in rapids, large tree trunks and branches floated along. A bit farther on, the water rushed down into a thundering waterfall which drowned all other noise and beat apart everything that washed down with it, beat it all to bits.

They had to go to the other side.

She felt strangely exhausted.

Madh had already gone to the other side. He was born here in the jungle, born and raised here. Nothing here was too difficult for him. He had tied a tough, clean rattan line over the river rapids; it went from shore to shore. Now Ben and the Orang-asli men stepped out into the river. They braced their feet and held on to the line. They were going to help them in the rapids, they were their stop blocks.

Nathan went first.

"Wish me luck!" he said, and pulled at the band under his hat. His eyes were large and happy.

"Here comes a Viking, and for a Swedish Viking, nothing is impossible!"

He stepped into the water and began to move forward single-mindedly. First it went fine, but then he slipped under the surface. Justine saw his joints, holding tightly to the line. She clenched her fists so that the nails went into her palms. Yes, she could see him again. He sneezed and shook his head; then he made his way up the other side of the river bank.

He stood there and waved his arms, hit his chest like Tarzan.

The backpacks were sent over. The men in the water lifted them from to hand and Nathan stood on the other side and picked them up.

"Do you want to go now, Justine?" asked Ben.

"Sure."

She sat on the slippery slope and glided into the water. It was deep. She felt a block of stone under her toes. But the water drew at her legs and ripped them off the stone. Ben grabbed her hand, showed her how to hold the line. His mouth was stern.

"Whatever you do, don't let go!"

She heard the thunder of the cataracts and the waterfall.

"Now what?"

"Quiet! Use your toes to search for a foothold."

She took a step. The water rushed around her, wanting to pull her down. She tried to make herself as heavy as possible. She saw Martina on the shore; she was on her knees with her damned camera. I hope she falls with it into the water; I hope she drops it and it disappears down into the cataracts.

One more step. A man was next to her; she crept under his arms. The water rushing past, one more step. Hold tight to the line. Now she was approaching the middle.

"Great, Justine!" called Nathan.

She felt the beat of her heart.

Right at the spot he'd fallen, she fell, too. It was a peculiar spot, where it was too far to reach the bottom. Her head was underwater, white and green whirls, her hands gripping tightly to the rope. The water attacked her, ripped and pulled her; she felt its power. With a violent effort, she moved her right hand farther along and let the left hand follow. Her right hand found a stone and she climbed on it and held fast.

"Just a little more, Justine. You're almost there!"

She took a deep breath; there was another arm to creep under, one more second of respite. Then out again, and through the last bit. Nathan reached for her. She got up, and the water streamed from her clothes.

"I did it!" she panted.

"You sure did!" he answered, but then turned for the next one.

When evening came, they made camp next to a wide and stony riverbank. The native men began at once to collect twigs and light fires.

Martina was changing film.

"They're lighting fires so that the animals won't come," she said. "The big mammals. The elephants come here to drink; we found their droppings over there, a few piles."

"Do we have to be in the middle of their private area?" said Steinn. "That's not very thoughtful toward the elephants. We can be anywhere in the jungle."

"We can't go any farther. Darkness is falling," said Ben.

They helped each other tie up the plastic shelters. Madh stepped out into the river with his fish net. Then Justine remembered the wild pig.

"What about that pig we shot?" she asked.

"He gave it to his family. They have six small children."

"Where is his family?"

"Somewhere here in the jungle."

Martina took her towel and a plastic bag with soap and shampoo.

"I'm going to wash off all this shit. What about you, girls? Let's take a ladies' bath together."

They found a small inlet where the water had made a lagoon. Justine had taken her swimsuit with her. Katrine and Martina slid into the water naked; they were as slippery and shiny as animals.

"Oh, if only I could live like this all the time! I wish I belonged to a tribe," said Martina as she poured shampoo into her cupped hand. "Away from civilization and all its demands; return completely to nature."

"Don't you already live like that?" said Katrine. "All your world travels and the like."

"Well, yes, in a manner of speaking. I'm never going to work nine to five. I can't settle down anywhere. I'm looking for something new all the time. New experiences, new people."

"Stephan and I have also traveled quite a bit. But once we get home this time, we're going to get married and have some kids."

"We're planning that, too," Justine said. "Getting married, having some kids."

Martina was already climbing out of the water. A leaf had attached itself to her stomach, right over her black field of hair.

She wrapped the towel around herself.

"You and Nathan?"

"Yes."

"I thought that he wasn't going to tie himself down any more."

Justine's throat burned.

"What would you know about it?"

"Nothing. That's just what I was picking up on."

Morning came again. Heinrich had given her a sleeping pill. She had fallen asleep immediately. During the night, she awakened a few times, and thought about the elephants, half dozing. At one point, she thought she heard the trumpet of an elephant from a distance. When she saw that there still was smoke from the fire, she fell asleep again.

They ate fish and rice. Nathan was sun-tanned; his eyes were two blue stones. He looked at her with those eyes. He said, "We're going to see the elephants."

A thud against her ear, like an ache.

"Why?"

"Martina is going to take pictures of them. Jeda and I are going, too."

"Who's Jeda?"

"He's the one in the green shirt."

He had gotten up, the golden hair on his legs. He said, "Martina and I are going with Jeda. He's going to show us the elephants. We can't all go, or we'll scare them away."

The words pierced her, exploded.

Martina was ready to go, her camera hanging over her shoulder.

They were gone until the middle of the afternoon. When she saw them appear again from between the trees, she knew everything was over.

A blast of cold went from the roundness of her heels, through the bones of her pelvis, her chest and right into her heart.

She could no longer speak.

She waited. Something was going on with her skin, as if it were shrinking. A throbbing pain in her head, as if something was clamped too tightly.

Nathan was walking along the riverbank in order to find a spot to piss.

No one saw her take Madh's blow pipe. No one saw her follow him, follow Nathan.

Part 2: Chapter Four

He stood and contemplated the water and the rapids. He stood and rolled a cigarette. He had formed his mouth to whistle, but she didn't hear anything but the thunder of the waterfall.

The dart hit him right between the shoulder blades.

He fell straight into the whirling, yellow water.

Chapter FIVE

Someone asked where Nathan was. Someone was asking with a whiny voice, Nathan, has anyone seen Nathan?
Maybe she was asking.
Maybe she herself.
She remembered voices, sounds.
And Nathan's backpack in the middle of everything.

Eventually, they had to decamp. She remembered the way the grass caught her shoes and undid the knots. How she had to stop again and again to tie them, how much effort it took to bend down, how the dizziness gripped her, and the heat. They had left the jungle. They walked over a steaming hot field; she broke a leaf, as big as the ear of an elephant. She held it over her head like a shield.

They had searched for a long time, even she did. Madh searched with her, his eyes were black, his blow pipe hanging on his hip.

Early the next morning, Ben came up to her. She saw him come. She stood straight and silent.
"I know you don't want to, but we have to go. We can't search any longer."
She started between the trees, as if she heard a sound.
She said, "The elephants."
"The elephants?" he repeated.
"The elephants can go crazy if you get too close."
He closed his eyes tightly.

"Poor little friend," he said flatly.

She was put on board a train.

Maybe she was alone.

Someone came with coffee in a mug, someone came with water.

"Drink," said a light, Swedish voice.

Martina's.

The windows were open; the heat swept in; a swaddled infant screamed. The mother's headscarf, held to her hair by two red pins. It looked like they went right into her temples.

Martina's fingers had white, clean nails.

The camera was no longer there.

She smelled her own body odor. A man came down the aisle, tottering. When he came closer, she saw it was Ben.

The train stopped for a moment. A village was out there. Two girls on a scooter; they smiled and waved.

The toilet was a hole in the floor. She got on her knees and threw up.

Then the city.

Ben said:

"I'll take care of the tickets. There's a plane tomorrow afternoon."

He had found a hotel. He put her in the same room with Martina.

"It's good that you're not alone. At least you can speak Swedish to each other."

He was extremely kind.

"Do you have a wife?" she asked.

He nodded.

"Yes, I do."

"What's her name?"

"Tam."

"Tam."

"Yes."

"Do you love your wife Tam?"

"I love her and respect her."

"Nathan!" she screamed, and then was quickly silent.

She got out of the shower; she was clean. She had showered for so long that the water finally ran cold. Martina stood in the room, her thin back, her sarong like a skirt. She was holding something in her hand; it was the mascot. She had untied it from Justine's backpack.

"What are you doing?" said Justine, her words coming like gravel and spikes.

"Nothing, just looking."

Justine bent over her luggage, unhooked her *parang*.

The pain in her head returned.

She remembered the strength of the blood as it hit her arms; she remembered it burned.

They brought her in to talk, again and again. Her head cramped. Some policemen and a woman named Nancy Fors. She was light-skinned; she was a Swede. She had been sent from the embassy.

The windows in the room had bars.

She repeated.

"I came out of the shower, and there was someone there, a man. She lay on the floor. Martina lay on the floor and I screamed, and he turned toward me. No, I don't remember his face, dark, thin. I ran into the bathroom. I slid and hit myself and the towel got wet. I heard him close the door. Then I went out. She was lying there, already dead."

"Where did you hit yourself, Miss Dalvik?"

She drew up her skirt and showed them, here, here on my thigh. She was full of scratches and strange bites.

There was a doctor in the room. He touched her leg and made her scream.

She remembered a syringe and the smell of ether.
Or was that later?
Maybe that was later.

"That man?"
"Yes."
"How old do you think he was?"
"I don't remember, I told you already."
"Was he thirty? Or just twenty?"
"He was dark and thin."
"Tell us everything again."
"She lay on the floor, and the *parang* was in her back."
"Did he threaten you, Miss Dalvik?"
"He didn't have time. I ran into the bathroom and locked
the door. He had killed Martina."
And it turned heavy and hard to breathe. The air didn't
make its way to her lungs. She tried to find oxygen and finally
screamed right out loud.

Then there was a hospital, because everything was white:
the sheets, the walls. Nancy Fors had a pleasant, long face.
She sat next to the bed every time Justine opened her eyes.
"Ben, the man who was in the jungle with you, asked me
to say hi."
She cried when she heard his name.
But mostly she slept.

Nancy Fors said:
"They've caught a man who specialized in hotel burglary."
"They have?"
"Yes, they wonder if you can come by and identify him,"
She had been sleeping for many days. Now she put on the
clothes that Nancy Fors chose for her, wide long trousers and
a patterned tunic with long arms.
"They're my clothes. I think we wear the same size. You
can keep them."

She looked through a peephole. A man was sitting there; he was thin with a hollow-cheeked face.

"They're wondering if he is the one," Nancy Fors said.

She said she didn't know.

She would have liked to say goodbye to Ben, but she wasn't going to get the chance.

She would never see him again.

Nancy Fors went with her on the plane, to be either her support or her guard. They went together all the way back to Stockholm.

part three

Chapter ONE

There were a number of interrogations back in Stockholm, too. Two Swedish citizens had lost their lives in Southeast Asia. Justine had been in contact with both of them. The first day, the telephone rang so much that she pulled the jack out of the socket. The police lent her a cell phone. We have to be able to reach you, they said. Make sure that the batteries don't run down.

But every time they mentioned Nathan Gendser's name something happened to her breathing; she had to loosen the clothes around her neck and she began to hyperventilate. She cried and ripped wounds into her arms.

She had been exposed to trauma. They gave her the name of a psychologist, but she didn't bother to contact her.

She did not dare refuse to answer the cell phone. One of the first days, Nathan's son Micke called. She let him come by the house.

There was a certain similarity between them, and as soon as she saw it, she had to start crying again. She rushed up from her chair in the blue room and left him by himself. Sitting on the bed in her room, she heard him wander about the house calling for her. Finally, she stepped back into the hall.

He was standing on the stairs, gripping the railing tightly. The bird was flying around the ceiling; he had been alone for so long now that unfamiliar voices made him excited. Justine called to him, but it took a while until he flew to her.

"Don't be afraid," she called down the stairs. "The bird is more afraid than you are."

Then she thought of the tigers and how Ben used the exact words: "He's far away from here; he's much more afraid of you."

She sat down on the top step, sit down, she told the boy, did you know that we saw a tiger's spoor?

"Do you think a tiger could have killed him?" he said thickly.

"More likely it was an elephant."

"An elephant. . . ."

"Yes, there were elephants near the camp."

"Jesus Christ! . . . Did you see them?"

"Not me. One of the guys with us in the jungle, Ben, said that he had never had experienced an animal attacking."

"Maybe he annoyed them?"

"Your father?"

"Yes."

"No, he didn't bother them. But maybe there was a sick or injured animal . . . you never know what could happen . . . the jungle is so . . . well, unpredictable."

"He was so into this job. I've never seen him like that. He thought he'd found his niche, we talked about me . . . eventually. . . ."

"How old are you, Micke?"

"Soon I'll be sixteen."

"Almost grown up."

He shrugged.

Suddenly, it all seemed to her a scene from the theater. She got up and went to him, next to him on the stair. The bird flew away to her room.

She placed her hand on the boy's head. The lines came just as they were supposed to.

"Go home and comfort your sisters. We can believe that your pappa is doing fine wherever he is. He was a man of adventure; he died with his boots on, as they say. He died when he was most happy. Out in nature, in the middle of a great adventure. How many people get to do that?"

And as she spoke, she realized that what she was saying was the truth. By sacrificing the one person she loved and valued more than any other, she had let him escape from trivial everyday life which sooner or later would overcome him, as it overcomes all of humanity. He would never be forced to return home, never need to grow old, never need to experience how his body broke down bit by bit, so that he finally would be sitting crippled and distorted by arthritis, forgotten and alone in a nursing home somewhere. She had helped him escape all that.

But the sacrifice was enormous.

The awkward boy fell to pieces; he cried loudly and violently.

She embraced him, as she had once embraced his father, felt his jacket and skin.

"He was so wonderful, Nathan, so strong and fine and courageous. I have never loved anyone as much as I loved your pappa."

She pushed him carefully away.

"Sometimes I used to play for him. I have a horn. . . . Maybe I could play a melody or two for you, if you want."

"What kind of horn?" he said, suspiciously.

"An old post horn which I received when I was a little girl."

"I don't know. . . . Can someone really play those things?"

"Oh, yes."

She got up and took down the instrument. It was covered by a thin layer of dust. She rubbed it with a fold of her skirt.

"I played for him a few times. He liked to hear me play."

She stood by the window and placed the horn to her lips. While she played, she saw the boy clench his fists.

When he had left, she broke down. A shrieking and cackling laugh rose from her throat. She wasn't able to stop it. It gushed out of her, forced her to cramp up. She pressed her tongue to the wall, the taste of stone, the taste of dust and stone. But the laugh kept coming. Until it finally hacked itself to pieces, until it transformed into crying.

Then there was Martina's parents. A very absurd story in itself.

Hans Nästman, a policeman who had spoken to her quite a bit, insisted on this.

"Of course I want to meet with them," she said. "It's just been so difficult. I've been so tired."

She did not want them in her house. She didn't say that to Hans Nästman, though. She said, "Can we meet in a room at the police station?"

"I'll take care of it," he promised.

He even came to pick her up. It was a normal, neutral car and he was wearing normal clothes.

"You have a nice place here," he said, and looked out over the lake. "And the boat down there; it's not exactly small."

"It was my father's."

"Not bad at all. Can you drive it?"

"I haven't driven it very far. Just around and about on the lake. But maybe I'll take a longer trip someday, maybe to Gotland or Åland."

"Well, you'll have to get more practice in. Have you taken a skipper's examination?"

He was speaking with a trace of dialect; it seemed like the Värmland one.

The bird was in the attic. For some reason she didn't want Hans Nästman to see him. She locked the door and followed him.

The car smelled new, a good smell. She thought about her old Opel and maybe it was just this moment that she decided to buy a new car.

Part 3: Chapter One

Too late, she noticed they weren't heading to the police station on Kungsholmen.

"Where are we going?" she asked.

"They live in Djursholm. They wanted to have you visit them in their home."

A pain in her head, as if her head were shrinking.

"What's wrong? Do you have something against it?"

"Not at all. It's just the smell in the car. . . . I just feel a little carsick. Maybe we could roll down the window just a little bit?"

Their last name was Andersson. She realized that she had never known what Martina's last name had been. Their house was as gray as a bunker with high narrow windows.

"I wonder if this is a Ralph Erskine," said Hans Nästman.

"What?"

"The guy who designed the place, I mean."

"No idea."

He walked closely behind her, so closely that he almost stepped on her heels.

"Nice area," she said, to have something to say.

"Yes, indeed. I wouldn't have anything against living here. But you can't complain. Where you live is just as nice."

The door was made from a massive piece of wood. There was a door knocker in the shape of a lion's head. Hans Nästman was about to use it when the door opened. A man wearing a dark suit was standing in the doorway.

"Not to bother with that," he said. "You can't hear it from the inside anyway. It's mostly there as a decoration."

He was thin and tanned; he wore his hair in a ponytail. He gripped her hand.

"Mats Andersson. Welcome."

Hans Nästman held onto her elbow, guided her into the house. She could sense movement in the house.

"Come in, my wife will be joining us soon."

He lowered his voice.

"This has been . . . how should I put it . . . difficult for her, naturally, for both of us."

They entered a large, longish room, decorated totally in black and white. There was a grand piano in the middle of the room. The sun burst into the room through narrow windows making a staff-like pattern. A row of black leather armchairs stood against one wall. Next to them, some kind of altar had been placed, with candles in silver candlesticks and a photo of Martina, happy and smiling, wearing a dress of lilac linen. One could see her nipples through the fabric.

The policeman went up to the photo.

"Yes," said her father. "That's her."

"I thought so. When was it taken?"

"Last summer, during one of those really hot days. She loved the heat; she never should have been born in a country like ours."

"So she was twenty-four when it was taken?"

Her father said, "Yes, she should have been. Excuse me for a moment; I need to. . . ."

And he disappeared from the room, and everything was silent.

They sat down beside each other on the armchairs. The grand piano's lid was lifted; it was a Steinway.

"Maybe you've heard of Mats H. Andersson?" the policeman asked. "He's a famous concert pianist. Or maybe you don't know much about classical music?"

Her eyes rested on the piano's emblem, it was embellished with gold and looked like a cognac cup. She suddenly had a longing for a glass of port or sherry.

They heard Martina's pappa talking out there, exhorting, like talking to a puppy. Then he stood in the doorway with a tray and some coffee cups.

"My wife will come in just a minute," he said, almost shrilly.

She entered, her head cast down. She was younger than Justine had imagined. She had Martina's dark hair and somewhat squinting eyes. There was something sluggish and slow about her.

"Marianne," she said and reached out her hand. "I'm taking Sobril right now. I assume it's not something I can hide."

Her husband entered with a coffee pot. When he began to pour, the lid fell off and knocked over one of the cups. Her face looked like a polecat.

"I can't stand that noise, I've said," she exclaimed.

His earlobes turned red.

"My fingers are anything but practical," he tried to joke.

The woman walked around the room. She was barefoot; there was a narrow ring on one of her toes. She threw her hair back; strange sounds came from her.

"To lose a child," she chanted. "To lose a beloved child."

"Was she your only daughter?" asked the policeman.

"Yes," answered Mats Andersson. "We also have a son. He lives in Australia. Of course, he's coming home for the funeral. Otherwise, he doesn't come home very often. Excuse me; I'm just going to get something to clean up the mess."

"The funeral, yes . . . you've received her back home, I've heard."

The woman stopped pacing.

"In a box! Like a piece of freight!"

She stood in front of Justine; she fell on her knees onto the white shag rug. Let her head rest in Justine's lap; she was warm and shaking. She turned her face to Justine's legs and suddenly bit down hard. Justine gasped; she slapped her hand on her mouth and stared at the policeman. He was there right away, lifted up Marianne Andersson and helped her to an armchair.

"How are you, Marianne?" he asked. "How are you?"

Her narrow eyes shone. She opened her lips, her mouth, but shut them again.

Her husband came back with a rag. Clumsily, he began to wipe up the spilled coffee.

Marianne Andersson said, in a completely normal voice, "Now, if we may, we would like to ask a few questions to the person who was the last one to see our daughter alive."

"Yes, Justine Dalvik, here," said the policeman.

"I really wasn't the last person to see her alive. That one is in Kuala Lumpur, the person who . . . killed her. He was the last one."

The woman turned to her.

"Don't play with words, please. It's difficult enough as it is."

"Please listen," said the policeman. "We are all deeply affected by what has happened. Our nerves are on edge. Justine Dalvik shared a room with your daughter. She has testified that she was in the shower when it happened."

"May I ask any question I want?" asked the woman.

"Yes?"

"There's a few things that I have been wondering about."

"Ask away."

"When you came out of the shower . . . were you naked then?"

"No . . . I had a bath towel around me."

"Was that man just standing there? Didn't you hear him come in?"

"No, I was in the shower, like I said."

"He didn't hear you in the shower?"

"I don't know. . . . Maybe he thought I was alone in the room. He heard the shower certainly. Maybe he thought he could rob the place while I was in there."

"And then he discovered that someone else was there?"

"Yes."

The questions came quickly and jarringly.

"Didn't my daughter try to stop him?"

"I don't know."

"Yes, but what do you think?"

"No . . . I think he caught her by surprise. They said there were no traces of a fight."

"But wouldn't he have fled the moment he saw someone else in the room?"

"I don't know."

"You don't know?"

"No, maybe she'd gone out for a minute and when she came back, he was there; maybe she had to go get something."

"You didn't try to defend her?"

"It was too late! It had already happened!"

"So what did you do?"

Her head was spinning. She looked at the policeman; he nodded encouragingly.

"What I did. . . . What would you have done?"

"I would have killed him. I would have strangled him with my bare hands. I would have cut him to pieces with my bare fingers. . . ."

"Marianne," said Mats Andersson. "Marianne. . . ."

"He was dangerous," whispered Justine. "If he killed one person, he might kill another."

"So what did you do?"

"I ran back into the shower and locked the door."

"Why didn't you run out of the room instead? Out to get help? It all appears very strange to me."

"I don't know. A reflex."

"If she could have reached a hospital! If she could have gotten there in time!"

"It was too late already!"

"How do you know? How many dead people have you seen? How can you be so sure?"

She gripped the coffee cup but her hands were shaking so strongly that she was not able to lift it.

"May I . . . ask something?" said her father. "How was she that day? What was her mood? Was she happy or sad . . . can you . . .?"

"None of us were what you could call happy."

"You have to remember what happened in the jungle," said Hans Nästman. "The group had to break camp suddenly, one of the leaders had disappeared, probably met with an accident, most likely dead."

"They never found him then?"

"No. When things disappear in the jungle, they tend to be lost forever."

"She was a wandering soul, our girl. I always felt on tenterhooks whenever she was out and about on one of her trips. That something would happen to her. Sooner or later, I would think, sooner or later . . . but you can't forbid them."

"No, you can't."

"Do you have any children, Commissioner?"

"Yes, two boys, eighteen and twenty."

"It's easier with boys."

"Don't say that."

The woman got up. She went over to the altar and lit the candles.

"You can go now, if you want," she said hoarsely. "Now I know what she looks like, that person who shared a room with Martina. I don't want to know any more. It's enough."

"What a strange and unpleasant woman," said Hans Nästman, when they returned to the car. "In my job, you meet a number of bizarre people. But someone like Marianne Andersson. . . ."

"Sorrow can affect you."

"Whatever."

She put the seatbelt on.

"What did she do to you?"

"Nothing."

"She hurt you. I saw it. She bit you, didn't she?"

"No."

"Justine, listen to me. You have to get a vaccination against lockjaw. Human bites are the most dangerous kind."

"I'm already vaccinated."

"Of course, of course. When you've traveled so far."

"We got all kinds of vaccinations. Nathan, too. But you can't vaccinate against everything."

"That's a wise saying."

He was silent for a moment. Then he said, "I saw that she bit you, Justine."

She sighed.

"I have the feeling you let her."

"OK, OK, maybe I deserved it. Maybe I should have protected her daughter somehow."

"Do you feel that way yourself?"

"I don't know. Maybe that's the kind of thing a psychiatrist needs to sort out. Please, can you just drive me home now? This has been an awful day."

Hans Nästman kept in touch with her.

"I imagine you want to know what's going on in Kuala Lumpur. And whether they ever find Nathan Gendser some day. But the man they caught for hotel burglary will only confess to burglary. He also insists that he never set foot in that hotel. Nothing can be proven. There are many fingerprints on the knife, but not his. He could have been wearing gloves . . . but it really is fairly hot in that country."

She didn't know what to say to him.

"I imagine they can put him in prison anyway if he doesn't have an air-tight alibi. A poverty-striken fellow with no money."

"I really don't want to talk about it that much," said Justine. "I would prefer to forget about the whole thing."

Chapter TWO

During the fall and winter, they left her alone.

She didn't forget, however. Nathan kept coming to her. During the night, he would come in her dreams; during the day, he moved behind her, so close that she could almost feel his breath, but when she turned around, he slipped away into a corner and disappeared.

Yes, Nathan came to her, but less and less often.

Then all of this with Hans Peter. That winter day of mild temperatures and the shine of rain on the window, when they had made love to each other for the first time, she knew he had to go, but she didn't want him to.

He said he had to go to work at his hotel.

They were in her kitchen. He embraced her, sat her on his lap.

"So strange . . . we don't really know each other . . . but still."

She threw her arms around him and burrowed her face into his neck.

"We know each other a little bit."

"Yeah. . . ."

"I want to . . . again," she whispered.

"Just a few minutes."

"A quickie."

She cleared the table until it was empty, leaned forward on it and lifted her dress. She had no panties on. He stood behind her, his hands running over her thighs and hips. She moved against him so he would get a hard-on; she felt him through the cloth of his pants.

At that very moment, the telephone rang.

"Fuck!" she exclaimed. "Fuck it all."

He had taken a few steps backward, lifted the receiver and handed it to her. She shook her head, but it was too late.

"Hello?" she said tensely.

"Hello . . . I'd like to speak with Justine Dalvik."

"That's me."

"My name is Tor Assarsson. I'm Berit's husband. I understand that you and Berit were schoolmates."

"Yes, that's right. Hi."

"I'm nervous about her. She's disappeared."

"She has?"

"She hasn't been home for over twenty-four hours."

"Uh-huh?"

Her headache started It ate itself into her forehead and when she turned, it seemed like the skin of her cranium was being pulled, as if her entire skull had shrunk.

"I'm wondering . . . she was going to your place. Did she show up there?"

"Yes, yes, she did. We sat and talked for a while during the evening."

"For how long?"

"I don't know, I wasn't paying attention to the clock."

"Was it late?"

"Somewhat late perhaps."

Hans Peter was observing her. He zipped up his pants; he smiled and shook his head. Justine tried to smile back.

"I have to admit that I am really worried."

"I understand. . . ."

"This is not like Berit. I'm afraid that something's happened to her. Something bad, something awful."

"Maybe she took a trip? Maybe she just needs to be alone for a while?"

"Did she say anything like that to you?"

"She didn't seem happy, if that's what you mean."

"She's had a rough time of it lately. And maybe I wasn't supporting her the way I should have. What did she say? What did the two of you talk about?"

"She talked about her job, that she didn't want to move to Umeå, or wherever it was."

"Luleå."

"Yes, that's probably it. She was unhappy and afraid about the future."

"Could she have done something to herself, do you think?"

His voice was rough; she could tell he was about to break down.

"I don't know. We really don't know each other all that well. At least, not as grown women. I have no idea if she's the kind of woman who would do something drastic. I just don't know."

"I've never thought of her as that type. She's been stable and strong in all ways, in spite of difficulties. But you never know. . . . She'd gotten to that age, I think, you know, menopause and all. I think her menopause had just started. Hormones can cause women problems, or so I've heard."

"That can happen, that women sometimes have complete personality changes."

"Though I haven't noticed any such tendency."

She heard Hans Peter go down the stairs. He was going soon. She noticed she didn't want him to go. For the first time, she felt that she did not want to be alone in the house; she wanted to go with him, go anywhere, just get into the car and drive.

"What did she say when she left?"

"When she left? Yes . . . she said she was going to walk up to Sandviksvägen and take the bus, I believe. But we had been drinking quite a bit. . . . I don't really remember what she said."

"Was she drunk?"

"Yes, pretty drunk."

"Do you think she might have fallen down somewhere?"

"I don't know. Wouldn't someone have found her by now, if that were the case?"

"Why didn't she take a taxi? She should have taken a taxi."

"Maybe so."

The man was breathing heavily.

"I'll have to call the police. There's nothing else left to do. Then I'll go out and look for her. I'll come around your place, too."

"I don't think I'll be home."

"Hmm. OK, here's our number and the number of my cell phone. If you need to reach me. If you remember something that you haven't mentioned."

He had put on his jacket.

"Well, we didn't have the chance for that lovely moment," he said as he hugged her. "I'm going to have the image of your beautiful ass in my head tonight. I'm going to have a hard-on all night."

"Oh, do you really have to leave?"

"Yes."

"It's so stupid that I forgot to disconnect the phone. I always pull the phone out of the jack. I don't like people calling here at all hours."

He pushed her slightly away.

"But Justine, don't do that! How am I supposed to reach you?"

"But you came here, didn't you?"

"But if I can't?"

"Well. . . ."

"Tell you what. I'll buy you a caller ID."

"What's that?"

"Don't you know? It's a little gadget where you can look at a display and see the number of the person trying to reach you. If you don't want to talk to Aunt Greta, you don't have to answer."

"I didn't know that there were such things."

"There are. Look, I've got to rush off now. I'll call you tomorrow when I wake up. I'm already longing to call you."

She was in the house. She was alone. She locked the doors and went through all the rooms. She washed the dishes and put things away. Then she turned out all the lights, and pulled the telephone cord out of the jack.

She stood by the kitchen window. She didn't want to go lie down, didn't want to close her eyes. The ache nibbled away at her brain, nibbled and ate.

She stood in the darkness and saw him come. He looked just as she thought: grey coat, white and blank face. Not even his worry was able to erase the look of an effective bureaucrat. She heard his steps on the outside stairs, then the doorbell which burrowed into the center of the house.

He waited a moment, then rang again. When nothing happened, he began to go around the house and toward the lake. She ran up the inside stairs. She saw him stand next to the edge of the ice. He took a few careful steps and then turned back. He had shrunk a bit more.

She felt incredibly sorry for him.

During the night, it began to snow. The thermometer showed a few degrees below freezing. She didn't get undressed; she wandered around the house and kept bumping into the walls as if she were blind. She had swallowed a few pain medication pills, but the pain remained in her head, barely affected.

It was two in the morning. She plugged in the phone and dialed.

He answered right away.

"Hi, again. It's Justine Dalvik. Sorry that I'm calling so late."

"I don't mind at all."

"You haven't found her?"

"No."

"Have you . . . called in the police?"

"So to speak. I was there and talked to them. But they're not doing much right now. They say that it's not unusual that wives disappear. Many do it to punish their husbands. But I think they were just trying to calm me down."

"I've been thinking a great deal. She actually talked . . . about your marriage."

"She did? What did she say?"

"I got the feeling that she was a little, how should I put it, disappointed."

"In me?"

"Yes."

"She said that?"

"She was crying and she appeared to be depressed. She said something along the lines of not having much in common these days. What do I have left, she said, neither a job nor love, something along those lines."

She heard him light a cigarette.

"She said that?"

"Something like that, yes."

He was crying now, mumbling something as if he had marbles in his mouth. It seemed that he might have hung up, but she heard him clear his throat and cough. Then he was back on the line.

"I'm so sorry," she said. "I shouldn't have called like this in the middle of the night."

"It's really OK," he said. "It's not troubling me at all, the opposite in fact."

"I can't sleep. I'm worried, too."

"I was out in Hässelby earlier. I rang the doorbell, but no one was home."

"No."

"What am I supposed to do? What in the hell am I supposed to do?" He was beginning to scream the last words. She heard him as if he were forcing himself back to normal.

"Excuse me . . . but I have been so worried that I have no idea what to do."

"I'm not surprised. Do you have any sleeping pills or anything like that? I mean, so that you can sleep tonight?"

"I usually don't use them."

"Maybe she did?"

"I honestly don't know."

"No. Well then, I don't want to trouble you any longer. I'll call if I think of anything else. Good night."

"Good night."

Every time she went to lie down, it came back to her. During the day, she was able to keep it at a distance. And right afterwards, she had fallen asleep. She was no longer totally drunk, but when she came out of the shower, she sat on the edge of the bed and drank a few more glasses of wine. She felt her foot aching again. Then she dropped off to sleep.

They had embraced each other. For a long time, they had stood and hugged, Berit's hot snotty face, her drunken crying, I've blamed myself. I've been so afraid; children are like that. I kept telling myself, children have no sense of empathy, but it hasn't helped, Oh, Justine, Justine, you have to forgive me.

She was somewhat shorter than Justine, and thinner. But she was strong. When Justine pushed her to the floor, she followed without resistance. Justine climbed on her chest, heaved herself forward, and began to press against her throat, and it wasn't until that point that Berit began to resist. Justine grabbed a book from the bookshelf, a Dostoyevsky, and she slammed the corner of the book right on the bridge of Berit's nose. She heard the cracking sound, felt the body underneath her go still. The whites of her eyes shone; she had fainted for a moment, perhaps more from the shock than the pain. Justine ran quickly up the stairs into her bedroom, got her long scarf, wrapped it a few times around the throat of the unconscious woman, and pulled.

She held on tightly until she had no more doubt.

She heard the telephone ring. She lifted the receiver; it was a man, Nathan? No, Hans Peter. Nathan doesn't exist anymore; his body was broken to bits in a waterfall on the other side of the ocean. That was a long time ago and all was forgotten. She silently put the receiver back in place.

She knew exactly what to do. Even though she didn't think about it in advance, it all came to her; a voice was leading her: get the cloth totes from the cleaning closet, the two white cloth totes with Konsum written on them. Then the scarf. Don't look at the body's face. Loosened the scarf from her neck—there came an unpleasant puff of air—tied it to one of the handles of the tote. Knotted it like a belt hard around Berit's waist.

The bird circled above her. Go and sleep, she told him; you can hurt youself here in the darkness. But he didn't obey her; he sat on her shoulder the whole time she dragged the body down all the stairs. He made her forget what she was doing for a moment.

He took off toward the upstairs once she started down to the basement.

"I'll return soon!" she called. "You know that I'll come back; then you'll get something good, a raw egg, a nice raw hen's egg, the kind you like, maybe even with an embryo in it."

She had left Berit in the hallway. There were stones in the basement, she remembered where they were. Her father had brought them home. He had bought them from a business acquaintance who had promised to help him build an outside grill. Nothing came of that outside grill. Flora was against it. She suddenly heard the nagging voice: you never finish anything you start. Are these supposed to be here in the garden until the day we die? It's slovenly, Sven. I will not have it.

One day, her father had gotten angry, and he carried every single stone into the basement. He did it in ten minutes; he was pale and enraged. Afterwards he took the boat and went out on the lake.

Justine carried up one of the stones. With a great deal of effort, she put Berit's coat on her body, and the ugly brown plaid cap. She almost forgot the gloves which were on the hat shelf. When she discovered them, she tried to put them on Berit's fingers, but stopped, sniffling, and pressed them into the body's jacket pocket.

Then she got dressed herself.

She dragged the kick sled to the stairs, and now came the hard part, struggling to get the lifeless body down and place it on the kick sled. She was conscious of the pain in her foot the whole time, but it was as if the pain didn't reach her. She steadied herself on it and it bit and ached, but it was a damped and suppressed pain. She would deal with that later.

She heaved her burden onto the kick sled. The runners slid slightly; the dead person's arms fell out against the snow. Justine tried to place them back in her lap, but they fell back, having no stability. So she had to go inside and look for some string. First she didn't find anything; she pulled out every drawer in the kitchen, dumped its contents onto the floor.

And now came the first moment of panic.

She went to the mirror. She saw her own face in there, and spoke her name out loud: "Justine. You deserve this, don't forget! Think about it the whole time!"

Her hands had begun to shake, she lifted them and gave herself two hard slaps on her cheeks: Calm, calm, don't become hysterical; you know what he thinks about that.

Then it was over.

Right after that she found the ball of string. It was in the niche by the window, she remembered using it the other day for . . . no, she didn't remember why. She lifted the scissors from the floor and went back outside.

Berit was sitting hunched over, ready to fall off. Justine tied her to the kick sled, her waist, her hands, her legs. The head hung, the strangled neck. Don't look at the exploded eyes, don't look. She drew the cap down as far as possible and went to get the stones.

Each Konsum tote could hold five stones.

The night was dark and misty. She was aware of an airplane high above her, heard its motor. With a great deal of effort, she managed to transport the kick sled to the lake. The runners cut through the snow the entire time. It was easier once she got out on the ice. She pushed the sled as far as she dared, frightened by the rumbling and sharp sounds coming from out there. She kept walking until her feet started to get wet. She saw a layer of water over the ice.

Then she stopped, and got ready to run. She ran, limping, at the kick sled, gave it a push, made it slide quite a bit forward. But it was not far enough. The ice still held. She would have to try going a little bit further. She lay on her stomach, pulling herself forward. The water seeped into her coat, but she wasn't freezing; it rather felt like burning. She placed her hands on Berit's backside and pushed again. The kick sled slid forward about ten meters. There was a breaking and cracking sound, then the kick sled tipped forward. She saw how it slowly slid into the water, saw the swinging runners, how everything sank and disappeared.

Back in the house, the pain in her foot resumed. She took off her wet clothes and hung them in the drying cabinet.

In the shower, she discovered the marks on her arms, marks and wounds from fingernails. It smarted like venom when she spread lotion on them.

But it wasn't until she went to the bedroom door that she noticed Berit's bag. It was still standing next to the chair where she had been sitting.

Chapter THREE

The following morning, she awoke with a heaviness on her chest. She tried to scream, but her throat was like a rasp. She kicked at the blankets and felt the bird; he had never gone into her bed before.

She had hidden Berit's bag in her wardrobe. When she came out in the upper hallway, she saw another bag, a dark blue tote with *Lüdings Förlag* on it, and a logo with a number of book spines. It had been thrown into a corner. She now remembered that Berit had brought flowers and a bottle of wine with her. She felt completely empty.

She folded the blue tote and put it in the wardrobe, too.

She spent the rest of the day with Hans Peter. She was able to suppress all those other events. She had thought about him; he was working his way into her consciousness. She felt a kind of tenderness when she remembered his collar bone, his neck, his hands. They were not like Nathan's; they were softer, milder. He gave her a happy contentment.

She had thought about taking care of Berit's bag after he left, but she didn't have the energy. Exhaustion knocked her out. She crept into bed; his aroma was in the sheets, his nearness.

Tor Assarsson called again on Monday morning.

"I just can't deal with going to work," he said. "I was hoping that you'd be home."

"I'm home."

"It is hellish. Everything is so damn hellish."

"I understand. Have you heard anything new?"

"No."

"Wait until the mail comes. Maybe she wrote you, from Rome or Tobago. Maybe she just picked up and left in order to get some distance."

"You think?"

"It's not completely impossible."

"Maybe you're right. Let's hope so."

He said he had to come over and talk to her in person. She was able to hinder that. "Wait for the mail first," she had said. "What time does it usually arrive?"

He said he didn't know. He was normally not at home during the work week.

She promised to let him come over after lunch.

She thought about Hans Peter.

First she had to deal with the purse and the tote. In some strange way, she hoped that they had just disappeared by the time she opened the wardrobe door. Of course they were still there. Berit's large leather purse stood on top of her gym shoes, just where she had placed it.

Her headache returned.

She sat on the floor with the scissors. She intended to cut the purse into small, small pieces, the purse and everything in it. When she took it in her hand, the way Berit had often held it, she realized that would be difficult. She didn't want to open it, but she realized that she had to. The small metal clasps released, and the purse yawned open with its dark secret contents. The owner's things, her life.

On the top was a cloth handkerchief with vague lipstick marks, then all the rest that she didn't want to see, but had to, all those personal belongings that would bring the picture of Berit back into her house: a wallet, worn out at the seams, the pocket with the bank card, the white plastic card from the *landsting*, an American Express card, a book club card that had expired a while ago, a pharmacy card. Justine lifted a flap and three person's eyes met hers: the husband, Tor, and the two boys, school age. There were almost a thousand crowns in the bill area. She began with those, clipped them to pieces; then the photos, the plastic cards, the small pieces of paper and receipts that were in the pocket behind the bills. Then she took the pocket calendar. She flipped through it and read sporadic notations: the dentist at one-thirty; don't forget to pick up shoes. At the very bottom, Berit's driver's license, loose. She did not look like herself in the photo. It was an old picture; Berit had her hair in a bun. It made her seem older. Keys, comb, mirror and lipstick. She started collecting it in a bag, sat for a while and tried to break the comb in two. It was a light blue plastic comb with a handle. She tried with all her might, but the plastic refused to give. A small bottle of perfume, *Nuits indiennes*; she rolled it into a small plastic bag to dampen the smell. The lighter was on the table. The cigarette pack was also there, five or six cigarettes left; she crumbled them to bits right onto the pile. Clipped the cloth tote into small pieces; tried to do it with the leather purse, but now she had to give up. The scissors had lost their strength.

What was she supposed to do with this? She sat on the floor with her legs straight. Berit's eye, cut loose from her driver's license, stared right into her face. She took it between her fingers and stuffed it into the bottom of the pile.

The telephone rang; she hadn't pulled the line from the jack. She was thinking of Tor Assarsson's and Berit's children. She had to be available, the happy and wonderful friend.

She spoke her entire name out loud, tensely.

"My dearest sweetheart!"

It was Hans Peter.

"I was afraid you'd disconnected the phone."

"No. . . ."

"I'm longing for you. My whole body longs for you; my palms miss the warmth of your skin. I want to hear your voice and embrace you."

"Oh, Hans Peter. . . ."

"What's wrong? You sound so different. Has something happened?"

"No, nothing."

"Are you sure?"

"I'm fine. Are you working today?"

"Certainly, but not until evening. May I come over right now? I want to!"

She froze from the sound of her own voice.

"I can't. I'm busy."

"When do you have time?"

She noticed the lessening of his enthusiasm.

"I'll have to call you."

"When?"

"Please, Hans Peter, there's a few things I really need to take care of first, and I can't talk about them now. But I will call you."

"Maybe I won't be in."

"No, but I'll try anyway. I have to go now. Sorry!"

She hung up the phone. This was not how she imagined things. She placed her hands on her eyes, and whimpered.

Should she burn up the purse? No. That would be too risky. She grumbled to herself and walked in circles. What to do? Then she remembered the transfer station Lövsta, on the other side of Riddersvik. Of course. Why didn't she think of this before? She was very tired; she was dizzy when she went into the basement. She found the roll of black garbage bags. She stuffed the purse and its pile of remains into one of the bags and tied it up. She strode about, searching in all the rooms; no, no more traces. She put on her coat and drove away.

She was afraid that someone would ask what was in the garbage bag. A man in overalls looked at her without any interest. She asked anyway, "Where's the container for combustibles?"

He pointed to one of the containers.

"Thanks," she said.

When she returned to the car: "Have a nice day."

He muttered something unintelligible.

As soon as she returned home, she dialed Hans Peter's number. Of course he didn't answer. Worry gripped her, began to transform into despair. She went into the bathroom and put on a thick layer of make-up, thick Kohl eyeliner and eye shadow. She put on a skirt, a cardigan and thick woolen leggings. Her foot was better after a night of rest, but it was still a bit swollen.

She tried calling again. No, now he was unhappy and hurt; he wouldn't answer, even if she called the whole day long. She could well imagine that he was the type who didn't forgive easily.

Someone was at the door. Was it him? There was a man outside; she saw him through the milky glass. It looked like Hans Peter. Was it him?

It wasn't him.

She knew who it was right away.

Tor, Berit's husband.

"You're Justine, aren't you?"

He looked scruffy; there was stubble like a cloud over his chin and cheeks, his eyes small and confused.

"Come in," she said softly.

He stood in the hallway, looked around.

"So she was here as late as last Saturday. I'm trying to think my way into her mind, imagine what she was reasoning and doing."

"Yes. . . ."

"Where did you go after she came in?"

"We went upstairs, I believe. We sat and talked up there for a long time."

"Let's do that, too."

She pulled herself up the stairs with the help of the railing. Her foot was aching again. He noticed, but didn't say anything.

"Maybe you would like some coffee?"

"No, I don't want coffee. I don't want anything."

The bird sat on the backrest of Berit's chair. When he saw the man, he screeched. Tor Assarsson jumped.

"What in the fucking hell is that?"

"Everyone asks," she said. "It's a bird. My pet."

He remained standing. Justine held out her arm, the bird hopped up onto it, and launched from there to the top of the bookcase.

Tor Assarsson stood with his arms over his head.

"How in the hell can you have a pet like that?"

She didn't answer.

"Do I dare sit down, or is anything else going to swoop down and surprise me?"

Justine was beginning to regret that she had let him in. He sounded irritated and provoked, probably was in shock.

She sank down on the edge of the chair.

"Were you sitting here?"

"Yes, we did, I believe."

"We've been married for many years, Berit and I. Now I understand how much she's become a part of me. Do you understand? And now it might be too late!"

"Did you wait for the mail?"

"Yes, but there was nothing. And, in addition, I found this."

He put his hand in his pocket and took out a passport. He threw it on the table with force.

"She can't have gone anywhere. At least, she hasn't left the country."

"What about the EU nowadays. . . . Do you need a passport anymore?"

"I think you still do."

"I'm sorry . . . but I'm afraid I can't really do anything for you."

"May I ask, were you really friends when you went to school together? Were you best friends, as they say?"

"Not really."

"Yes, I got that from her. She was hinting at something along those lines. You were bullied, weren't you?"

"It was a little difficult for me, but I haven't really dwelt on it very much. It was really quite a long time ago."

"She hinted that there was something she wanted to bring up with you. She had a bad conscience; she was suffering from it."

"She did?"

"Did she do it, say anything to you?"

Her thoughts whirled around her brain, was it the right thing to do to answer honestly now? Was it?

"I believe she said something like she hadn't been so nice all the time."

"She said that?"

"I think so."

"And what did you answer?"

"I don't remember. . . . I probably said something like I hadn't exactly been an angel myself."

His shoulders sank. She observed his shirt; the collar was wrinkled. He wasn't wearing a tie.

"The boys," he said heavily. "What am I going to say to the boys?"

"I know that you're worried," she whispered. "But it hasn't been that long yet. Try and be patient. Maybe she's calling you right now; maybe she's on the phone."

"I have everything sent to my cell." He patted his jacket pocket. "I'll hear right away when the phone rings at home. Where did she say she would go? Which words did she use exactly?"

"Oh, I don't really remember."

"Did she just look at her watch and say something like, oh, I really have to go?"

"It must have been something like that."

"I was out at the cabin the whole weekend. Otherwise I would have reacted earlier. Why, why the hell did I go out to the cabin!"

He rubbed his fingers against his forehead.

"I really don't understand all this. I just don't get it."

"I can imagine. . . . You think you know a person. And then you realize you really don't."

"That's true; that's really true."

Justine's telephone rang. She got up.

"Please excuse me!"

Hans Peter, she thought. *Kind, sweet, dear Hans Peter.*

But it was a different Hans, Hans Nästman.

Chapter FOUR

The wind had picked up. Clouds of dry snow were blowing through up there, like wisps of smoke. Her face got warm.

"Good day again, Justine Dalvik. Do you remember me?"

"Yes, of course I do. Why are you calling? . . . Is there any news about Nathan?"

"No."

"All right."

"And no news about the murderer of that young girl?"

Justine held her breath. Behind her in the room, Tor Assarsson was pacing about. He had opened the balcony door now and was lighting a cigarette. An ice-cold draft swept across the floor.

"Just a minute!" she said into the phone. "Close it!" she hissed to Tor Assarson and pointed to the bird.

"Do you have visitors?"

"Yes."

"You had a visitor on Saturday evening, too, didn't you?"

"Yes."

"I would like to talk to you about that."

"Why? Don't I have the right to have guests in my own home?"

"Certainly you do, Justine, certainly."

"Then, well, I don't understand. . . ."

The call was cut off, and she realized he was speaking on his cell phone, which had come into shadow. She regretted her reaction; she had gone straight to the attack. That was not good. She hung up the phone, bent down and got her jacket. Then she went out on the balcony with Tor Assarsson.

"You have to be careful with the doors and windows. The bird can impulsively fly out."

Smoke streamed from his nostrils.

"That'd be just fine!"

"Absolutely not!"

"A bird like that should be free."

"Yes, but he wouldn't manage. He doesn't know how to defend himself against wild birds, and other animals that might hurt him. He's been with people his whole life, since he fell from his nest. He is imprinted by people, by me."

The ashtray was on the floor. She realized that she had forgotten to empty it. The gusts of wind made the ash swirl a bit. Tor Assarsson put out his cigarette among the many half-smoked butts left by Berit.

"Whatever. It's really none of my business."

He left. At first he said he would call a taxi, but then he changed his mind a moment later.

"I'll walk along the route she took. I'll go and take the bus. Do you know how often they go?"

"Sorry, I never take the bus."

"No. You have a fine new car, I noticed."

"Yes, I just bought it. I have some things to do, or I would give you a lift to the subway station."

"No, no, I'd rather walk. As I mentioned before, I want to think my way into what Berit was doing last Saturday."

She followed him to the door, handed him his coat and scarf. Took his ice-cold hand into her two warm ones.

"Tor," she said, using his name for the first time. "We'll cross our fingers as hard as we can. That Berit will show up unharmed. That she's not hurt and everything will be like before. And if we think of her as hard as we can, it'll certainly happen."

He cleared his throat.

"Thank you," he said.

As soon as he left up the hill, she returned her jacket to its place. The telephone rang immediately.

"Hello?" she called, but heard only static noise.

"Hans Peter, is that you?"

It was the policeman. He was muttering and swearing. The words came in bits.

"Hello? Dammit all . . . I'll soon . . . in Hässelby. In about . . . minutes."

She went up to the balcony, took the ashtray and emptied it into the toilet and had to flush four times until all the butts disappeared. Then she called for the bird, and placed him in the attic. A strange calm came over her. She put a pot of coffee on and set mugs on the table.

Hans Nästman came alone. He parked right behind her car and walked up the gravel path. She opened before he rang the bell.

He didn't look like his usual self. He was a great deal thinner.

"Good day, Justine. I haven't forgotten you, as you see."

"I haven't forgotten you, either."

"That's a good thing."

"I've made coffee."

He nodded.

They sat at the kitchen table, just as she had earlier done with Hans Peter. She had cleared off the surface and was filled with a physical longing, and then the phone.

"You've changed," she said.

"So you noticed?"

"Yes."

"I've been sick."

"It looks like you've lost a number of kilos. Nothing serious, I hope?"

"A colon tumor."

"Oh."

"It's gone now. The tumor. And I hope it's gone forever."

"This horrible illness, cancer."

"Yes, you learn to value life in a completely different way after something like this."

She poured the coffee.

"I apologize. I don't have any coffee cake."

"Wonderful! Too many cakes and cookies all the time in these situations."

"You've come here for a reason, I take it?"

"For the sake of Berit Assarsson, your former classmate."

Her stomach turned to ice.

"Berit, yes."

"Justine, now don't get offended, but it seems that bad luck follows you around. People in your vicinity tend to disappear or die."

"This is supposed to be my fault?"

"Your fault? I didn't say that. But listen: First it was Nathan Gendser, your male companion. He just disappeared in the jungle and no one has heard from him since. Then Martina Andersson, a young and beautiful photojournalist with an open interest in this Gendser. She was found murdered in cold blood with a jungle knife. In your shared hotel room."

"An open interest?" she repeated.

"Of course, I've been talking to the other people in your group. You must have noticed something like that."

"She was flirty, but that was mostly her way; young women like to do that. And Nathan was also flirty, and I have to admit that it was hurtful to me sometimes. And of course he was flattered by Martina's attention. He was a real guy when it came to her."

"And now we have this woman Berit. Her husband has just reported her missing. It was in that context that we came across your name. She was with you right before she disappeared."

"And you somehow suspect me? Are you going to put me in jail?"

He looked at her over his glasses.

"I just want to talk with you about it."

"Is this an interrogation, or what?"

"Don't take it like that. I just want to ask a few questions."

Part 3: Chapter Four

She pressed her hands to her face. Her heart was pounding so strongly that she almost imagined that he could hear it.

"OK," she said in a low voice. "Nathan . . . I still haven't gotten over it, if that's what you think; every time his name is spoken . . . we were going to get married. I would have been his wife by now. It hurts me. I see him lying there in the rain forest, maybe hurt . . . dead . . . how the wild animals. . . ."

Hans Nästman waited patiently until she finished. He leaned back in the chair, and when she took her hands away from her face, he gave her a friendly smile.

She had to tell about Saturday evening; he wanted to hear every little detail. He let her show him exactly where they sat, what they said, what they ate and drank. He asked about her foot.

"I fell when I was out running. I've probably sprained it."

"Her husband said that she felt some kind of regret. Her childhood seemed to catch up with her. She had apparently been a leader and had bullied many classmates. Including you. It seemed to weigh heavily on her mind."

"Yes, she . . . mentioned something along those lines."

"How do you remember that bullying?"

"I told her all children do things like that; I wasn't exactly a saint myself. I could be a bit nasty, too. Isn't that part of childhood? I mean, think about it. How many kids did you hit on the chin when you were a boy?"

"She looked you up in order to talk about it."

"Well, not just that. We were classmates; she was rummaging around in her roots, trying to make things fit together, so to speak."

"Hmm. But why would she disappear right now? What do you believe about it?"

"Well, I don't know . . . but it's just Monday. Certainly, she'll show up soon!"

"She'd never done anything like this before, her husband says."

"Nora Helmer in *A Doll's House* didn't do anything like that either until the day she left husband and family."

"I haven't read *A Doll's House*."

"Ibsen."

"I know that."

"I said the same thing to her husband, who was here earlier. Berit is certainly depressed. She was seeing her life as one big failure: the marriage, the boys who didn't want to have much contact with her any longer, and then all that with her job. Her boss was going to move the entire business up to Norrland. You can well imagine. . . . She's not young anymore, of course; she's my age. But maybe you don't know the value of a woman who is our age? In the job market . . . and other markets for that matter?"

There was a noise from the attic. A screech and some thuds, as if someone had fallen over. The policeman jumped up.

"What was that?"

She sighed.

"I have a bird. He's up there. I usually let him fly free in the house, but I am so damned tired of explaining him to people who come here. So I put him in the attic before you arrived."

She went up the stairs and opened the door.

"Hello?" she called. "Are you coming?"

She didn't hear him. She entered the darkness and saw a stack of her father's old bound magazines, *Arbetsledaren*, which had fallen from a shelf. The bird sat in the middle of the books, biting the covers and giving her wrathful looks.

"Leave those alone!" she scolded. "Pappa would have been furious!"

"What is that?" asked Hans Nästman. He was standing right behind her now; he was holding the railing. If she kicked her leg backwards? The stairs were steep; he would lose his grip from sheer surprise and fall headfirst onto the landing. He was weak and fragile after his illness; he wouldn't be able to resist.

She didn't do it.

The bird flapped over their heads.

"He's angry," she said. "He doesn't like to be locked up."

"No," said Hans Nästman. "Very few do. And still, crimes are committed."

She was finally alone again at four-thirty. She went straight to the telephone and dialed Hans Peter's number. Still no answer. Maybe he'd already gone to work? What was the name of that hotel where he worked, something with roses? She got out the yellow pages and looked under Hotels, she found it right away, Tre Rosor on Drottninggatan. She wrote the telephone number in a notebook.

She started the car. He couldn't have reached the hotel yet; he didn't start work this early. She drove toward Fyrspannsgatan and parked alongside the cemetery. It was a gray day. The wind ripped at her hair and clothes, made her freeze down to the marrow of her bones.

First she went to the wrong building. After searching around, she finally found Hans Peter's entrance. She realized that she had never before been inside a rented place. She stood outside for a long time and read on the board in the entryway the names of the residents. In the distance, she heard the dampened sound of footsteps, then the sound of running water. A vague, almost unnoticeable smell of marble and stone. She saw his name, too long to fit completely, H. P. Bergman, fourth floor.

There was no elevator. She slowly walked up all the stairs. His door was directly on the right; she saw his name again.

No, he wasn't home. She rang the bell many times and when he didn't come, she peeked through the letter slot. His smell, the smell of Hans Peter and everything that belonged to him. She called a few times but finally realized that the apartment was empty.

Should she sit and wait? Or had he already gone into town? Maybe he'd done that. No sense in staying. She had her notebook with her, so she ripped out a page and wrote his name on it: *Hans Peter*, she wrote, *I long for you so much, so very very much. Please forgive me if I hurt you. Justine.*

She folded the paper in the middle and stuffed it through the letter slot. It fell down to the welcome mat. She saw it lie there and caught a glance of the edge of his winter coat, which was hanging on a hook.

She suddenly began to cry.

Chapter FIVE

The bird was in the kitchen. She'd forgotten to give him food. Where was it? Any frozen ground beef in the freezer? No, not even that. It was twenty to six.

"I'll be right back," she said. "I'm just going to do some shopping."

She drove to the shopping center. There was an incredible number of cars for a Monday evening, but she found a place next to the shopping cart storage.

In the bank window to her right, she saw a photo of a house that was for sale. This is where the real estate agent wanted to place her house, too. She got angry just thinking about it.

She hadn't been here for a while. The library was being rebuilt; the personnel and the books were at another location for the duration. She stopped next to the pet store. A large guinea pig sat all alone in a big cage, displayed in the store front window. Once the store had been filled with all kinds of animals and was owned by a woman who called the animals her friends. They had been her whole life. Finally, she was forced to sell after contracting an allergy.

Impulsively, she went into the pet store. A man was standing at the counter, pricing cans of fish food.

"Can I help you?" he asked.

"That guinea pig."

She looked toward the cage. The animal had his front paws on the bars and sniffed at the air.

"He looks lonely."

"He's a she."

"*She* looks lonely, then."

"Yes, we've sold all the other small animals and birds. Just that guinea pig is left. We are going to concentrate solely on reptiles in the future. Snakes and lizards and the like. It's very popular these days."

"Really."

"Do you want the guinea pig?"

"When I was little, I really wanted a pet. A girl in my class had a guinea pig. They weren't sleek like this one, but black and full of cowlicks. They had babies, I remember. They used to toddle around on the floor after their mamma."

"These little guys are pleasant and peaceful. They don't need much."

"They don't?"

The man opened the refrigerator door and rustled a plastic bag. The small animal was ready and began to shriek with a heart-rending voice.

"She thinks she's getting some lettuce."

"Isn't she then?"

"I guess."

He held out a piece of lettuce to the guinea pig who elongated herself to grab it with her teeth.

"It'll be hard to lose her," he said.

"Are you fond of her?"

"No, not really, but nobody seems interested. If someone doesn't take her soon, I'll have to feed her to the snakes."

"You can't do that!"

"Eat or be eaten, the law of the jungle."

"How much does she cost?"

"Tell you what, if you really want her, you can have her."

"I can have her?"

"Sure. You really seem to like animals."

"Well . . . thanks. I just need to get some groceries."

She bought raw liver and two kilos of ground innards at the meat section. She picked up a large package of eggs, some onions, and two packages of white tulips. At the produce section, she took lettuce and a whole heap of vegetables, cucumbers, carrots, tomatoes.

The cashier joked with her.

"If I didn't see all that meat, I would swear that you've gone vegan," she laughed. "Those militant vegans. I've read how they set sausages free."

"I'm on the side of the sausages," Justine joked back.

"And how is your mother?"

"Well, it is what it is. Unchanged."

"Well, we all have our fate. To think that she was always so attractive and well-dressed. I used to admire her so much. I remember as if it were yesterday. She was so rich and distinguished, one would think, and yet she would come and shop here, a normal grocery store."

"Yes."

"There was something humble about her. She never acted stuck-up or superior. A wonderful woman, Mrs. Dalvik."

Justine packed up her groceries.

"You probably go and visit her, right? Can you be so kind and say hi from Britt-Marie? If she's able to. . . ."

"Oh, yes, I can say hi to her from you."

The bird flew toward her the minute she entered the house. He landed on the cage, tilted his head to the side, and looked curiously at the guinea pig.

"This is the new member of our family," she explained. "She was nearly fed to the snakes, but I saved her at the last minute. If you are nice to her, maybe she'll be your playmate."

The bird plucked itself beneath one of his wings, apparently uninterested. A soft, downy feather fell onto the guinea pig's back.

She put liver and eggs into his bowl. He flew there directly.

She carefully lifted the guinea pig, felt her small paws with her fingertips.

"You look like a rat," she whispered. "If you had a tail, it would be hard to tell the difference. I think I'm going to call you Rattie. Yes, Rattie's the perfect name for you."

She let the animal to the floor, and it scurried directly to the cabinet and tried to squeeze underneath it in order to hide. The bird flew there. He was bloody and sticky around his beak.

"Be nice to Rattie!" she scolded. "You are going to be friends, keep that in mind!"

He shook himself, took a few hops, and pecked lightly with his beak on the guinea pig's round back. Rattie whirled around and raised herself onto her hind legs.

"It'll be fine," she said. "You'll get used to each other."

At eight o'clock, she called the hotel. A man's voice answered. She asked to speak with Hans Peter.

"He's not here."

"But . . . doesn't he work there?"

"Yes, but he's not here now."

"Why not? Did he say why?"

"Can I take a message?"

She hung up the phone.

She woke up many times during the night. The same dream; it returned in quick sequences. Hans Nästman, with a cleanly washed, thinned face. He stood next to her bed; he didn't move, just stood there. When she tried to get up, she found that she was chained to the bed with a rattan rope. Hans Nästman smiled and showed all his teeth. It's over, Justine; you are to come with me now, and not make a fuss.

"You can't prove anything!" she screamed. "Get out of here, leave me in peace!"

He took a step toward her; his hand had neither skin nor fingernails.

"Nothing needs to be proven, my friend. Now Hans Peter Bergman is also missing, and that's enough to take you in."

She woke up from her own screaming. There was flapping and screeching in the room. She turned on the light and saw the bird flying around in panic. He calmed down in the light, landed on his branch, still thin and frightened. She had to get up. She had to call, call home to Hans Peter. It was a quarter to three. No one answered.

The day was quiet, without sun. Dry snowflakes in the air. She took the guinea pig with her in the car. She wrapped the animal in a blanket, and it rolled up and went to sleep almost immediately.

She came to the ward and went to the desk. A nurse sat, flipping through a binder.

"Good morning. I'm Justine Dalvik, and I thought I'd visit my mother."

"Your mother?"

"Flora Dalvik."

"Oh, yes, Flora. Good morning. It'll be great for her; every change is so welcome to our residents."

"How's she doing?"

"Very well. Yesterday she was up the entire day."

The nurse was named Gunlis. Justine didn't recognize her. Gunlis closed the binder.

"I'm fairly new here. I don't think we've met before. I'll take you to her. What do you have there, by the way?"

"A little guinea pig, which I've just gotten. I wanted to show Mamma, I hope that there's nothing against it."

"Oh, no, quite the opposite. It makes things a little more human in the ward, a little less clinical, if I may speak freely. I've always advocated for it, but it's hard to make changes in the daily routine. Wouldn't it be wonderful with a house cat wandering around visiting the residents, who rubbed their legs in a friendly way, who jumped in someone's lap and began to purr? I think the residents would have greater quality of life if things were less sterile."

She lowered her voice: "But you can hardly dare say anything like that. You risk losing your job."

"Really?"

"Well, of course you can't. What would it look like if the workers had opinions? May I look? What a sweet little nose peeking out here! It doesn't bite, does it?"

"No, of course not."

Flora was sitting in the wheelchair. She lifted her head, her roving gaze.

Gunlis went up to her and dried off her chin.

"Look, Flora, look who's here for a visit. And a little grandchild, too. Or you could almost say so. Right?" she laughed.

Justine bent over the wheelchair.

"Hi, little Mamma."

She stroked her chin, petted the dry, cold hands. She placed the towel with the guinea pig on Flora's lap; unwrapped it carefully. There was a hoarse, gasping sound from the old one's throat.

A telephone rang in the distance.

"I have to go answer it," Gunlis called. "Oh, I really wanted to see it!"

The guinea pig had pooped. The blanket was full of long, hard pearls. Justine emptied them into a garbage can. Then she let the guinea pig crawl around in Flora's lap. She saw drops of sweat appear on Flora's upper lip. The gasping sound had become faster, even more rattling.

"Isn't she sweet? Her name is Rattie. No, it's not really a rat. It's an everyday old guinea pig. You know that I always wanted a pet. You remember, don't you?"

Flora had closed her eyes. Her skin had taken on a pale gray tone. Justine lifted up the guinea pig, carefully wrapped it in the towel again. The nurse returned.

"Was she happy?"

"I think so . . . but it's so hard to tell."

"She looks a bit tired . . . but certainly it made her happy. It's sweet of you to come by with your guinea pig. Thoughtful, even. May I pet it?"

The other bed in the room was missing sheets. There were no personal articles on the bed stand.

"Didn't my mamma have a roommate?" Justine asked.

The nurse pulled her a bit to the side.

"Yes, but, unfortunately . . . she's not with us any longer."

"That's sad to hear."

"Yes, but that's life, isn't it? It has to end sometime."

Justine gestured to the woman in the wheelchair. Flora had opened her eyes and had a strong look of fear in them.

"Unfortunate for my poor mamma. I believe that they got along fairly well. As much as can be expected."

"Yes, it's very sad. But a new person is coming this afternoon. The beds don't stay empty for long here."

"Bye-bye, Mamma," Justine called. "I'll come back soon. Maybe take you home for a little while. Maybe even tomorrow, if that works for you?"

The old person's lips jerked, gurgling noise from her throat.

"She's trying to say something," said the nurse.

"She had such a pretty voice," sighed Justine. "What bad luck that she can no longer use it."

"Others have it worse," said the nurse.

"Too true, there's always someone worse off."

She drove to Fryspannsgatan. He must have come home; he must have read her note. She rang the bell, but still no answer. When she opened the mail slot, she saw a magazine and some envelopes lying on the floor. She couldn't tell if her note was still there.

She went home but felt restless. She paced around the house, finally ending up in the room that had been her father's and Flora's. A violent rage came over her. She flung open the closet door and ripped out everything that had belonged to Flora: her dresses, her shoes. The clothes carried memories, and Flora appeared, materialized, her mouth white and closed. *Take off your clothes, you good-for-nothing. I'm going to give you a whipping.*

She lifted one of the dresses, it had been hanging so long that the cloth had puckered, was fragile. She grabbed the fold, and with one pull, she ripped it all the way to the waist seam. She kept going, from the bottom up, until the skirt was nothing but long strips. But Flora's hand came to her; it slapped her head, hard and ringing.

"You've never been completely normal. Take your clothes off so I can hit some sense into you. I'm going to stuff you into the wash tub. . . . You'll sit there until you learn how to become nice and compliant, you spoiled little monkey, until you do exactly what I want."

Flora was still there inside her; she was in the memories of the house. She would never let go of her grip. Even in her look, there was a certain strength beneath the fear, Justine had seen it when she had visited, a triumphant scorn.

Justine's body began to shake; her throat became thick and harsh. She had to leave and drink some water.

Then she got some plastic garbage bags, She threw everything into them: shoes, jewelry, clothes. Everything which could remind her of Flora.

Then she saw her father's suits, and she stepped into the closet and burrowed her face into them. She was crying now, bellowing and ugly; then she ripped them off their hangers and stuffed them into the bags as well.

The next afternoon, she drove back to the nursing home. She had slept heavily and without dreams. She had drunk quite a bit of wine before she finally could fall asleep. She felt feverish; her forehead hurt her as though a clamp was tightening around it.

Gunlis appeared in the hallway. Her eyes were bloodshot.

"Well, good day to you again!" she said, and yawned. "Oh, excuse me!"

"It doesn't matter. I'm also a little tired. But I thought I would let Mamma come home for a short time today. Would that be all right?"

Gunlis placed her arm around her.

"That's a silly question. If more of our residents had relatives who cared, the world would be a very different place. Wait here, and I'll get her ready."

Justine sank onto a bench. The floor was as shiny as a mirror; it appeared to be unbearably long. Farther down the hallway, a man with black skin was pushing a cleaning cart.

A hunchbacked, very wrinkled man came out of one of the rooms. He came shuffling toward her, supported by a walker. He stopped right in front of her.

"Nurse . . . do you work here?"

"No," she said, turning red.

"You ought to be glad of that. This is not a good place."

Gunlis had returned.

"What's going on, Martin? Is there a problem?"

"I want to go home; that's the only thing I want. Why do you keep me imprisoned here?"

Gunlis shook her head.

"My dear Martin, we're not keeping you prisoner here."

The man spat. The spit landed on the nurse's shoes, a brown, sticky gob.

Tears came to her eyes.

"Martin!"

He glared at her threateningly.

"Don't you touch me; you can be contagious. The radioactive material is spreading with the speed of the wind. It's spreading and is going to kill us all. . . ."

Gunlis grimaced. She disappeared into the washroom, Justine heard her flush and rinse with water. A girl with a ponytail came out from Flora's room.

"Are you the one who's picking up Flora?"

"Yes."

"I've dressed her and placed her in her wheelchair."

"Great."

"Can you take her down yourself?"

"Certainly. I've done it before."

Flora was wrapped in a blanket. A coarse knitted cap was on her head. She stared at Justine; her eyes never left her. Gunlis came out just as Justine was starting to leave.

"Forgive me," she said. "I lost my head for a moment. I'm still a bit tired, I'm afraid."

"It's not so pleasant to be spat upon."

"He can't help it. He thinks he's a prisoner. I wish that he also had someone who would come and take him on fun outings. Or what do you think, Flora?" She bent down and adjusted the knit cap. "Have a great day, you two!"

Chapter SIX

She talked to Flora; the whole time, she talked to her. She had fastened Flora's seatbelt, and was now approaching the Vällingby roundabout. "Do you know where you are, Flora? It's been awhile since you were outside. Do you think it looks familiar, farther on, by the small houses between Åkeshov and Ängby? They're in the middle of building noise barriers, yes, so the people won't be bothered. We never have to worry about that kind of thing; we're never bothered. We have always kept to ourselves. We have enjoyed peace and quiet, haven't we, dear Flora? Do you know that Martin, the one with the walker, he thinks that he's being held prisoner. To think what it would be like to always long to get out. Maybe I can set up some kind of system; get a minivan and drive around picking up old people who are all by themselves and want to get a little joyride. Wouldn't that be a great idea? You've always said a person needs a mission in life. I thought you could come home for a while; it's been so long since you were home. You haven't been home since you got sick, little Flora. Won't it be nice to come see the old place, even though you wanted to sell it? But we're not going to do that, of course. The house is going to stay mine. I am going to live there. It's my house, but now you can come and visit, now you are my guest. What a generous step-daughter you have, Flora. Didn't you hear what Gunlis said? Every resident should have someone like me. Do you see the palace there, Hässelby Palace? So beautiful and frozen it looks, Hässelby Palace. This part is just the same as always; nothing much has happened here in Hässelby Gård. What does the thermometer say there? 100 degrees? They're crazy. I wonder if that thermometer has ever shown the right temperature. You can fly to the moon but can't get a thermometer to work. Do you think I'm talking too much? Yes, I am, I'm sure, but I have to speak for two now, you understand; you can't speak so I have to speak in your place. Look, there's the cemetery, where Mamma and Pappa are buried. Look how well-kept it is. There was a burial yesterday. They throw away the flowers afterward, the wreaths and the coffin arrangements, what a great waste. I wonder what will happen with you, I mean, if there is any special kind that you want. I've been thinking about graves and maybe it's better with ashes spread in the *minneslunden*, the field of remembrance; that could be nice, too. The forest on our left, it was huge when I was a child; the perspective changes. I played there sometimes. I found a dog there once, but I think it was already dead, I remember that strange smell, though then I didn't know how death smelled. OK, hold on, we're turning on to Strandvägen. The bathhouse is gone, that fine bathhouse, and the water slide that was here for a while; nothing like that is left. But you know that. Flora, do you see the ice? It looks thick and like it can bear weight, but you have to be careful; a few hundred meters out it's open water. But look here to the right. They've torn down one of the summer houses, the one that was so rotten and ramshackle. Now there'll be another villa. They're tearing down all the old stuff. Now we're getting there, Flora. Are you happy?"

She drove up to the house and parked. The old woman sat straight and unmoving. When Justine loosened the seat belt, she fell straight to the side, and Justine had to catch her and lay her down across both seats while she unbuckled the seat belt. Then she lifted Flora's tense body and carried it up the stairs.

"Sorry that I can't go any faster; my foot hurts. Do you remember when I broke it? Do you? After that it's never been the same. No, I'm not complaining. I can both walk and run, but I twist it easily and sprain it. . . . No I really am not complaining, not like you. I can come and go just as I please. How does it feel now, Flora? I'm going to put you in your favorite chair, where you sat with Pappa all those years ago. You can look out into the mist if you want. You can imagine that it's summer and you're sitting on the balcony and the sun is round and hot, and Pappa is in the boat down there. I'm just going to take off my jacket and lock the car. If the phone rings, answer it. No, that was stupid of me, just plain thoughtless of me. Sorry."

She took a long time. She made coffee and prepared a coffee tray. The bird was in her room; the door was shut. She heard him cawing in there, how he heard her voice and wanted out.

Flora sat just where she'd been left, her head slightly turned toward the window.

"Would you like some coffee? I can help you. Open your mouth and sip. Is it too warm? No I don't think so. Are you sitting here and thinking about old times, how we used to have it, you and I? . . . What is that? The sound you mean? I have a pet living here, you know; you met Rattie yesterday. I call her that even though she's not a rat. She was with me in bed last night for a little while, but I was afraid I might suffocate her, so I put her back in her cage. She was warm and soft. I have a bird, too. You'll meet him in a minute, but drink up now; he's such a bother when we're eating . . ."

A sharp ring, the telephone.

"Is it you?" she said breathlessly.

"I guess I should always answer yes to that kind of question," said a hearty voice. "Jacob Hellstrand, the agent."

"I don't have time and I'm still not interested."

"I have developers who are ready to pay whatever you ask. You'd be crazy not to grab this kind of offer."

"Don't you understand that no means no!" she yelled, and slammed down the phone.

She went to Flora. Flora's saliva was running down her chin and on to her neck. Her pupils glowed and burned. Justine stuck her face right into Flora's.

"Do unto others as you would have them do unto you. Have you ever heard that passage, Flora? Jesus said it, and it's a good rule to follow, even today."

She lifted up the old woman, carried her in her arms like a child.

"Let's go for a tour of the house; that must interest you. Here's the kitchen, just as it was; here's the blue room. I've honored your memory, as you can see. And then the basement, oh yes . . . we're going there, too. Do you remember what you had down there, Flora? Do you remember what was hiding behind that door? Do you remember?"

Flora had begun to make noises. She threw her head around; the high-pitched wail intensified to a muddled, long drawn-out howl. They had come into the room with the washtub. Justine climbed carefully up onto the cement block where the tub was standing. She lifted Flora slightly into the air and then lowered her gently into the tub.

Then she went to get the bird.

She was at the funeral director's when the telephone rang. They had a fine, thorough conversation, the coffin had been ordered and they had chosen some beautiful songs that the old woman would have liked. It would be a simple ceremony, simple but dignified. The director had promised to sing, and he knew someone who played the flute.

"And how would you prefer the obituary?" he asked, right as she stood up to go.

She gave him a weak, sorrowful smile.

"Let's not bother with it. I'll write to those concerned. It will be more personal that way."

But the telephone rang. She had long since given up hope.

"I got your little note," he said, and happiness flowed into her like honey. But she was silent.

"Justine? Are you still there?"

Everything broke through; she had to place the receiver to one side. She heard his voice, how he called and pleaded.

"Yes, I'm here," she said at last.

"You don't have to ask for forgiveness! Like you wrote in your note. Not at all, it's me...."

"You just disappeared," she snuffled.

"I called before, but you weren't home. Or maybe you'd taken the phone off the hook."

"You could have called again."

"It wasn't easy ... you understand."

"What happened? I even called the hotel."

"My mother. I had to go right away."

"Your mother?"

"She'd always been so healthy. But . . . she just had a heart attack."

"Oh no, that can't be true!"

"Yes . . . but things are going better now. She'll come through. We've been staying at the hospital, Pappa and me. You have to know.... I've missed you and have been longing for you, too."

"Are you sure she's going to be all right?"

"Oh yes, yes. At least for a while."

She was crying again, had to go get some kitchen towels.

"What's going on with you, Justine?"

"You must come over, I'll explain everything."

He arrived at her house within a half an hour. He embraced her, kissed her, rocked her back and forth. She let herself be heavy and limp.

"Come," she whispered. "Let's go upstairs."

She opened the door to the bedroom.

"We can be in here. I've redecorated a bit. This used to be my parents' bedroom. I think it's better that I have it now."

She crept onto the bedspread. He lay behind her with his clothes on.

"Tell me what's going on," he whispered. "I'm here now. Why are you so despairing?"

"It's just that . . . you must understand, Hans Peter . . . that bad luck follows me around . . . evil deeds."

"What are you talking about?"

"A policeman was here last Monday. He told me that. *Everyone around you seems to encounter bad things,* he said. Oh, Hans Peter, I'm so frightened. What if it's true? What if something bad happens to you?"

She felt his lips on her neck, but his breathing was shorter. He was on guard.

"Why did a policeman come visit?"

"The man I'd been with, Nathan, I mentioned him to you; he just disappeared in the jungle. We never found him. We had to leave without him . . . it was . . . terrible. And then . . . when we were going to return home to Sweden, a crazy guy burst into our hotel room and a girl who was traveling with us, we were sharing a room, she and I . . . he stabbed her to death . . . she died immediately. You probably read about it in the newspapers. And now . . . now a classmate of mine has disappeared. She was here visiting me, you know, a week ago Saturday. . . . She never arrived home. The policeman was here searching for her . . . but now . . . now I really don't know anymore . . . last Tuesday . . . I took my foster mother here. She is old and paralyzed. She lives in a nursing home, and I thought she would be happy to come home. . . ."

"You don't have to tell me if you don't want to."

"Suddenly she was just sitting there dead. We were in the basement. The bird came. I watched him fly, and suddenly . . . she was just dead."

"Dearest little Justine."

She turned toward him, cried into his blue shirt.

"Leave me if you must. I understand completely."

"These must just be unhappy coincidences. It's not your fault, little silly."

"But why did he say that, the policeman?"

"Yes, well, it wasn't a smart thing to say. We know he's wrong, don't we?"

"Yes . . ."

He was breathing normally again. He took hold of the plaid bedspread and wrapped it around them both.

"You're not working tonight, are you?"

"No, Justine, I'm with you. I'm staying here."

He stroked her hair, kissed her neck, her ears.

"You're not going to just disappear?"

"I'm sorry, Justine, forgive me. I should have tried to call you again, but Pappa was beside himself. I've always been their support in life."

They lay pressed against each other for a while. He embraced her. He was heavy, living. She felt calm returning, like sleep, but without sleeping.

"Do you have a handkerchief?"

He searched in his pocket, took out a wrinkled tissue.

"It's clean," he whispered. "Even if it doesn't look like it."

"I believe you," she said and blew her nose.

Then she let her hands go toward his narrow, hard hips.

"Hans Peter," she said, in order to massage his name into the room.

About the Author

INGER FRIMANSSON was born in 1944 in Stockholm and grew up in various places in the middle of Sweden. Today she lives in Södertälje, a town not far from Stockholm, with her husband Jan. As a young girl Inger Frimansson won a number of literary competitions, among them, the so-called Little Nobel Prize in 1963. She started her career as a working journalist, and she made her debut as a writer of serious fiction in 1984 with her novel *The Double Bed* (*Dubbelsängen*). In 1997, she published her first full-fledged psychological thriller, *I Will Fear No Evil* (*Fruktar jag intet ont*).

A significant breakthrough in her writing career occurred in 1998 with the publication of *Good Night, My Darling* (*Godnatt, min älskade*), which was voted Best Mystery Novel of the Year by the Swedish Academy of Mystery Authors. The jury's citation included this appreciation: "A psychological thriller about senselessness and revenge that doesn't loosen its grasp of the reader's attention for the length of the book."

In autumn 2002, *The Island of Naked Women* (*De nakna kvinnornas ö*) was published, a thriller about vehement passion and unprovoked manslaughter. *Hidden Tracks* (*Mörkerspår*), 2003, followed with more rave reviews from the critics, as did the recent *The Shadow in the Water* (*Skuggan i vattnet*), awarded with The Swedish Academy of Mystery Authors Award for Best Swedish Crime Novel 2005. She is the only female crime author ever to receive this award twice.

Inger Frimansson's novels are translated into several languages and are published in various editions in Norway, Latvia, Holland, Finland, Denmark, Spain, Bulgaria, and Germany.

Order List: Books from *Pleasure Boat Studio: A Literary Press*

(Note: Caravel Books is a new imprint of Pleasure Boat Studio: A Literary Press. Caravel Books is the imprint for mysteries only.)

Falling Awake: An American Woman Gets a Grip on the Whole Changing World— One Essay at a Time • Mary Lou Sanelli • $15 • **an aequitas book**

Way Out There: Lyrical Essays • Michael Daley • $16 • **an aequitas book**

The Case of Emily V. • Keith Oatley • mystery • $18 • **a caravel book**

Monique • Luisa Coehlo, Trans fm Portuguese by Maria do Carmo de Vasconcelos and Dolores DeLuise ISBN 1929355262 • 80 pages • fiction • $14

The Blossoms Are Ghosts at the Wedding • Tom Jay • ISBN 1929355351 • essays and poems • $15 • **an empty bowl book**

Against Romance • Michael Blumenthal • ISBN 1929355238 • 110 pages • poetry • $14

Speak to the Mountain: The Tommie Waites Story • Dr. Bessie Blake • ISBN 1929355297/ 36X • 278 pages • biography • $18/$26 • **an aequitas book**

Artrage • Everett Aison • ISBN 1929355254 • 225 pages • fiction • $15

Days We Would Rather Know • Michael Blumenthal • ISBN 1929355246 • 118 pages • poetry • $14

Puget Sound: 15 Stories • C. C. Long • ISBN 192935522X • 150 pages • fiction • $14

Homicide My Own • Anne Argula • ISBN 1929355211 • 220 pages • fiction (mystery) • $16

Craving Water • Mary Lou Sanelli • ISBN 192935519X • 121 pages • poetry • $15

When the Tiger Weeps • Mike O'Connor • ISBN 1929355189 • 168 pages • poetry and prose • $15

Wagner, Descending: The Wrath of the Salmon Queen • Irving Warner • ISBN 1929355173 • 242 pages • fiction • $16

Concentricity • Sheila E. Murphy • ISBN 1929355165 • 82 pages • poetry • $13.95

Schilling, from a study in lost time • Terrell Guillory • ISBN 1929355092 • 156 pages • fiction • $16.95

Rumours: A Memoir of a British POW in WWII • Chas Mayhead • ISBN 1929355068 • 201 pages • nonfiction • $16

The Immigrant's Table • Mary Lou Sanelli • ISBN 1929355157 • $13.95 • poetry and recipes • $13.95

The Enduring Vision of Norman Mailer • Dr. Barry H. Leeds • ISBN 1929355114 • criticism • $18

Women in the Garden • Mary Lou Sanelli • ISBN 1929355149 • poetry • $13.95

Pronoun Music • Richard Cohen • ISBN 1929355033 • short stories • $16

If You Were With Me Everything Would Be All Right • Ken Harvey • ISBN 1929355025 • short stories • $16

The 8th Day of the Week • Al Kessler • ISBN 1929355009 • fiction • $16

Another Life, and Other Stories • Edwin Weihe • ISBN 19293550117 • short stories • $16

Saying the Necessary • Edward Harkness • ISBN 096514139X (paper) • poetry • $14

Nature Lovers • Charles Potts • ISBN 1929355041 • poetry • $10

In Memory of Hawks, & Other Stories from Alaska • Irving Warner • ISBN 0965141349 • 210 pages • fiction • $15

The Politics of My Heart • William Slaughter • ISBN 0965141306 • 96 pages • poetry • $12.95

The Rape Poems • Frances Driscoll • ISBN 0965141314 • 88 pages • poetry • $12.95

When History Enters the House: Essays from Central Europe • Michael Blumenthal • ISBN 0965141322 • 248 pages • nonfiction • $15

Setting Out: The Education of Lili • Tung Nien • Trans fm Chinese by Mike O'Connor • ISBN 0965141330 • 160 pages • fiction • $15

Our Chapbook Series:

No. 1: ***The Handful of Seeds: Three and a Half Essays*** • Andrew Schelling • ISBN 0965141357 • $7 • 36 pages • nonfiction

No. 2: ***Original Sin*** • Michael Daley • ISBN 0965141365 • $8 • 36 pages • poetry

No. 3: ***Too Small to Hold You*** • Kate Reavey • ISBN 19293550x • $8 • poetry

No. 4: ***The Light on Our Faces: A Therapy Dialogue*** • Lee Miriam WhitmanRaymond • ISBN 1929355122 • $8 • 36 pages • poetry

No. 5: **Eye** • William Bridges • ISBN 0-929355-13-0/24 pages/chapbook/$8
No. 6: *Selected* **New Poems** *of Rainer Maria Rilke* • Trans fm German by Alice Derry •
ISBN 1929355106 • $10 • poetry
No. 7: *Through High Still Air: A Season at Sourdough Mountain* • Tim McNulty •
ISBN 1929355270 • $9 • poetry and prose
No. 8: **Sight Progress** • Zhang Er, Trans fm Chinese by Rachel Levitsky •
ISBN 1929355289 • $9 • prosepoems
No. 9: **The Perfect Hour** • Blas Falconer • ISBN 1929355319 • $9 • poetry

From our backlist (in limited editions):

Desire • Jody Aliesan • ISBN 0912887117 • $14 • poetry (an Empty Bowl book)
Deams of the Hand • Susan Goldwitz • ISBN 0912887125 • $14 • poetry
(an Empty Bowl book)
Lineage • Mary Lou Sanelli • No ISBN • $14 • poetry (an Empty Bowl book)
The Basin: Poems from a Chinese Province • Mike O'Connor • ISBN 0912887 206 •
$10/$20 • poetry (paper/hardbound) (an Empty Bowl book)
The Straits • Michael Daley • ISBN 0912887044 • $10 • poetry (an Empty Bowl book)
In Our Hearts and Minds: The Northwest and Central America • Ed. Michael Daley •
ISBN 0912887184 • $12 • poetry and prose (an Empty Bowl book)
The Rainshadow • Mike O'Connor • No ISBN • $16 • poetry (an Empty Bowl book)
Untold Stories • William Slaughter • ISBN 1912887 249 • $10/$20 • poetry (paper/
hardbound) (an Empty Bowl book)
In Blue Mountain Dusk • Tim McNulty • ISBN 0965141381 • $12.95 • poetry
(a Broken Moon book)

Orders: Pleasure Boat Studio books are available by order from your bookstore,
directly from PBS, or through the following:

SPD (Small Press Distribution) Tel. 8008697553, Fax 5105240852
Partners/West Tel. 4252278486, Fax 4252042448
Baker & Taylor 8007751100, Fax 8007757480
Ingram Tel. 6157935000, Fax 6152875429
Amazon.com or **Barnesandnoble.com**

Pleasure Boat Studio: A Literary Press
201 West 89th Street
New York, NY 10024
Tel: 2123628563/Fax: 8888105308
www.pleasureboatstudio.com | pleasboat@nyc.rr.com